DEATH OF THE "DREAM"

I pushed and pulled my way into the tunnel with the bunch and, like them, stopped cold in my shoes when I saw him. There in the dimly lit corridor lay Dream Weaver.

Not really lying, but sitting in a heap against the tunnel wall, his legs splayed, his arms limp, his hatless golden head flopped onto his right shoulder. His eyes were wide open, staring as if in disbelief and a sight no man, or batboy, would ever forget.

But most ungodly, and perhaps the ultimate scarilege, was the sight of the team insignia lying over his heart. Due to a pea-size hole in Weaver's chest that still gurgled blood, it was a circle of crimson, a stain so vivid that it washed the beloved CUBS crest into a ghastly, sickening, unreadable circle of warm, glistening doom.

For unimaginable seconds none of us—players, reporters, bystanders—breathed or spoke or moved. Dream Weaver sat in a freeze-frame heap before us: murdered.

Then all hell broke loose.

Bantam Crime Line Books offer the finest in classic
and modern American mysteries.
CRIME LINE Ask your bookseller for the books you have missed.

Murder
in
Wrigley Field

Crabbe Evers

BANTAM BOOKS

NEW YORK · TORONTO · LONDON · SYDNEY · AUCKLAND

MURDER IN WRIGLEY FIELD
A Bantam Crime Line Book/April 1991

CRIME LINE and the portrayal of a boxed "cl" are trademarks of Bantam Books, a division of Bantam Doubleday Dell Publishing Group, Inc.

ISBN 0-553-28915-2

Published simultaneously in the United States and Canada

Bantam Books are published by Bantam Books, a division of Bantam Doubleday Dell Publishing Group, Inc. Its trademark, consisting of the words "Bantam Books" and the portrayal of a rooster, is Registered in U.S. Patent and Trademark Office and in other countries. Marca Registrada. Bantam Books, 666 Fifth Avenue, New York, New York 10103.

PRINTED IN THE UNITED STATES OF AMERICA
RAD   0 9 8 7 6 5 4 3 2 1

To the memory of Bill Veeck, who built the scoreboard, planted the ivy, reveled in the bleachers, and left his sweet spirit in Wrigley Field.

"Wrigley Field is a Peter Pan of a ball park. It has never grown up and it has never grown old. Let the world race on—they'll still be playing day baseball in the friendly confines of Wrigley Field, outfielders will still leap up against the vines, and the Cubs . . . well, it's the season of hope."

—E. M. SWIFT

"When the snow melts away
Do the Cubbies still play
In their ivy-covered burial ground?"

—STEVE GOODMAN

Prologue

In legend his name was Dean "Dream" Weaver, but that was only an alias.

For when he stood out on that hill, his cap back on his wheat-colored hair, his anvil-broad shoulders outlined against the benign summer sky, he was the Grim Reaper.

It did not matter if a latter-day Murderers' Row stood poised at the plate.

It did not matter if a gusting hitter's wind rippled the ivy along the outfield walls like fur on an animal's back.

It did not matter if the ball was hopped or the bat corked.

For when Dream Weaver kicked and his golden arm dealt, he was Famine, Pestilence, War, and Death— Johnson, Feller, Koufax, and Ryan—in a single rider on a snorting horse.

Except today, this cruel day, when that horse faltered and its rider grew pale . . .

That is how Grantland Rice would have described it. Now I am not Granny nor am I accustomed to borrowing his lines; but I am not above putting a little spin on a phrase or two. In this case it was demanded and— I'll even concede—appropriate. Besides, I knew Rice a little, and he was a thoroughly smudged member of the profession of ink-stained wretches. I never made much of those stories about how he borrowed all that Four Horsemen business. Granny was "still stepping along at the top of his stride" the day he collapsed at his type-writer, and I can appreciate that.

My own hand would have written something to the effect that Weaver, that big, gifted ox of a southpaw, was found shot to death in the tunnel leading from the dug-out to the clubhouse.

Single slug. A line shot that cleared the bases: aorta, spleen, pancreas, and kidney.

That's how Duffy House would have put it. No bull-shitting around. I'm too old for that. Nine column inches of the cleanest prose this side of Red Smith—delivered on deadline and digested with your morning coffee. Did it for thirty years, and I could do it again in a minute.

But these new editors wanted Drama and Gran-deur, Pathos and Poetry—"These are the saddest of possible words/Tinker to Evers to Chance"—Tristram and Isolde, and if I wanted to sell them some prose on the Weaver thing, they said, it had better be dressed their way. So I gave it the Grantland Rice touch.

I do not mean to sell the event short. The Weaver demise was yet another day of Cubs' infamy, as grievous as Hack Wilson's dropped fly balls in the '29 Series, as insulting as the Babe's called-shot round-tripper off Charlie Root in the Series of '32, as desperate as the Swoon of '69, the fifth game of the '84 playoffs—and, if you stretch matters, as haunting as Brock for Broglio.

I know, because I was around for all of the above.

1

Dream

It was a postcard summer day, warm but not sticky, with a breeze off Lake Michigan—bright as only June can offer. My father used to quote the poet James Russell Lowell on days like these:

Oh, what is so rare as a day in June?
Then, if ever, come perfect days.

Old James R.'s observation may have preceded organized baseball by a few years, but he knew a good game day when he saw one. It was a day the Good Lord meant for baseball, and this being Wrigley Field on one of those sixty-six dates when those infernal beacons perched on the roof were not illumined, it was daytime baseball—as the Good Lord meant it to be played.

People are fond of invoking the whims of the Good Lord when they refer to baseball and Wrigley Field, and they are probably right in doing so. What they invariably omit, however, is that the aforementioned deity, after setting the green, perfect stage for this country's pastime amid the ivy and the red brick of the venerable arena on Clark and Addison streets, always seems to take a pass on the proceedings that follow. We speak, of course, of the inexorable fate of the Cubs, and need we say more? Only to observe that the denizens of this park have not tasted the full sweetness of victory since 1908.

But I am a sucker for the place, this curio, this Wrigley Field. Hardly a person is now alive who remembers that it was built in 1914 for $250,000 as Weeghman Park, to be the home of Charles Weeghman's Chicago Whales of the newly formed Federal League. The Chicago Whales? But Weeghman's Whales and their league folded after a couple years, and Weeghman quickly bought control of the Cubs franchise. The club opened in his park in 1916 against the Cincinnati Reds and has been there ever since. The original capacity of 14,000 was increased to the classic 39,008 and the name changed to Cubs Park in 1920. It became Wrigley Field, after new club owner William Wrigley, Jr., in 1926. It should be duly noted that its dimensions—355 down the line in left field, 353 in right, and 400 in straightaway center—are almost perfect, so much so that most of the new parks, those freakish domes mainly, have virtually reproduced them.

On that day I walked from the concourse into the light and was temporarily blinded, like a vision, I guess. My eyes adjusted and I once again took in the ballyard: the white chalk on red clay, the natural carpet of clipped grass, the ivy-covered outfield walls, the aged Chicago apartment buildings beyond them with rooftop fans just waiting for a souvenir. There is no more beautiful sight, not to any claret-blooded American raised on Charley Grimm and Ernie Banks. The words slip off your tongue: *Let's play two.*

To my right was the redbrick wall over which Hack Wilson leaned to pen an autograph for the son of Al Capone. Al smiled. To my left was the spread of left-field bleachers where Gabby Hartnett hit the homer in the gloamin'. Looking down from on high, of course, was the drab-green scoreboard built by young Will Veeck in 1937, when his daddy ran the club and which, to this day, offers manually kept line scores of every game in progress. Utterly amazing. Oh yes, the ivy was planted by Will in 1938.

The tradition oozes out of this old field like sap from a maple, and you lose yourself in wistful reveries. Pick your club, your year—usually the one when you held on to your father's hand as you walked in for the first time —your idol or your bum. KiKi Cuyler, Hank Sauer, Swish Nicholson, Ron Santo. Tinker to Evers to Chance —"Trio of Bear Cubs and fleeter than birds . . ." to further quote from Franklin P. Adams; or "Banks to Baker to Addison Street," to borrow from Jack Brickhouse.

Anyway, on that pretty day the Bruins, as we scribes used to call them—never *Cubbies*, for godssakes, that being a wretched misnomer applied by slick merchandisers—were two games over .500 and a mere three games out of first. Anything was possible. June, of course, is a time when teams have not yet unraveled. The won-loss monkey is not yet on the manager's back, so he waxes sanguine. Spring training's phenoms are still seeing fastballs. Million-dollar rotator cuffs have not yet torn.

The first-place New York Mets, with one star just out of substance abuse rehab and another one headed there, two as-told-to boohoo books on the East Coast best-seller lists, and a half dozen intrasquad feuds, were in town for a weekend quartet.

It was pregame, that loose time of fungoes and pepper, batting practice and barbering. The cage was up, and Billy Williams, Cooperstown resident and Cub batting coach by virtue of a placid, glass-smooth swing that hung many a frozen rope between back-pedaling outfielders, was trying to somehow transfer his former skills to the jittery swats of his young Cub batsmen. With dubious success. The Cub regulars, in groups of four, were hitting three and laying down one. While waiting, they gave grumpy interviews to visiting reporters. A coach slammed ground balls to backup infielders. Pitchers not scheduled to pitch jogged wind sprints across the outfield just slow enough so that when a serious game-time sprint presented itself, a hamstring would pull like a plucked banjo string.

Reserve outfielders shagged flies and bantered with tattooed young ladies in the bleachers. Other team members, alone and seemingly oblivious to the filling stands, were in various contorted postures, stretching

Crabbe Evers

quadriceps, hamstring, groin, and lower back muscles. And once in a while, with the randomness of a shooting star, one would streak from the sidelines into the open space of center field, and then walk back as though nothing had happened.

After letting my eyes wander over this scene for about a half hour, I meandered in the direction of the Cubs' bullpen along the left-field foul line. The starting pitcher, who had just emerged from the dugout, was doing his own set of muscle stretching and loosening: a few touch-your-toes, a couple of wind sprints, some arm windmills. Standing together, waiting for him to get ready, were a reserve catcher and the new pitching coach, a minor-league hand unknown to me but who had already mastered the look of worry and the oft-repeated mantra of Wrigley Field: "Keep it low. Keep it in the park."

In a few moments the starter was throwing to the reserve catcher, who wore a mask but no cup. The hurler looked good as he loosened up. His fastball tailed, his curve and slider snapped off like angry wasps, his change-up seemed to hesitate in midair. Such stuff cleared the look of worry from the face of the pitching coach as I watched. He even grinned from time to time.

Which was understandable. The coach was standing in the shadow of Dean Jamie ("Dream") Weaver, who was not just another thrower. His blessed left arm had been clocked at 101 miles-per, hence the term "aspereen chucker." Weaver was, quite simply, faster than any man alive. Attached to that gifted wing was a body the Good Lord almost never gives to one person all at the same time: Dream was 6' 2", 190 pounds, with hulking shoulders, no waist, simian arms that dangled nearly to his knees, and hands the size of four-pound lobsters.

He had the looks of a movie star—a little Paul Newman, a little Robert Redford. Even his hair was a dirty blond color, his chin cleft, and he possessed that horsey smile that started brushfires. To say that women went crazy about him is to say that Jim Palmer looked good in underwear. Incidentally, I heard the Jockey people wanted Dream to replace Palmer until he told them he didn't *wear* undershorts.

As might be expected, Dream had the intelligence of most left-handers raised in Southern California, being exposed to too much sunshine, too many carefree young ladies, too much loose change, God-knows-what sweet-smelling smokes and powders, and music that is not music at all. All of which ruled out his being a Rhodes Scholar, or the necessity of becoming one, yet supremely qualified him for life as a superstar.

Dream *was* bright enough, however, to keep his shirt half-buttoned and that platinum smile pasted on his mug whenever he was in over his head. Plus, he had that awesome arm of his, which took a few years of minor-league ball to develop. In baseball it usually does. The speed had always been there; but for three or four seasons Dream was Steve Barber, Steve Blass, Sudden Sam McDowell, and Ryne Duren all rolled into one. He couldn't have found the strike zone if it wore a brassiere. Well, maybe *only* then.

He would stand out on the hill, kick his leg, uncork a pellet, and pray. Everybody prayed. The ball was likely to scream not just over the catcher's head, as Duren did it, but in the direction of the batboy, the on-deck hitter, the photographers, even clear into the pressbox. As one old-timer said of the great Johnny Vander Meer in his early days: "He was fearsome—fast and wild. You were afraid not only of being struck out but of being struck, and the fear of the latter often caused the former."

Batters stood in the box and shook like palsied schoolboys. Guys who hadn't been to church in years suddenly remembered the sign of the cross better than Jose Cardenal. It took three years, a few hundred walks, scores of hit batsmen, all of whom nursed doughnut-sized welts, and even the fractured skull of a Cuban, who then and there gave up all thought—*Aiii Caramba* —of being the next Minnie Minoso, before Dream found the plate. But when he did, he was Sandy Koufax without high holidays. And the world was his taco.

Weaver himself had no idea what happened or why

he found the groove. Or why his fastball had a wicked tail on it. He just kept smiling and hearing pistol shots come from the gloves of his catchers. His heat won him 27, 23, 24, and an incredible 32 last year. The Cy Youngs came his way like two-bit bowling trophies. And the money—the first $5 million contract—the fame, the endorsements, TV programs, and invitations to the White House.

To all that I would add girls, but Dream, even when he was a cockeyed lefty in the bush leagues, never lacked for girls. When he hit the top there were simply more girls. Compared to Dream Weaver, Broadway Joe was a eunuch, Reggie Jackson a recluse.

I had stood in the midst of these pregame warm-ups thousands of times, usually in relative safety behind the batting cage, drawing country bromides from a coach or a manager, jawing occasionally with a player who had something to say, scribbling indecipherable notes that would somehow turn into deathless column-inch prose in the next morning's *Daily News*.

But not this day. In my emeritus state, I was the guest of Arnold ("Red") Carney, the voice of the Cubs and an old friend. Red had promised me a free clock-radio of some quality if I would jabber with him on his pregame show. Red talks like the backs of old baseball cards read, with a measure of opinion half-cocked or otherwise, so he and I can always get in a couple of good innings on the current state of The Game. Just about sixteen minutes before the National Anthem, I stepped onto the infield gravel and headed for a pair of folding chairs set up near third base. Red was already there, miked and perspiring. He spotted me and waved me over.

But as I passed in front of the dugout I was side-swiped by a stumbling dervish of a Cub batboy.

"Hey!" I yelled, more in surprise than ire, as I held my hip and tried to keep from falling on my keister.

The kid yelped and gasped and sent little gobs of spittle flying from his chops. His face was white and his

eyes were wide and struck with what can only be de-
fined as unvarnished fear. He continued to stumble and
flail his arms, as if something evil possessed his soul or
something buzzing had invaded his shorts. He gasped
and yelped and made no sense at all except to point at
the dugout tunnel. Then, just as his spikes caught on a
dropped bat and he sprawled backwards, the sound
finally peeled from his lips—a shriek, a howl, a cater-
waul: "Dream!!"

A crowd of coaches, reporters, security, and a
player or two gathered around him, jostling me and my
hip pointer, and trying to grasp what was going on with
the kid. Then somebody, a P.R. guy, I believe, wised up
and went where the boy had pointed.

"In here! My God! Hurry, for Christ's sake!" came a
voice from the tunnel.

At that the crowd left the prone, stunned batboy
and stumbled its way down the dugout steps and into
the dark portal. Like a well-lit mine shaft, but a shaft
nonetheless, the narrow—no more than four-foot wide
and seven-foot high—concrete passageway leads due
west from the dugout beneath the box seats for about
twenty feet, where it turns north for several more yards
to the clubhouse. It is a short, claustrophobic run, and
dark once you get away from the light of the field.

Those few yards between the light of the field and
the spray of the shower room are a no-man's-land
where players cop a smoke between innings or managers who have been ejected from the playing field and
should be pouting in the clubhouse furtively linger and
pass marching orders out to their coaches. How the
umpires love to catch them and tack on even heavier
fines.

When you make the turn to the clubhouse you are
out of sight of most everybody and everything but the
clubhouse door. Bare lightbulbs light the space. Damp-
ness oozes from the concrete. Most of those who daily
pass through this area—players, security, club personnel, umpires, and reporters—pay it little mind because
they have much more pressing things to think about.
Only uninitiates and poets find significance in the tun-

nel. Let me amend that, for on that day it offered sublime appeal to a psychopath.

I pushed and pulled my way into the tunnel with the bunch and, like them, stopped cold in my shoes when I saw him. There in the dimly lit corridor lay Dream Weaver.

Not really lying, but sitting in a heap against the tunnel wall, his legs splayed, his arms limp, his hatless golden head flopped onto his right shoulder. His eyes were wide open, staring as if in disbelief, and a sight no man, or batboy, would ever forget. His jaw drooped in the rictus of death, exposing flawless white that ordinarily comprised a grin, a toothsome, all-American grin that oozed spirit and supreme confidence. Now it was petrified in a stunned, rugged grimace like that of a fighter pilot, of a stallion, of a golden kid who had just seen his wonderful life pass before his eyes before he felt it sucked from him.

But the most ungodly, perhaps the ultimate sacrilege, was the sight of the team insignia lying over his heart. Due to a pea-sized hole in Weaver's chest that still gurgled blood, it was a circle of crimson, a stain so vivid that it washed the beloved CUBS crest into a ghastly, sickening, unreadable circle of warm, glistening doom.

For unimaginable seconds none of us—players, reporters, bystanders—breathed or spoke or moved. Dream Weaver sat in a freeze-frame heap before us: bug-eyed, murdered.

Then all hell broke loose.

2

On the House

I was trapped inside the Cubs' clubhouse among the scrum of reporters, TV crews, club officials, players, and cops. When word of the murder got out, packs of newshounds, not to mention a few thousand extra fans, descended on the ballyard like ants on a banana. The clubhouse and the front offices were soon cordoned off, followed by the ballpark itself and the street out front. If you were in, as I was, you were in, even though you could hardly move, and that was it. Not only that, but the cops announced that anyone anywhere near the scene of the crime was not to leave until he had been interviewed by detectives.

It was now a good hour after the discovery of the crime. Dream Weaver's corpus had long since been removed to the morgue. Due to quick action and the uncommonly good sense of the president of the National League, the game had been cancelled. In a small but significant gesture of civility, nobody even suggested a moment of silence, a game face, and "Play ball!" Instead, of course, everybody was running around trying to find who could come up with a different way of saying "Omigod!" and "What's going on in this world?"

In the meantime, no detective had taken my statement and I was getting sick of waiting. I squeezed over to the cop who seemed to be in charge, a plainclothes guy from 11th and State who only shows up when something big happens. I told him of my impatience. I half

expected him to tell me to go to hell, but he nodded like
he knew what I was talking about. He gave me the
name of the detective in charge.

"I liked that piece you did on Moose Moryn," he
added.

I hadn't written about the Moose in thirty years.

The homicide dicks, I guess, were doing about as
much as they could, which amounted to trying to figure
out who could get into the tunnel and pop the kid. It
took timing, access, coincidence—the kinds of things,
not to mention motive, that sleuths thrive on. I stood
there and took a few notes; for what reason, I was not
entirely sure, but the habit was hard to break.

Through the hubbub and camera lights I spotted
Red Carney. He was on the air, grabbing anybody he
could. I had never made it over to him or his program,
and it hit me right then that I had blown the clock-
radio. Red was functioning—he's a pro—but you could
tell that he was stunned, his face flushed and his eyes
red. He hadn't got his moniker by accident.

I watched and listened as he got ahold of Cub manager Fred Merkle. Merkle—a brushcut, plug-chewing
veteran of countless clubhouse interviews concerning
every conceivable kind of win, loss, and even a few
draws—was at a complete loss on this one. He was a
mess, stripped of his stopper, his meal ticket, his stallion. The blasted reality of it was just starting to sink into
Fred's knubby head. With Red's arm around him, his
hat pushed back, Freddie searched for the right words.

"He was Kid Natural, we all knew that, Red. Just a
heckuva talent and a heckuva fine kid. I never had one
like him. Maybe I'll never have another one like him
again. Look. Here's my scorecard for today. Still in my
pocket. His name right there. That's all I had to do
when his turn came up. That's all I had to do! And now
for something like this to happen . . . geez!"

He paused and turned away, seemingly overcome
by a spasm of grief and also in need of emptying the
juice from his cheek.

"I had him wrote in as my starter. What a genius
that made me. Rest of the game I sit there and say, 'Way

to go, Dream.' 'Chuck 'em, kid.' 'Hone, babe.' Then somebody comes over and says they shot him. 'What the—?' I says. For crying out loud, some nut shot him?!"

He turned his head again, too choked up to talk.

"You'll hafta check with somebody else, Red," he said when he turned back to the mike. "I know about the game of baseball. This kind of thing I don't know."

With that, Merkle pushed off and fought his way through the crush of reporters and crews who wanted him to say the same thing over again to them.

Next up was George Rohe, the Cubs' general manager. He was the man responsible for signing and keeping Dream Weaver in a Cub uniform. Rohe didn't look good either: his normally pressed summer suit looked like one of mine after I'd sat in the press box for three hours, his tie was off center, and he had the look of a man who had just watched his house burn down.

"My feelings aren't any different from anybody else's, Red," Rohe said. "I'm shocked and stunned and— but wait a minute—"

With that he grabbed the microphone.

"I *do* have something more to say. This is an outrage, that's what. This is a ballpark, dammit. This is Wrigley Field and the Chicago Cubs, not some damn gangster hangout. What kind of a world is it that something like this can happen?

"We lost something besides a young man here, Red. We lost some of our dignity."

He pushed the microphone back into Red's hands and went off. Red was pretty much handcuffed by that piece of oratory, and he blustered and tried to fill in the airtime while searching the crowd. When the radio station switched to its regular news spot, and Red was off the air, he spotted me.

"Duffy, for cryin' out loud!" he said, motioning me over.

He was perspiring fiercely, something that masked the genuine tears that leaked down his cheek.

"Why, Duffy, why?" he wailed. "Greatest arm in the whole doggone game. Holy cow!"

It was Red's turn now, and for a moment the crowd around us quieted and listened.

"Ya know, he was my boy. Deano—that's what I called him, just Deano—he was *somebody*. They coulda whacked some damn middle reliever and who'da cared? Huh, Duffy, huh?" he said, looking at me but expecting no answer. His mug was now a pudding of wet tears. He was an old friend, and his grief played on me. Such sorrow is the stuff of fires, floods, and earthquakes, not sports, and it devastated Red.

I put my arm around him and we stood shoulder to shoulder for a while, exchanging mute condolences, until a couple of young newsies tried to poke microphones and recorders into our faces in an attempt to capture our timeless remarks. I pushed them away. As if we had anything to say other than the obvious. The worst passed. Red recovered. I nodded a nod that told Red I'd see him later.

Shoving my way out of the mob, I found a detective. He told me that, unless I had anything extraordinary to tell him, he would interview me later. I caught a cab over to the building that housed my old newspaper to sell my version of the story. After I had embellished the prose with the aforementioned Grantland Rice touches, the boys bought it, put it and my mug on the front page just like old times, and that was that.

My dear mother brought me into this world in the early twenties, shortly after the Great War, in those dour yet earnest days when Americans were recovering from the great influenza epidemic and bracing themselves for the prospect of Warren Gamaliel Harding. Worse yet, the Great American Pastime was on the ropes, since the Black Sox had dealt it a pretty mean haymaker the year before. Right at the bell, however, the Great Bambino administered smelling salts. George Herman Ruth—the Sultan of Swat—with his masterful clouts and his mincing home run trot, rescued The Game from the dead-ball era and the dark night of scandal. Fifty-four homers in 1920! Why, Home Run

Baker had set the prewar, dead-ball roundtripper standards with nine, ten, twelve, and eight, respectively. The Babe would paste better than ninety-three in just a couple of seasons.

Ah, baseball. The ballpark. The lay of the green grass and the cut of the diamond. A simple game with its grand characters that somehow diverts harried minds from epidemics and political scandals. Even in those besmirched, say-it-ain't-so-Joe, bad old days, The Game didn't have the complicated problems of today: the blizzard of cocaine and the sea of alcohol, doctored balls and corked bats, naked ball girls, the Yanks going bad and the Blue Jays getting good, those ungodly domes being built and Wrigley getting lit. One wag suggested that the promotional line should be changed from "Baseball Fever: Catch It!" to "Baseball Colic: Shake It!" But the baseball of the 1920s was as fine a time and as colorful a setting as any for Frank and Estelle House to bring me, their firstborn bambino, onto the scene.

I started with the old Chicago *Daily News* when I was fifteen, rubbing up against the legacy of Sandburg, Hecht, Lardner, and some of those other big-name birds. But I didn't slobber all over them like the rest of the world did. I knew I couldn't touch them in the poem, play, or novel business, so I didn't try. I was more interested in the likes of Pat Malone and KiKi Cuyler. Look for no Ivy League silver-spoon-in-your-chops sports journalism from this corner. No sir. Knocking around this hog-butchering town as many years as I have, you don't cotton to the George Plimpton thing. You do your job, the athletes do theirs; and *your* job is to cover how well they're doing *theirs.* Never do you want the tables turned.

Then again, doing my job hasn't exactly put me in the public library either. Reminds me of something Heywood Hale Broun told me once. He said his daddy, the great Heywood Campbell Broun, once took the family down to the morgue of one of the New York papers he worked for. Spreading his arms wide, the elder Broun said, "There's a life's work. And none of it between hard covers."

Well, I've decided to remedy that—at least on my own behalf. I've been sitting here trying to write my memoirs. When turned out to graze after a half-century on the beat, a broken-down old fart of a sportswriter like myself doesn't have much else to do. I go back to the days when you could break in as a kid with nothing but a grammar school education and a keen nose. Of course, those were the days when you could come onto a paper, like I did, as a copy boy and rise through the ranks on the basis of some talent and a lot of good old hard work. Not like today, when you spring full-blown out of the famous Medill Journalism School onto the sports scene writing like Brent Musberger talks.

In my day, if you were any good, you picked up the tricks as you went along. I gleaned my share, enough so that for the last thirty of my years on the *Daily News* I presided over a daily sports column called "On the House." Now, writing a column is really very easy: you just open a vein and let it bleed out onto the paper. Red Smith said that, and I wish I had; but we both, for better or worse and for a lot of years, did it.

"On the House" was not all that original a title, given that my name is Duffy House. My book will probably be called *One More On the House*, which ain't too original either, but why start now? It was Charlie Miller, my editor on the *News* back then, who came up with the title. Charlie didn't think it was inspired either, but he was in a hurry and figured the column wouldn't last two weeks anyway. A lot he knew.

Nevertheless, I'm not just stringing together a bunch of the old "On the House" columns. Too many retired columnists have done that, God knows, and every manuscript has the running title *The Bases Were Loaded and So Was I.* Or should have. For some reason these fossils get long in the tooth and thin in the belfry and think the same people they aggravated in the morning paper over the years are just dying to see all that baloney collected between hard covers.

As far as I am concerned, I would just as soon -30-

the whole "On the House" business and start from scratch. I wrote my columns during the heat of the moment or, at the latest, in its afterburn. They were timely and shortsighted; hell, they had to be. The fans saw the game and I wrote about it, and together we digested the thing, savored it, then went on to the next one. It was never much more significant than that. Or at least I never thought so. I'd just as soon let the columns be. If someone wants to collect them, bind them between hard covers, well, they have my permission. But I have never felt moved to do it.

Instead, I've been writing new stuff about the old stuff. I've told a few yarns about some great guys who have long since passed from this earth, not to mention the playing field. I've thrown in a few pet grumps and some common sense to see if I can't leave the folks thinking. My druthers are to call the book *I May Be an Arsehole but I Can Tell You a Thing or Two.* But I tried that out on a few people and they didn't think much of it except for the arsehole part.

So I'm retired, away from the daily grind. And that could be taken to mean "old." But writing my memoirs doesn't mean I'm holed up in some study somewhere, never getting out and finding out who's doing what to whom. Put out to pasture, maybe. But part of that pasture has ivied walls on one side and sits on the corner of Addison and Clark. I can still smell a good series brewing a week off. I don't get my baseball out of the TV cabinet. Yeah, I have to be there, to see what kind of stuff the pitcher's got, catch the signs, the pigeons, the whole ball of wax.

To their credit, the current editors of the downtown rags knew this, even four years after my last "On the House" column. So they knew old Duffy was good for a sentimental touch, a tribute to Dream Weaver that would transcend the jargon of the sports section and sparkle for the reader of the front page. That's where the Grantland Rice touch fit in.

The grist for the piece came from the fact that, thanks to a tip from Gordie Goldsberry, the Cubs' gifted farm director, I had ballyhooed Weaver when he was still a teenager in Covina, California. I said in *The Sporting News* that this kid was golden if he could harness his 100-mph fastball. Some genius, huh? When he won his first twenty and the Cy Young, *Sports Illustrated* asked me for the sidebar piece. There was, of course, that big inside piece in *Esquire* that raised all the eyebrows among the Emil Verban Society, that East Coast–Washington, D.C., set of Cub boosters who wished they had thought of it. In fact, you could say I had pretty much written the book on Dean Weaver.

But who am I kidding? None of that would have counted for more than a drag bunt and an extra paycheck, a brief interruption of my Geritol days, had not Weaver's murder sent the game of baseball into unrest, disarray, and what people like me would call a damned mess. The game of Ruth, Gehrig, Hartnett, and Ernie Banks was coming apart at its red-threaded seams. And that is when my phone rang and my ears were blistered. I would have hung up after two syllables had not the diatribe come from the big boss of baseball, the commissioner, occupier of a seat so hot that his blood was boiling and his breath was fire.

3

Grand Canyon

"Duffy!"

"You got him," I said.

The Underwood manual stopped dead in its hunts and pecks when the phone rang. It was only a few short days after the Weaver murder and I was back into my memoirs. I expected any number of callers—editors, publishers, the boys down at the Press Club—but I didn't expect this one. The line held baseball's nibs. Direct dial to yours truly.

"This is Chambliss!"

"Heard of him," I said.

Chambliss was Granville (Grand) Canyon Chambliss, former head of the Chicago Board of Trade, presently Commissioner of Baseball. Now I knew Grand before he made his fortune in the soybean pits, and I knew he would be the one commissioner worth his salt on account of not only did he have more money than most of the owners but because he truly did not give a shit. That's right. Baseball was not Armageddon, as far as Chambliss was concerned, just a pastime become a business.

And the business was getting as loony as the bean markets, which meant Chambliss was in his element. You can hire only so many sportswriters, retired generals, labor lawyers, and California golden boys to be the High Hoo-Haw of Baseball before the public gets the idea the office of commissioner is nothing but a popcorn fart unless the guy running it has some *cojones*. Grand Canyon was rich in that department, thank you.

"Unhook your colostomy bag, Duffy, and get your butt into my office tomorrow morning," Chambliss said.

"Bed and board at the Algonquin and expenses?" I ventured.

"The YMCA, Chock Full o' Nuts, and carfare," he said.

He had me. On my terms, of course.

I walked into his office the next morning with no idea what was on his mind. I was only hoping that he was not interested in my doing some phony P.R. for the Great Game.

I should not have worried.

"Duffy, cut the small talk, sit your butt down, and listen to me," Chambliss said as he gave his secretary the slit-throat signal and closed the door.

Grand was a short, bowlegged pug of a guy who reminded you a little of Herman Franks and a lot of Popeye Zimmer. Even with all his money, he always looked a mess, five o'clock shadow at noon, satchels under the eyes, a wardrobe on loan from Bill Veeck. But he had drive, the guts of a burglar, and the gumption of Charlie Finley. Pacing and waving as if he were still in the trading pits, he let me have it.

"Duffy, dammit, I'm gonna tell you a lot of things you already know and some you don't.

"The game of baseball is horseshit. That you know.

"Worse right now than it was in '19 with the Black Sox. Worse than the strike of '81, the drug trials of—hell, pick a year. It's as bad as when that dame plugged Eddie Waitkus in the Edgewater Beach Hotel."

"Room Four-twelve," I added.

"That's right," he said.

He went on.

"The Weaver thing. Good God Almighty—murdered right in the ballpark. Look at this—"

He held up a three-day-old copy of the Chicago

Sun-Times. THE DEADLY CONFINES, blared the headline. I remembered the edition well.

I didn't interrupt; Chambliss was just warming up. "Look what they're writing. They've torn into that kid's background looking for a killer and they've found every floozy, every neighbor lady, every one-night stand, every hustler, gambler, riverboat captain, and pool shark who ever crossed his path. Miserable, miserable stuff. And never mind what it's done to that kid, who got around, for Pete's sake. No offense to the memory of Dream Weaver, but all this uproar in the press and the television has done no good at all for big-league baseball. No good at all. And I'm no Pollyanna.

"Good God Almighty, Duffy, I thought we had problems with the d.h., free agents, cocaine, gambling, Astroturf, and Steinbrenner. Why, all that was charming compared to this."

He paused, and the room ceased to vibrate. Then he lowered the volume, swung one leg over his desk, ran his hands over his ears and started in on a new level.

"I'm talking character, fiber, what these steroid cases have in their *souls.* Let me give you a for instance. You remember those guys on the Yankees who swapped wives? Pupich and Pudderson, or whatever their names were. Just up and traded wives like they were a couple of fielder's gloves. Check that—they probably *wouldn't* have traded their gloves. And they smiled and cuddled for the cameras like they'd done nothing amiss.

"But baseball, hell, the national game, the sport of Gehrig and DiMaggio and Clint Courtney, just swooned. Dragged down to its lowest level. You can talk all you want about Babe Ruth having the clap, or Johnny Bench playing ping-pong on his wedding night, but it didn't match what those two guys did.

"See, if you look at it in the grand scheme of things, what they did spawned this Dream Weaver thing. It's all part of it."

His face was taut. The blue vein in his temple throbbed like a jackhammer.

"You with me, Duffy?" he said.

"Every word," I said.

"So did I fly you in here for me to let off steam?" he said.

"Not on your life," I said.

"It's been days since Weaver caught his lunch, and we've got nothing but diddly squat. The Chicago cops tell me what they got, and they have their top guys on it because of the heat. But they got nothing so far. A list of security guys, vendors, wives, girlfriends, gamblers, dope dealers, reporters, and even two of the Mets, for crying out loud.

"But that's only half my problem. Even if they do pinch someone and prove that he or she was in the right place at the right time, it won't end this thing.

"That's what I'm driving at, Duffy. I've put out some feelers of my own and what's coming back bothers me. Some people believe Weaver's private life didn't have a thing to do with his murder. That the *Game*, capital G, *our* game did it."

At that, Grand stopped and leaned over my chair, putting his foot on the cushion like a manager contemplating a pitching change. His voice descended into depths bordering on conspiratorial.

"Which means, Duf, we got trouble in Abner Doubleday's game."

He hung the words like black bunting.

"Now, if I was smart I wouldn't shake that tiger's tail. I'd let it lie, just ease back, put on my best Ford Frick act and stonewall the damn thing. Sing 'Take Me Out to the Ballgame' and hope that it'd blow over.

"Baseball fans are forgiving, you know. Just ask all those nose cases on the Mets. But I been thinking long and hard about it. I got caught up in history, you know what I mean, Duf? I sit in the same damn chair as Frick, Bowie Kuhn, and Happy Chandler, none of which gives my butt much inspiration.

"But wait a minute, I say to myself. Mister Kenesaw Mountain Landis also sat here, and that says something. I got to thinking what he did after the Black Sox scandal —hell, the damn gamblers *owned* the game back then! So he grabbed the sport by the sack and twisted until people's eyeballs crossed.

"So I started thinking like Landis would have thought, and first off I decide I can't just sit here on my ass. I've got no choice, Duffy. I've got to chew some nuts on this thing. What would happen if, thanks to me, the world found out the true story? No matter where it leads. Get past the fact that Dream Weaver was less than a choirboy and deal with cold truth.

"The more I thought about it the more I liked it. I mean, I loved it. I'll dance on Dream Weaver's grave if I have to—especially if he was stupid enough to have people around who could kill him—as long as I get to the bottom of what happened. All the facts, the dirt, the conspirators and accomplices. Even if it ends up in a couple dozen indictments. But this great game will survive this—it's survived everything up to this point—and I will *not* have it drug into the dirt as being somehow responsible for the Weaver murder.

"If we get some indictments, *I* want to be the cause. This office. Not some twenty-four-year-old reporter who'd sell his soul to sling mud in my eye so he can get into *Sports Illustrated*. And that's where you come in."

"That's what I was afraid of," I said, coming out of my reverie.

"I don't have to educate you," he said. "I'll give you carte blanche to find out everything Dream Weaver was up to and who wanted him out of the way and whether or not we can stop it and save the damn game."

"And your job," I said.

"That too."

"Just checking."

"We'll even solve the murder along the way, and end all the mystery," Grand said. "The last thing Dream Weaver will be in my league is a martyr.

"That's where you fit in. There ain't a better investigator on the face of this earth. Not a person who knows more about the history of the game and has a greater respect for it. That's crucial. I want someone I can trust. So what do you say?"

I hesitated for about three seconds.

"Forget it. Hire a gumshoe," I said.

"Gumshoe. Gumshoe, he says. Okay. So call yourself Gum-Shoeless Joe Jackson," he said.

"Good Lord."

"Couldn't resist," he said.

"Yellow Pages," I said.

"Not a one of them could do it. No private eye could get around the league—in the locker rooms, the hotels, the joints—without blowing the whole thing.

"But *you*. Why, Duffy House can walk into any sports gathering in the land and get an earful without anybody thinking twice. Research, call it research. Old buzzards like you are always writing books—*Great Games Played on Tuesday, The Life of Van Lingle Mungo*. You could even say you're doing your memoirs. This office will back you up."

"Thanks," I grumbled. The man had just insulted my life's work.

"Let me run through this again," I continued. "You want me to run an investigation of the life and death of Dream Weaver. With emphasis on what enemies and whose shorts he was into, and whether his fall was anything bigger than it looked."

"Sold," Chambliss said.

"And you don't care where the chips fall."

"You got it. And if you can pinch the killer, all the better. I'll take credit where I can get it. In the meantime, keep it secret. Report everything back to me."

"Out of the question," I said.

"Then you'll do it?"

"For two-hundred bucks a day, expenses, and a ghost job with your office when I'm done," I said.

"Done," Commissioner Chambliss said.

"One more thing," I said. "What if this thing gets nasty? What if all of a sudden I'm rubbing nosehairs with hoodlums or somebody like that?"

"Pack a gun or something, Duffy. Or bluff 'em. I don't give a shit. Besides, who would want to pop a washed-up sportswriter, huh? Who do you think you are, Jerry Holtzman?"

"Yeah," I said, and meant it.

4

Petey

There were plenty of reasons for me to stay in Manhattan, plenty of joints to visit, numbers to call, memories to dredge up. Not that I'm Joltin' Joe, or even Broadway Joe, for that matter, but the sidewalks of the Big Apple will still part for Mr. House, thank you. I closed Mr. Toots Shor's fish and chips joint many a night, and shared many a vodka and tonic with Red Smith at his favorite bistros. I could have shown my mug at a half dozen watering holes now, not spent a dime, and left stinko.

Nah, I'm no stranger in that town. But once I'd walked out of the commissioner's office, I said to hell with it. The exhaust that passed for air on Sixth Avenue hit me in the puss and with it came second thoughts. A pang of regret? An attack of ethics? Conscience? I didn't know. I only knew that my head began to reel and my breath came up short, and I felt something sear into my chest that made angina feel like a kiss.

What in the hell had the commish talked me into! An undercover investigator? A snitch? A snoop? A spy? A dumb ass? Pick one, pick 'em all.

I had just given the okay to becoming proctologist to the national game. After decades of viewing things from the press box, of fencing with the honorable and the up-and-up, of calling the shots as they caromed, I was going off the record, and for the Other Side. The commish was a friend, I could rationalize—oh, how I could rationalize!—but he was still the commish, the guy in the office I had spent a lifetime watching, not watching *out* for.

I couldn't help wondering whether the arteries were clogging. Had I become so stationary in my retirement, so anxious to get back into the center of things, that I'd become a mole? Could I live with myself in an official, league-authorized trench coat?

I needed a beer, but I hailed a cab instead. Dinner that night with Chambliss, which he had suggested, was out of the question, unless, of course, it was for the purpose of telling him I did not have the stomach for his job. As I walked, oblivious to eight million lugs around me whose stories weren't as good as they thought, as easy a mark for a pickpocket as any jamoke on the avenue that day, I decided to get back home. I'd sleep on it, and if I woke up and looked in the mirror and saw something fish wouldn't eat, I'd cable the commish and tell him to get himself another boy.

On the flight back to Chicago I drank too much.

In three hours I was in front of my building. The new one, not the old home on Hoyne Street. After Wilma died, I had sold the old homestead and moved into this Outer Drive joint, fourteenth floor. Apart from a view of the Sheffield Avenue entrance of Wrigley Field, the less said about this overpriced shoebox the better. It sways in the wind, and I can hear my neighbor flush his toilet. Then again, there are no walks to shovel or grass to mow. And without Wilma, the old house had turned big and empty and full of things that made me stare off into space every so often. At my age, and with some good lines left in my Underwood, I figured I needed a change of scenery.

I bought this condominium, I should mention, because of Henry "Biz" Wagemaker, doorman, gentleman, and former outfielder of the Chicago American Giants. Henry spotted me when I first walked in, introduced himself, and lit up like the Comiskey Park scoreboard when I said I remembered him hitting bingles off

Satchel Paige and Bullet Joe Rogan. With Biz filling its lobby with that much baseball history, the building had me.

Biz was gone for the day when I returned. I nodded at his relief, a young fellow named DeWayne, who did not have Biz's history but had a sharp eye for anything going on in the area. I pushed the right elevator button. As usual, I encountered no one in the hallway before letting myself into 1403. The inside of my mouth was cotton. My head was banging. So I didn't see it—the bundle, that is—and it caught my foot like a shortstop's outstretched tag. I landed on my can.

"It" was a bloated red canvas bag, like something the Cardinals might carry on the road, that had been dumped just inside the door of my previously uncluttered living room. I rolled over and clutched my hip, the same one banged by the hysterical batboy. It was busted, it was fractured, hell, the damn thing was broken, as Dizzy Dean used to say. Okay, maybe it wasn't, but it hurt like a sonuvagun.

"Let me guess," came a voice from the kitchen. "Pete Rose headfirst into Ray Fosse, All-Star game, Nineteen Sixty-Nine."

"Nineteen seventy," I writhed.

She came into the room and stood over me, shaking her head and extending her hand in aid. I spotted that carrot hair, the same lovely locks of my kid sister Betty, which made the present owner Betty's girl, Petey.

"Fosse was never much after that, was he?" she said.

"Journeyman," I growled, ignoring her outstretched hand.

She sat down on the floor next to me, tucking her feet under her fanny as if she were in for a bedtime story. It had been a good twenty years since I'd tucked her in, and I don't have the faintest idea where the time went in between. I do know that the redhead looking into my face was all grown up now, smelling of some sweet southern flower and batting a pair of green eyes that could get away with a lot of lies.

"You ever do a piece on how Rose felt about ruining a guy's career?" she said.

The pain of my hip seemed to be subsiding; I would walk again.

"That collision ushered in a whole decade of jock violence," she went on, pursing her lips in cogitation.

"The start of the 'me generation' in sports," she added.

"Horsefeathers," I finally said. "It didn't do a damn thing but separate the kid's shoulder."

She leaned over, put her forearms on my shoulders, and grinned.

"I'm *here*, Uncle Duffy," she said.

Petey was one of those little arrangements you forget about. Not that she was forgettable, but when Betty had called a few months back and asked if her daughter could bunk in with me for a few weeks until law school started and her apartment became available, I said sure, fine, no problem. Then I forgot about it.

After all, what are big brothers for? My little sister Betty could always disarm me with a simple pickoff move. Her nerve did not always put her in the good graces of Wilma, the late Mrs. House. And it looked like Petey had her mother's spunk, energy like an engine stuck on high idle, so that sometimes you have to kick it to get the revving down to where you can shift into gear.

So here she was, no longer the two-year-old redtop munchkin who used to uppercut me in the privates and dive under the covers, but now a twenty-two-year-old college graduate, Oberlin, Phi Beta Blah-Blah, soon to be a first-year law student at Northwestern University School of Law.

She smiled, a smile you couldn't put a price on, and I saw that little girl I knew way back when. Her name was Petrinella, which was a family name and a mistake no matter what, and everybody called her Petey, which you knew they would. Back when I was reading her bedtime stories, the family hadn't yet moved from Chicago to Cincinnati, which they did when Petey was about three. The water must be good down there, because in nineteen years the kid had gone from peewee cutes to queen of the Rose Bowl parade.

Petey had the good looks on my mother's side: the flame in the hair, the tight skin, a nose so upturned you could hang a hat on it. Sort of like me, back a few years, or at least I thought so. And she had that smile—just like her mother and her mother's mother—like Christmas and New Year's. She was smiling it right now.

"I see you stole home on the doorman," I said.

"Like Jackie Robinson," she said.

"Way before your time."

"Why don't you lock your front door?"

"I'm superstitious," I said.

"You're great!" She laughed, and gave me a hug and a peck on the cheek that all but erased the pain from my hip. She had on a little T-shirt that exposed her stomach when she leaned over, a tummy you could have landed a Piper Cub on.

"Where are we gonna go tonight?" she said.

"I was on my way to bed now, and San Diego in the near future."

"Ugh. Boring on the first count. Chicago's better this time of year on the second."

"Well, that settles that," I said.

"Good. On the first night of the rest of my life in Chicago I want to gambol—that's g-a-m-b-o-l. Take me to all your old hangouts. Introduce me to the guys with ink in their veins." She beamed.

She sounded as if what she'd just proposed was a good time.

"I'll stay real close and cuddle once in a while so people will think you got lucky," she said, and cackled.

"Dress like that and they'll think cash and carry," I said.

"You're nasty," she said.

Suddenly she scissored her legs together and, in an exercise only Russian gymnasts are supposed to be able to do, stood straight up and went into the kitchen.

"San Diego?" she asked from the refrigerator.

I could hear the telltale clank of my bottle of prune juice, and I pretended I had not heard her inquiry.

"Are you really going to San Diego?"

"Sooner or later. A little favor for the commissioner."

"Of Baseball?"

"No, Streets and Sanitation," I said.

"Good line," she said, reappearing with a glass of geriatric rocket fuel. "Chambliss? He's a Chicago guy, isn't he?"

"Same one. And don't drink too much of that stuff," I said.

"Ugh, it's all you have. Doing what?" she asked.

"League matter."

"Tell me," she said.

"Can't do that. Privileged information. If you're going to be a lawyer, it won't be the first time you hear that line."

"I'm going to law school, but who says I'm going to practice?" she said, sitting back down again, her jeans so tight they whistled, the five long brown toes on her bare feet showing no signs of polish or varnish.

"Huh?" I said.

"Oh c'mon, Uncle Duffy. Law school is just something to fall back on. What I really want to do is write sports."

"No you don't," I said.

"Yes, yes! I do declare," she declared. "*You* know that. I've read every word you've ever written, Unk. You're my idol! That's why I came here. To Chicago. God, where it gets positively arctic, when I could have gone to any law school in the country."

"Stop it, kid," I said. "I'm a dried-up old fart who spent fifty years writing for fish wrappers. Winos stuck my day's work into their pants for insulation. Parakeets shat on it. Millions of words and gone in a day. I could go on."

"Wrong, wrong, wrong," she replied. "You made people's mornings. They drank their morning coffee with you. You were a friend. Like Red Smith and Jim Murray and all those great guys. I got scrapbooks full of your stuff."

Suddenly she was two years old in a pair of Dr. Dentons snuggling up for her fix of Mother Goose.

"Doll," I said. I cupped her earnest and lovely skull and let her keep her delusions. "Join the profession and I'll kill ya."

She kissed me fat on the forehead.

"So where we going tonight?" she said.

"Stick with me, kid," I said.

5

Red

I have haunted a few places in my time, once even had the wind to keep up with Harry Caray. So it was no toil to show Petey around. After she spruced up a little and changed her clothes, we grabbed a cocktail at Rickey's in Marina Towers, watched the bridges part, and the boats bob in from the lake. Then we shuttled over to Miller's Pub for a steak. I figured Petey would get a kick out of Jimmy Gallios and the best sports photo gallery this side of Cooperstown. I was right. She took in the place with a gush and a sigh. She looked at a black-and-white shot of Moose Skowron, a Chicago boy, and positively swooned.

But it was her table manners that won me. Petey knew how to eat and how to talk, together and separate. She filled me in on the family, on her schooling, on her plans. I listened to every word. She had been educated well, raised better, and knew how to speak in complete sentences. On top of that, she had the style to throw out a hip and pull it back in again. The looks shooting over to our table were not on account of my sportcoat. The world was eating out of her hand, and I have to admit, I kind of liked the way it rubbed off.

Before I knew it, it was near midnight and Petey was showing no signs of turning into a pumpkin.

"It was two minutes to twelve and Cinderella was dancing with a wonderful man. 'But I've got to go,' she said. 'What did you say your name was?' 'Peter, Peter, the pumpkin eater,' the man said. 'Care for another dance?' Cinderella said."

I laughed too loud.

"That's filthy," I said.

After all that beef and too much beer, I had to walk a little. We ambled over to Michigan Avenue and sauntered in the fresh night air. The Boul was alive with people and cars and summer racket. Light splashed off the limestone of the Wrigley Building, that monument to chewing gum and bad ballclubs. Across the street was the gothic tower of the Corporation, an outfit that had decided that, since it already owned everything else, it might as well buy a team. Neat, it said in so much corporate jargon. And the team became the Corporate Cubs. It made you long for the Wrigleys.

But I kept those curmudgeonly thoughts to myself as we walked. In no time we were at the end of the Boul, and I swung Petey into the Drake Hotel and its subterranean Cape Cod Room. Normally a place to grace for a cup of Bookbinder red snapper soup better than you can find in Philly, the Cape also had a bar that Red Carney liked to close.

I had not seen Red since we'd slobbered together at the ballpark after the Weaver debacle. Figuring he had regained his faculties and his color, I wanted to barber with him. One look at Petey, though, and he paid no attention to me.

"Now *this* is a pretty lady," Red barked in a voice that had kept him on the air for forty years.

Petey beamed as her knuckles were nibbled. I made the introductions.

"Where in hell have you been hidin' this beauty, Duffy?" Red bellowed.

Then he took Petey's arm and cradled it as if it were a swaddled infant as he led her around the nearly vacant restaurant to meet the maître d', the table captains, the waiters, and the busboys. Petey smiled and giggled. I groaned, figuring Red was half in the bag. He wasn't, just a little lonesome late at night, and easy game for something as convivial as Petey.

In time he settled down and insisted on a nightcap.

Petey ordered Irish coffee. Red had another beer. I went for a club soda to settle the linings.

"It's been, what, a week now since it happened, and the worst thing, Duffy, is that it's business as usual. Criminy! Oh sure, the team's got the black armbands on and we do a minute of silence at every park we go to. But that's it," he said.

His tone had lowered, bordering on off-mike and solemn.

"Maybe it's even more of a business than you and I ever knew," he said.

Like me, Red was old school, and it didn't take much to get him to spout reservations about the new school.

"It's a kid's game, Red. We're all kids in different bodies, with the young and strong ones playing out our fantasies," I said.

"But these guys are heroes too," he replied. "Always have been—but haven't always acted it, for sure. Youngsters idolize them—that's the way it should be—and they turn around and ruin that trust with drugs and astronomical salary demands."

It was Red's familiar complaint: salaries, strikes, contract renegotiations, hold-outs, drugs. They were all part of today's players, and they were way out of line as far as he was concerned. I'd remind him of early player strikes or about how twenty-one-year-old Ty Cobb was a contract holdout in 1908, for God's sake. Wanted five thousand—a king's ransom! Or Honus Wagner's career almost ending in 1909 over money. Just about every legend of our youth was involved in contract disputes at some time or another.

But Red would always counter with "Aw, Duffy, you know it was different then . . ."

"Your utility infielder makes four times as much as the President," he went on.

At that, Petey, who had been listening intently, piped in.

"There was a time when Babe Ruth made more money than the President, I think it was Coolidge—"

"Herbert Hoover," I injected.

"—yeah, Hoover, and the press asked him how he could justify making more than the President himself and you know what the Babe replied? He said, 'Why not, I had a better year than he did.'"

Red couldn't help breaking into that horse laugh of his, indulging Petey's bromide in spite of himself, his belly softly shaking up and down.

"But those guys back then had some team loyalty, young lady. Today you don't find that. If they don't think they're getting enough they go free agent and move to greener pastures," he said.

"Not unlike a certain broadcaster I know, who has been with a few stations in his day," I reminded.

Red scowled.

"I think it's the owners who don't have loyalty," Petey said, leaning into the subject. "They'll trade a guy in a minute if they think they need something. It doesn't matter if he's hard-working or important to the team. Remember how the Reds got rid of Tony Perez after all those great seasons? That just killed our team."

"Perez? Who'd he play for?" Red said.

Petey punched him. "And the owners will degrade a guy in the papers when they do it," she added.

"That's an occupational hazard when you get that kind of dough," Red countered.

"Sure, we all know salaries are out of hand," I said. "And it's no mystery who got them there."

"Naaaa, I know where you're going now, Duffy . . ." Red grumped.

"Right from the beginning of free agency—the Messersmith thing—the owners talked up a storm with those wooden teeth about taking a stand against runaway salaries. The next minute they turned around and outbid each other. That's what drove the offers up. Owners have always been like that. Even in 'the good old days' . . ."

"Yeah, but now you got players with free agency and attendance bonus clauses and unions and the ten-year-trade rule and they're still holdin' out. *That's* where the fans have lost patience with them. And who can blame 'em for bein' pissed off! Excuse my French, young lady," Red said.

"What fan, as a worker, wouldn't ask for twice the money he was making if he thought he could get it?" Petey said. "Or if he thought another company might give it to him."

"But not the kind of money we're talkin' about here, young lady. Hey, what is this, gang up on the play-by-play man?" Red said.

Petey laughed and clutched his arm. She was a clutcher, and Red loved it.

"The fans always lose, Red," I put in. "Not just because of higher ticket prices or player strikes. How about when the owner decides to move the franchise to another city because he gets a sweetheart deal? You've seen a few of those in your time."

I sensed my spiel was verging on the long-winded. Red was feeling his hops and inhaling Petey's fragrances.

"It's a business, like you said first thing," I added. "But if the money wasn't there, there wouldn't be a spectacle. And nobody would employ your inimitable pipes to ballyhoo the whole thing, and all those people wouldn't show up to sing along with you in the seventh inning, for cryin' out loud."

"Hey, now yer talkin'!" he bellowed, and quaffed another inch of beer.

He scratched and stifled a belch, smiled lazily at Petey, and tossed in his chair.

"So whattaya hear lately about this whole thing?" I asked, lowering my voice.

Red knew what I was getting at.

"They got coppers turning this thing inside out. But if they got anything, they're keepin' it a state secret," he said.

"Rumors?"

"C'mon, Duf. I hear everything from the Mob to the CIA to drugs to some floozy poppin' him. And you can pick your reason for that last angle," Red said.

It was warm in the Cape Cod, and he pressed his beer glass against his cheek then drained the contents.

Beer to Red Carney was the same as it was to Bill Veeck: a vital bodily fluid.

"Kid ran with a fast crowd, no question. You know that, Duffy. You got your gambling like what messed up Denny McClain, or your drugs, and you got your broads. No offense, young lady," he said, patting Petey's forearm.

"What's the line from the front office?"

"No comment on top of no comment. They'd just as soon this thing went away. Too many cops, too many questions. Gettin' so there's too many tributes and eulogies and the whole mess."

"Rohe won't talk about it. He sent down orders for everybody else—starting with Merkle and his coaches and me and all the guys in the booth—to button up. Veddie"—he turned to Petey—"that's my producer, Veddie Marsden, said Rohe didn't want any more references to it on the air. No what-ifs or boohoos, no speculation whatsoever. 'Red's baseball and that's it. He ain't Perry Mason,' Veddie said Rohe told him. But don't quote me on that, for cryin' out loud."

He went for his beer, but the glass was dry, and he motioned for a refill.

"So it's all just layin' there like yesterday's fried chicken," Red said. "We were playin' .500 ball before it happened, and we been playin' .500 ball since, so whattaya got?"

"Who do *you* think killed him?" Petey said. Her eyes had never left him since he'd begun.

New suds arrived and Red wet his whistle, then erased the suds from his lip with the tip of his ruddy tongue.

"Darling, if you ask my honest opinion, which you just did, I think we got another Waitkus thing here. Now that was considerable before your time."

"*The Natural.* Robert Redford," she said.

"If you say so," Red said. "See, Eddie Waitkus wasn't the only guy to get plugged by a dame. Billy Jurges took it from a dolly in the Carlos Hotel on Sheffield Avenue right here in Chicago. Most people don't know that.

"The more I think about it," he went on, "getting shot right there in the *ballpark*, for Pete's sake—the more I wonder about just what Weaver was up to. Somebody wanted him and wanted him bad. The kid messed around—everybody knew that—and I gotta think it was some chippie done it. Some crazy dame, like in that 'Fatal Extraction' movie, with a lot of mascara and guts and something pretty damned lethal hidden in her handbag.

"I mean, that's another thing gets me. A kid with that kind of talent has got to mind his *p*s and *q*s. He's got no business taking chances and leaving himself open to something like that. There's too much ridin' on him, for cryin' out loud."

"That's a lot of blame put on the victim," I said.

"How else you gonna call it, Duf?" he said.

"Won't try," I said.

At that the lights dimmed and we picked up. Red needed no escort home; he lived in the hotel. The only thing he needed was a good-night kiss from Petey. She laid it right on his forehead.

"Be still, my thumping ticker," Red said.

As I hailed a cab on the corner of Michigan and Oak, Petey breathed in the air off the lake. The beach was but a few hundred yards away. Then she squeezed my arm and sighed.

"What a dynamite place!" she said. "What an absolutely great place!" And she said it again and again.

I had to admit that sometimes the old town was just that. Once upon a time I would not have added the qualifier. I felt downright blessed to be living, working, and part of the bustle. Then I got old. The air got stale, the politics rancid, the ballclubs worse. What other people saw as energy and locomotion I saw as a pain in the ass. Cabbies got foreign. Shoeshine boys ground polish into your socks. Old ladies slept on the bus benches. Bleacher seats went from fifty-five cents to three bucks.

But Petey Biggers, all twenty-two years of her, honeymooning in the few months before she'd be swallowed by the law books and oral examinations, standing next to me this mild Chicago night, inhaling the air and gushing spit and vinegar, was a tonic. A spritz of youth.

I found her pretty brown arm and squeezed back.

She padded into my room, I guess because she couldn't sleep and saw my light. It was on because I couldn't sleep either. Sleep is not precious when you get my age. Not that I'll miss anything, only that the battery needs less charging. She couldn't sleep, I suspect, because the bulbs go off in her bright little noggin like scores in an arcade.

I was reading. Travis McGee for another go-around. Old John D. passed on too soon for my money. Yet not even *his* prose could jog my thoughts from the mess I'd taken on with the commissioner. Park it or drive it, fish or cut bait, shit or get off the pot. You know all the scolds.

And now I had a cub, so to speak, a cute thing I could love like a daughter—which she almost was—who wanted in. Yes, she did. I could see it in her eyes in the bright downtown lights. I could see it in her eyes on the way home in the cab. I could see it as she batted her peepers at me now. She didn't say a thing. She didn't have to. A girl that sharp gets the wheels turning and you can hear the gears hum.

Here she was, dressed in pajamas so skimpy and scandalous, even if she was my niece, as to not be pajamas in my book at all. She had on a pair of underthings you could have stuck inside the cap of a ketchup bottle and still had room for ketchup, out of which poked her golden, freckled long legs which looked so sleek and toned that you'd be tempted to tape them and enter them in the Preakness.

What with my sex drive long since gone the way of Lon Warneke, I harbored no indiscretions. But I didn't look the other way either. This little package was right there in front of me. She, on the other hand, was as casual as a greenbean.

"I've been adding things up, Uncle Duffy," she said.

She sat on the edge of my bed.

"I read your piece on Weaver's death. It was so good. Every paper in the country picked it up. Then today you tell me that you're on your way to San Diego. Doing a little work for the commissioner of baseball, but you don't say what. Then we go see Red, and you grill him on the murder. By my math, that means you're not retired anymore."

She stopped and looked at me as if she expected a diploma.

I yawned.

"Don't give it another thought. You're here on holiday."

"And you're digging into the Weaver thing," she said.

"Just curious, like everybody else."

"San Diego?"

"You're not going."

"I'll pay my own way . . ."

It had already gone too far. She'd had this in her head from the first. But Petey was a child of television, so it was "lights, camera, action" and cue the opening scene. It was "C'mon, Unk, we're off on a mystery adventure." To her, faces get punched, *wham!* and guns go off, *bang!* But nobody really gets hurt, nobody bleeds.

"I've got two months to kill and I'm not going to do it reading bad novels on the Oak Street Beach," she said.

"Read good ones then."

"But I could help. I'll be your point woman."

"You'll be nothing of the kind."

"I can communicate, Uncle Duffy. I love your face, but remember, I got almost fifty years on you. People can talk to both of us, but we hear different things."

"I have no idea what you're talking about."

"Yes, you do," she said. "Plus, I'd be great company."

"You think I'm a lonely guy? You think that a fella my age, wife gone, retired, living alone, not a care in the world, a thirteen handicap, needs company?"

"Yup."

6

Jimmy Slagle

The first order of business was the details. I wanted to know what the police knew, which, I figured, might be related to me in picaresque style by Jimmy Slagle, a young but increasingly influential member of the Chicago Police homicide corps. He was a double-knit sportcoat-and-tie replica of his old man, Shorty, an affable leech from the Southwest Side who first buddied up to me when his beloved White Sox went against the Dodgers in the '59 Series. His kid, Jimmy, was also a Sox fan, which meant he did not care if the Cubs lived or died, a fact that cast some doubt on his objectivity in the Weaver case. Sox fans are like that.

"Not even the Pope sees that file," Jimmy said over the phone.

"To the memory of your father and Nellie Fox," I said.

"So okay. Don't think I don't appreciate you tryin' to get Nelson into Cooperstown." He paused. "But what I really need is decent seats to wrestlin' at the Rosemont."

The first retort that burst into my mind is unprintable.

"Done," I growled, though I wasn't sure just how.

"When can you come down?" he asked.

I slipped out of the apartment the next morning while Petey was still sleeping. If you want to beat youth, do it before noon. Jimmy Slagle was waiting for me. He had his father's same misaligned ears, thin but wet hair, and a habit of clearing his throat in such a way that you shielded your eyes. Come to think of it, he was a sawed-off dead ringer for Earl Torgeson.

"I'm trustin' that you don't know me on this," he said, which was as much of a caveat as he had ever mustered.

"This thing is still tight as a Dutchman's ass. The press has the old man's nuts in a sling. He gets the updated file on his desk every A.M. It's like it's the only homicide in town. Hell, I can remember when a Cub pitcher got murdered every day and nobody raised a stink. Y'hear what I'm sayin', Duffy?"

He was jawing at me in a windowless conference room deep inside the Sixth Area station out on Belmont Avenue. The place was new, and nothing like the cop shops I used to visit when I was a cub. I remembered stone buildings with high-ceilinged rooms, wooden desks, black telephones, and alleged felons standing handcuffed to a ring in the wall. This place had fluorescent lights, cubicles, carpeting, telephones that buzzed instead of rang, and no felons that I could see.

Jimmy tossed a two-inch-thick folder on the table. It was chapter and verse on the murder. Nary a name, hunch, or opinion had been left out. Even yours truly was included.

To make a long, stilted narrative—"Perpetrator gained access . . ."—short, Weaver's murder was quick and efficient and accomplished by someone who knew how to thread a needle. In other words, potting Weaver at that time in that place took some doing. Illustrating that fact was a carefully drawn floor plan of the scene of the crime and the adjoining area beneath the stands.

As drawn by the detectives, the tunnel out of the Cubs' dugout on the third-base side of the field is L-shaped. It leads west beneath the box seats for twenty-one feet, then turns north for another twenty-one feet to the clubhouse. Weaver was shot just around the bend in view of the clubhouse door but out of sight of the dugout. When the tunnel gets to the clubhouse door, however, the fun begins. There it leads north once again on an upward grade for seventy-five feet until it reaches a steel door opening to the concourse. Before it gets there, alas, it passes two doors to the umpires' room—add four more suspects—and a large, cavernous storage shaft that follows the curve of the infield all the way around to the first-base side of the park.

This maintenance passageway is damp, dark, even eerie, and cluttered with supplies, building materials, landscaping equipment, and just about anything else that is used, stored, or discarded in a ballpark. It is low, maybe eight feet high, but about ten feet wide. Large enough for a jailbreak or, at least, a single escapee. The shaft is not the sewers of Paris, just the dreary, functional underbelly of an old stadium and a place all but unknown to the general public. It is a place, I must admit, I had passed thousands of times on my visits to the clubhouse and had paid little heed. Someone else, perhaps, had done just the opposite.

I studied the floor plan. It allowed for four separate routes into the dugout tunnel: the dugout itself, the clubhouse, the maintenance shaft (which has a half dozen entrance points before it ends at the tunnel leading between the visitors' dugout and clubhouse on the first-base side of the park), and the door leading directly out to the concourse. The report indicated that the detectives on the case were partial to that door, and for good reason: when Weaver was found, it was unlocked. Unfortunately, when its round knob was dusted for prints, it had produced nothing but smudges.

As for stadium security, things got even more interesting. One guard is always assigned to the tunnel just outside the umpires' room at the junction of the maintenance shaft, and one is stationed near the dugout opening. These are members of Cubs' security, which means they look like vendors but for their pith helmets. Their job consists mainly of checking the credentials of those going into the clubhouse—not what you would consider hazardous duty. Reporters, photographers, club officials and P.R. guys, and various privileged guests come and go through the area until an hour before game time, when the clubhouse closes to all but team personnel.

It was somewhere in the neighborhood of a half hour before game time when Weaver was killed, so plenty of people had access to the area. Including the ball girl, a pretty lady with butterscotch legs and a cherubic smile, who usually perches herself on a stool in the tunnel a few minutes before game time. That day, however, detectives had found that the ball girl was out on the field posing for photos with some diehard fans who'd come all the way from Copenhagen. The dugout security guard had left his post five or ten minutes before the incident to assume the backstop gate post because the guard there had taken an errant baseball in the chops. The guard stationed near the umpires' room had left his post to get a pair of sweat socks for the home plate ump.

In all, the two tunnel security posts were apparently untended for anywhere from three to ten minutes, and the tunnel itself was as empty as Bill Faul's cranium. It was not a grievous lapse in security, given the areas involved, as much as it was coincidental. Detectives found it hard to believe that the killer could have known the two were both absent. As for the two guards, they were scolded and transferred to bleacher duty.

Weaver had come in from the bullpen after doing some warm-up tosses. He had told the pitching coach he needed a fresh tin of snuff. The clubhouse was virtually empty when he came in and extracted a can of gum cancer from a refrigerator. He was observed by clubhouse man Yosh Kawano and a *Sun-Times* beat writer named Goddard, a good man. Weaver's disposition seemed normal—an emotional range somewhere between quietly determined and phlegmatic—and he did not say anything to either of them.

The perpetrator—the usage, I admit, is kind of infectious—had somehow slipped into the L-shaped section of the tunnel and confronted Weaver on his way back to the field. There were no signs of a struggle. The can of snuff in Weaver's back pocket was still chilled when they found him.

Nobody could explain to detectives when, how, or why the concourse door was unlocked. The killer could have left it so. If it was somehow unlocked before the incident, however, the tunnel was open to anyone in the ballpark with guts or knowledge enough to open the door and walk in.

As of my reading, there were no eyewitnesses. After the killer, the batboy—assuming they were not the same—was believed to be the next person on the scene. The batboy, a good Catholic boy from a neighborhood high school, was not considered a suspect and, according to the papers, was currently acting as though his stumbling on the corpse of Weaver was tantamount to discovering the Shroud of Turin.

Just about anybody and everybody else was a suspect, however, particularly a bevy of young ladies whom Weaver had apparently loved and left with great consistency. Or the departed could have been killed by a coach or teammate (though most were accounted for on the ballfield), an opponent (a Met, for godssakes, though that seemed unlikely), an umpire, a member of the media, a club official, a vendor, an usher, a security guard, or, lastly, a fan.

Those were the mechanics. Oh yes, the autopsy showed that Weaver's stomach contained a Big Mac, several dozen masticated sunflower seeds, the juice of his snuff, and a hard-boiled egg in what must have been an ungodly stew. And wonder of wonders, there was no trace of drugs.

The rest of the file dealt with the ongoing investigation. The dicks were talking to anybody and everybody who had anything to do with Dream Weaver. They were looking for leads, tips, hunches, insights, breaks, and maybe dumb luck. Most of all, they were looking for a motive. Nobody seemed to have one. Except, that is, the aforementioned dames.

"That's where it juices up," said Jimmy Slagle, who had never left the room. Then he grinned, exposing his wet lower teeth, and jabbed the reports lying in front of me.

"Broads, ya know? Catch the stats on 'em. Blondes, brunettes, redheads . . . Ol' Dream went through 'em like the lower end of the batting order," he said. "The guys are calling this the Snatch Detail."

He had been waiting to use that one, and he laughed so hard he began to cough.

"Talk to one and you get the name of another. Broads and more broads. And those broads give us the names of more broads.

"We put six guys on the case and we still haven't checked out the action just here in town. And the rest of the National League is still out there. All of them are lookers, *whew*, you hear what I'm sayin'? He liked blondes. Young, nineteen through, say, twenty-three. 'Course he made exceptions, mostly brunettes and redheads."

"Shut up now, Jimmy," I said, trying to concentrate on the file.

"As far as we can find, he didn't like boys. You probably heard those rumors too. No way. That was put out by some doll he threw out one night. In fact, he was touchy about the subject.

" 'Course, you probably heard he was supposed to be havin' a fling with the general manager's ol' lady. We knocked that out of the box first thing. If you ask me, the tootsie *herself* put out that story. What a piece of work she is."

"Shut up, Jimmy," I said.

"No drugs. No coke, no chemicals, not even pot as far as we can tell. Champagne was about it. We hit that angle pretty hard, what with all the noses in sports nowadays, and we came up empty. So that's about it. I'll shut up and let you read for yourself," he said.

"But you know, Duffy," he went on seconds later, "we ain't got on record a single dose of the clap or any of them incurable social diseases. Can you *believe* that? The guy had to be blessed. You and I get the action Weaver got in a week, and we'd be clapped up in no time. They shoulda called him the Titan of Twat!"

The line convulsed him, and he slapped the wall a couple times until he got it out of his system.

"So anyway, I'll get out of your hair. Right now we're checking out the cranks, kooks, and cornballs. We got plenty of those. Like the 'No Lights' crowd. They're still makin' noise. We had a guy over on Bradley, respectable, doctor, in a classy house, coupla dogs, who writes this letter saying if the lights ever go on, he's going to personally pick off somebody big. Like Dream Weaver. Yeah! He flat out named Weaver. 'Course it was in 'eighty-eight during the flap, but we had to check him out. We go over and talk to him and it turns out he's a little half-cocked, but no shooter. His wife now, that's a different story. Smart lady but wacko! Claims every Cub fan takes a piss in her front yard before they go home at night. Je-sus."

"That all, Jimmy?"

"Yeah, I guess, except that we're hittin' his buddies and mopes and hang-arounds. That's no joke either. A guy like Weaver has friends he never heard of. Starting with the fat guy who worked for him—"

"Obie Blintstein," I said.

"Yeah. He ain't been that helpful. He was in on Dream's action, and maybe he don't want to fink on some of the dollies, you hear what I'm sayin'? There's a few other slants. But nothing to get excited about. We're drawin' blanks the size of home plate. So who knows how long we're gonna stay on it like this?

"Horniest damn investigation I ever pulled though, Duffy. Like running through this big field of tits, you know what I mean? And every once in a while you stub your toe, fall flat on your face, and end up with a mouthful. You know what I mean, Duf?"

I looked up at this human mosquito, Jimmy, son of Shorty, thought of Torgeson, the Earl of Snohomish, and how Kluszewski came in at the end of '59 and took his job.

"What was that, Jimmy?" I replied.

* * *

For the next thirty minutes I sat in that little room beneath the hum of the fluorescent lights, copying names, addresses, and phone numbers of males and females out of the file. It made me feel like a snoop, like some kind of piker working for a grocery store tabloid who had just copped Dream Weaver's personal datebook. I wondered if I was taking down a list of suspects in the murder of a jock with a set of hyperkinetic gonads or a survey of infidels responsible in part for the erosion of American Sport. I chose the latter. I had to think loftily with regard to this part of the job. Hell, I had to carve out some self-respect.

I told Jimmy Slagle that I would be keeping in touch. As far as he knew, I was doing an article, maybe even a book, on the Weaver killing. It was my cover. I knew very well that there would be plenty of books on the kid.

As I told the commish, the work of an operative is not my bailiwick. To begin with, I was not sure I wanted to duplicate what the murder dicks had already done. I was not sure I wanted to jaw with Dream's floozies concerning his prowess. Kiss and tell is not my idea of good conversation.

Oh, it might give me a clue as to what Dream Weaver was up to off the field. But would it tell me who killed him? Would it provide any insights apart from the state of hanky-panky currently practiced in the big leagues? Would it be worth my time? I didn't think so. I just was not buying the distaff angle.

What I did decide right then and there was that I had a problem with this whole thing. My problem was that normally I would not pay a lick of attention to a ballplayer's private life. I was not trained that way. When I started writing forty-five years ago, a sportswriter had to be concerned about what a man did *on* the field, not off. And we didn't apologize for it, thank you.

Let me give you a for instance. After he became a cripple, Franklin Delano Roosevelt was never photographed from the waist down. It just was not done: news photographers did not take advantage of the president of the United States because of a disease he had no control over.

The same went for sports figures. We did not report on Babe Ruth from the waist down either. We all knew what he was doing—some of us were even doing a little bit of it ourselves—and we knew how he loved to carouse and that some of his injuries were probably of the social-disease variety rather than anything related to muscle and bone. Professional athletics has always had its share of drinkers and womanizers, and it always will have. Guys in uniform have always snuck out of the fans' sight lines to cop a cigarette. We didn't think the public was interested in that; and the public seemed to agree.

But you couldn't get away with that today. This is a much more critical age. Or hypocritical, if you ask me. I began to sense that in the last years of my column when the letters from my readers started asking different questions, questions that led me to believe that people thought I was holding something back. People feel they have a right to know just about everything, and that today's reporters should give them what they want. Even editors, who have been known to have the spinal columns of Bowie Kuhn, started hitting me for soiled laundry.

I'm convinced the villain is television. These practitioners of the new sports journalism are starting to sound more and more like broadcasters. Call me crusty, but those were two very different genres when I came up. These current "journalists" all sound like they were the team managers of their high school football squads. Those perfectly unathletic guys who walked around with a ball in one hand and towels in the other. They always referred to athletes by clubhouse nicknames, calling Carlton Fisk "Pudge" and Dave Righetti "Rags." A kind of buddy-buddy cadre of show-biz hounds.

Unfortunately, these guys, and women too, are less interested in what goes on on the field than what a celebrity had for dinner or what lady he is currently squiring. They hate players like Steve Carlton, who wouldn't speak to them in their language. Articulate athletes they quickly portray as arrogant, and those who don't fit the norm they dub "flakes" or worse.

And the effect they have had on the King's English, oh lord. My old friend Red Smith, God love him, had little patience with the language abusers already in his day. "Murder of the mother tongue," he wrote, "is a form of matricide committed with premeditation by coaches and players, encouraged by writers and broadcasters as accessories after the fact. . . . Eager to crash the inner circle and eagerer to prove themselves in the know, they borrow the coachly barbarisms and employ them in tones of arrogant authority." Now that nails it to a tree, and nobody drove a nail better than Red. How the use of the "sports present" would have curled what hair Red still had. For example, "If that drive isn't caught by the third baseman two innings ago, it's a whole new ballgame." Good grief!

But alas, they don't stop with the homicidal homily; these birds want dirt and scuttlebutt. Too many seem to think that not only do they have to get under the skins of athletes, but under their sheets. A guy gets sued for divorce nowadays, and two-to-one you'll see a reporter get cozy with the estranged missus.

And for what? A legitimate story? No. He wants a byline full of boohoo bellyaching—which nowadays passes for journalism—and she wants a bigger settlement. Plus a little something barbed up the poor sap's giggy.

Sportswriters today seem to think they have every right to bait an athlete to get a story. They deliberately pick a fight. My old friend Jimmy Cannon had a name for them. He called them chipmunks because of the noises they made. A chipmunk isn't happy unless he's insulting someone.

But if you ask me, the noble art of sportswriting was changed not so much by sportswriters themselves, which is unfortunate, but by an interloper. I mean Jim Bouton and the book he wrote. Now here was a sore-arm pitcher and a guy with no class whatsoever telling stories out of school. He put Mantle on motel roofs peeping into open windows. The Mick, the Commerce

Comet, for crying out loud. Bouton's garbage got so much play that sportswriters went green. Players too. It wasn't long before the mimic was on.

I once put together an article for a baseball magazine called "Dames and the Game." It was a look at some of the trouble ballplayers got into with women. But it wasn't a bunch of gossip or locker room talk. I wrote about the Babe, Eddie Waitkus, Bo Belinsky, and a lot of other saps. I *reported* these events, events that actually damaged athletes' careers, not just anecdotes that might have gotten them in dutch with their wives. There's a big difference.

Now I don't know if Grand Canyon Chambliss is right when he says that baseball went sour when those two Yankees swapped wives, but I can appreciate his point of view. It just ain't the same game anymore, and Chambliss is concerned about it. Whether or not what he talked me into doing would make a pisspot's worth of difference was anyone's guess—which was making me grouchier than I usually am.

My problem in this Weaver thing was the private, dirty-linen side of it, and I had to get over that if I was going to make a dent in it. I figured I could. The reporter in me is still alive and kicking, even though I've never been a journalist of the ambulance-chasing persuasion or a bedroom bird-dogging detective. My head is still screwed on straight, and I can put one foot in front of the other. The youth movement in America, as Casey Stengel used to say, is for kids.

But I also figured that a little help might be in order. Just looking at that file of floozies convinced me. That's why I gave in to Petey. I could dig into the baseball business of this crime against the national pastime. I could grill every player and manager and club official as if I were trying to scoop a nine-player off-season trade. But I was queasy about the female side of it.

* * *

I added all kinds of qualifiers, disclaimers, caveats, and deductibles when I talked to Petey. I must have said, "But I'm warning you, young lady . . ." about eight times. But none of it kept Petey from jumping around the room deducing, contemplating, scheming, and replaying just about every game of "Clue" she could remember.

7

Obie

It was time to hop a plane to San Diego.

We got out to O'Hare for the 10:20 nonstop to Padretown and Obie Blintstein. Obie was Dream Weaver's Man Friday, a onetime fan and hanger-on who had become Dream's friend and loyal companion, then his social secretary, housemate, and gofer. No, there was nothing fishy about it. In his earlier days Obie had been married, the father of two lovely girls, and a hard-working haberdasher. And a baseball fanatic. A little Obie, a star of Little League he could dote on and cheer from the stands, was not to be, and Obie's daughters and wife had no interest in 3–2 counts.

He met Dream when the big hurler started custom-ordering his shirts. The two of them got along like a tailor and his chalk. When Obie casually mentioned one day that he was sick of selling clothes, Dream said, "Hell, come to work for me." Obie's daughters were grown, the wife had converted to Seventh-Day Adventism, and Obie said why not?

Almost every big star has somebody like Obie somewhere on the premises. Well, not just like Obie, for Blintstein had become a fifty-six-year-old overweight matzo ball, 300 pounds of help and companionship. He had thrown himself into Dream's career and the demands the public made on his charge. Consequently, Weaver's death shattered him, cold-cocked him, dropped him right out of the sky. It also ended his meal ticket, which was no mere trifle. That said nothing of his world of freebies, corner booths, first-class aisle seats, and the company of the famous and beautiful.

Aside from all that, Obie had been a valuable source to me. When I set out to do the Weaver profile for *Sports Illustrated,* I speculated that Obie might be the key to the story. If I was lucky, Weaver would come alive through Obie's eyes. I was lucky. Tapping Obie was like plunging an auger into Old Faithful. He invited me in and showed me around. He jabbered and clucked, dropped anecdotes, and, most significantly, he loosened up Weaver himself. "Can't live with him and can't live without him," Dream always said.

Obie was Dream's keeper, and a smart one. He knew that if I wrote a hell of an inside piece on Dream —and he cannily weighed the efforts of the right writer in the right publication—it would be nothing but good for the kid. I didn't have to pry or lurk or steal the trash from out back. I was an ally, and one not offended by Obie's bulk or his loud shirts or his giggle. In return, he was my entrée with Weaver at a time when the rest of the press was being kept at arm's length.

For the trip, I took along my battered briefcase. It had plenty of room for a toothbrush, a change of underwear, and a clean shirt. Petey slung her grip, which was the size of a batbag, over her shoulder and walked sideways down the aisle of the airplane.

Inside the satchel, I was to learn, was a second pair of cowboy boots, jeans, two blouses, a trench coat, a white business suit, her cosmetic case—including hair dryer—a radio with headphones, a copy of *An Unfinished Woman* by Simone de Beauvoir, a current edition of *The Sporting News,* and a bag of Dutch licorice.

We didn't talk much at first. We had fresh newspapers, and the stews were quick with the drinks. I sipped my Jack Daniel's and Petey read her *Sporting News* as if she were editing it. But I couldn't keep quiet.

"This Weaver thing . . ." I began, "from what I read in the police report . . ."

I paused.

"Lay it on me, Uncle Duf," Petey said, her head still in the paper.

"Okay. He got around, as you probably can imagine."

"That I can," Petey said.

"Baseball Annies, groupies, ball girls, stewardesses, secretaries—"

"Stockbrokers, doctors, lawyers, CPAs, insurance brokers," she added.

"—yeah, well, let's just say he had his share of women."

"Or they had him."

"All right, I'm gonna lose this one. Let's just say kids are different nowadays: sex is like egg noodles to you. Even with all these diseases and incurable viruses that treat penicillin like it was a soft fastball—"

"Great simile, Unk."

"—whatever—Weaver's appetite for the opposite sex went off the map."

She put down her paper and took a swig of my drink.

"Part of the game, Uncle Duffy. Pitcher serves it up and dares somebody to hit it. Can't blame the ladies for taking a few swings," she said. "Remember what Casey said, 'Good pitching will always beat good hitting—and vice versa.'"

"Just never mind," I said.

"Okay, now I got one for you," she said. "From what you learned doing those pieces on Dream, is there anything in his past that we can go on?"

"Good question. I've been knocking that one around, thinking to myself that maybe there might be some ghost that came back to haunt the kid. Fact is, however, I once wrote that it was almost as if Weaver didn't have a past."

"How do you mean?"

"Well, in writing the profile I did for *Sports Illustrated,* I found that he didn't have much of a family. His folks were California teenagers. The father vanished while Dean was an infant, so Dean never knew him. The mother latched onto another guy, got pregnant again, and Dean became sort of the odd kid out. The extra baggage. He bounced around, lived with an uncle, went to a boys' school for truants, then fell in with the whole California beach and surfing scene."

"Sort of like a kid named George Herman Ruth, plus the surf, that is," Petey said.

"Hmmmm. Anyway, even with nobody pushing him, no father or mentor to speak of, he still turned into a ballplayer. It's remarkable really, but somewhere he must have developed a good dose of discipline and resolve. Because nobody makes it on just a live arm . . ."

"Any coaches?"

"There you go. Dean told me in great detail about a coach he had in high school. The guy's last name was Gonzalez, if I remember, but Dean called him 'Chewy.' Always Chewy this and Chewy that. Little Mexican guy come up from Monterey who worked with Dean's high school team. Did it on his own time. I made a lot out of it in the piece, because Chewy seemed like the one person responsible for keeping Weaver on track when he could have disappeared into gangs, drugs, and a life of crime. His background could well have destined him for the underside of this society. But Chewy worked with him, inspired him, developed his technique—and his head, for that matter. Gave him a little stability, I think, when that commodity was in short supply. He died a few years back, I seem to remember."

"What a switch," Petey said. "A Mexican immigrant being the force behind a California white kid, instead of the other way around. Kind of puts some English on the American way, huh?"

"Well, Dream always gave Chewy Gonzalez all the credit. In the beginning he dedicated his awards to him, and when he signed his first big bonus he went out and bought the guy and his family a new house. Just like that. Dream would have done anything for Chewy. Loved to talk about him.

"Anything about his father or mother," I continued, "whew, you had to pry it out of him with a crowbar. You gotta figure that his mother basically abandoned him too."

Petey turned to me.

"Don't chew on this too hard, but maybe that gives you an idea of what he was looking for in all those women," she said.

"And never found, I'm sure," I finished.

It was a good talk. I liked having Petey, her sound, percolating brain, in the seat next to me.

Obie Blintstein was expecting us. Most every cabbie knew the whereabouts of Dean Weaver's house, so I didn't have to scrape my memory. I'd done a column on Weaver and Obie when they built the joint, high above the Bay, a cross between a hacienda and a Palm Springs country club. I called it a jock version of the Playboy mansion—right down to the pinball room, the Leroy Neimans, and the cavernous, multilevel swimming pool. One end of the pool even had beach sand and one of those machines that creates a three-foot surf. The other end was a tangle of waterfalls and slides. Throw a fastball as wicked as Weaver did and you can have a room full of naked nymphs slithering around like river otters.

Today there was no surf, no slithering, no nymphs. Just that looming, lonely house, and man-mountain Obie with a face as long as an avalanche, bidding us enter. We were friendly callers, unlike the reporters, attorneys, and insurance operatives who'd beat a trench to the door since Dream's demise. I patted Obie on the arm, which was a mistake. He clutched me, and wept into my shoulder, a slobbering sumo wrestler attacking a helpless old man.

The only thing that brought him back was his first look at Petey.

"The towels are in the other room, babe," he said, sniffing and smiling.

Petey, to her credit, smiled back.

"It's been a nightmare, Duffy," Obie said.

He shuffled in with his fat man's shuffle, pushing his expanse ahead of him with the rustle of the fabric whispering on his thighs. Only Obie's garb had any spark.

Over the bay of his belly was a Hawaiian shirt, an enormous explosion of silken blues and oranges that would have blinded a parrot. His trousers were pineapple yellow.

"I'm what you call a fat man," Obie said to Petey. "I say that so people don't feel self-conscious."

"You're not Peter Pan," Petey replied.

Obie giggled. "Loads of pan, no peter."

Petey laughed beautifully.

Her spirit was welcome. Under normal conditions Obie was jolly, good for bonhomie, bons mots, and bonbons, a man born for bloat, and exuberant fat guys are fun to have around. He was a laugher, a shill, a teddy bear and, most important, no threat to Dream Weaver. At first I thought it odd that a kid like Dream would have a guy like Obie around. But then it made sense. Obie was a presence, a caretaker, a mother, and even, if you stretched things, a wife for a guy who badly needed all of the above but had no leaning toward marriage.

As for me, I liked the guy because he was closer to my age. I could talk to Obie and read Dream's generation. He also was a marvelous set of eyes and ears. Dream could run hot and cold, mercurial, phlegmatic, all those adjectives that make for a tough interview. Obie, if you had his private number, which I did, always answered the phone. Through the Dream years Obie was invaluable to me, and I never betrayed him, never let him down.

He was also very adept, I came to learn, at entertaining Dream's dates—just as he was beginning with Petey right now—until Weaver was ready for them. Obie would look into their lovely green or brown or amber eyes, and they would look upon his wattles, part in love and part in pity, not even hearing the slight gasps as he spoke because what he said to them was usually kind and understanding and occasionally even touching. He loved to jabber with pretty young women, and they jabbered back as if he were Santa and they were three-year-olds.

Then Dream would appear, all showered and talced and reeking of testosterone, and Obie would relinquish the floor, wave, and melt into the draperies so Dream could take over. At least, that's how I generally understood it.

"It's been death around here. A kind of quiet this house hasn't *ever* known," Obie said.

He turned to Petey. "Dream had it built, you know."

With that he went right into the tour for her, padding on kelly green carpet so thick you thought you had stumbled into the rough at Pebble Beach, and showed off the paintings, the autographed bats and balls, the trophies, the golf tourney mementos—this one from Bob Hope, that one Andy Williams—the still photos of this television program and that special—yeah, that's Heather Locklear, and George Winston, very good— the All-Star programs and souvenir dolls, the pennants.

And we were only in the bar area. The den/trophy room looked like a museum, with cases full of glittering tribute to the best pitcher in baseball. There were souvenir baseballs everywhere—for no-hitters, twenty wins, All-Star games, strikeouts, you name it. Trophies of all sizes, every alloy, and a few sleek crystal and marble creations. One of Dream's massive basketlike gloves was propped up with nothing to catch; behind it the shirt of a Cub uniform.

In one corner of the room sat a pair of battered wooden seats, with a pockmarked home plate in front of them.

"Those are from a Little League park in San Ysidro. It was the first park Dream ever pitched in. They tore it down, built another, and named it 'Dream Weaver Field,' " Obie said.

I ran my hand over the wooden slats of the seats. Their being here was a token of sentimentality in Dream's soul that I had not been aware of.

The walls were ablaze with three-foot-high technicolor photos, paintings, and reproductions from *Sports Illustrated*, the cover of *Time*, the front page of the Chicago *Sun-Times* with WHAT A DREAM!!! in three-inch headlines. There was a photo of Dream and the President of the United States after an All-Star game, an artful photo—close up—of his left hand fondling the seams of a baseball, and several others.

No medium had overlooked the Great Left Arm, no honor eluded it. Every mention was collected and collated in this ample room, including a few words of my own. And its curator was Obie, who beamed in its midst.

All that was missing was the final and most dramatic headline, a headline which, in some papers, surpassed the type size and space given the same reports for FDR and JFK. That banner was as yet unmounted. If it ever would be.

Petey looked and listened and commented with appropriate awe, adding a tidbit here and a stat there. She knew her beans.

"I once got the same tour from Johnny Bench down in Cincinnati," I said. "And I thought *he* had the metal."

"A lot burned in that fire he had," Petey said.

"My heart just ached when I heard about that," Obie added.

I looked up at him and I swear his eyes were beginning to moisten. He was a bowl of emotional pudding. I should have known better than to let him take us into the trophy room. What we needed was popcorn and Mountain Dew and a little loose talk. I hoped his lips had not sealed with his master's coffin.

"Oh, I just don't know," Obie said some minutes later as he reclined onto an overstuffed sofa. He laid the best of Orville Redenbacher between his lips a puff at a time.

His voice was a sad monotone, so meek, so wan.

I had asked him what he now thought about it all, more than a week later, and what, if anything, might yet develop.

"Oh, I just don't know," he repeated. He stared off.

This wasn't Obie, not the jabbering jellyroll I once knew.

"All that's been said and written," he went on, still staring off, "the only thing wrong with Deano was that he liked girls."

He smiled weakly at Petey.

"Mucka-mucka," she said.

"Hey!" Obie exclaimed, suddenly coming alive. "You *know*."

"A girl at school told the story. I always wondered if it was true," she said.

"Definitely! Mucka-mucka!" Obie yelled.

"What the hell?" I said.

"Code, Uncle Duffy," said Petey. "At home games sometimes you could hear it from all corners of the stadium. Is that true, Obie?"

"Oh my yes, it got so bad Dean had to put a stop to it."

"Mucka whatta?" I said.

"The truth can be told now, I guess," Obie sighed. "That was a little password among some of our friends. Some of the girls who used to come over and party. And well, Dream didn't just have parties, he had *parties*.

"It was one night when we had a hot cassette going on the giant-screen TV, Bruce Springsteen howling on the stereo, about a dozen babes running around and Dean was in the middle of it all as usual when he took this little blonde—she couldn't have been more than ninety pounds—and held her up in the air with one hand like one of those college cheerleaders at a bowl game, except this babe probably went to a college of cosmetology. But when she got up there just about high enough to hang on to the chandelier she started yelling, 'Mucka-mucka!! Mucka-mucka!!'

"Nobody knew what it meant, but it caught on, and afterward whenever things really got going people started screaming 'Mucka-mucka!! Mucka-mucka!!' Heck, even when things weren't going, some little doll would whisper 'Mucka-mucka' and then look out.

"Then it spread to where whenever Dean was pitching and going well, maybe with a three-two count in an important situation, someone would yell 'Mucka-mucka.' If you looked real hard you could see him kinda smile because you knew he heard it. You'da thought it would have destroyed his concentration, and I think maybe it did finally, because he told me to tell the girls to cool it.

"Even so, there wasn't one time that I can remember after a mucka-mucka when he didn't bear down and fire a pellet, just as if he wanted to get things over with and get home to do a little mucka-mucka-ing."

"Right out there on the mound!" exclaimed Petey. "Wonderful."

"Wonderful?" I said.

Obie looked at me and shrugged, then he started to giggle. It shook him from his melancholia. He started telling the stories, some of which I had heard, most not. Petey hung on every word, sitting on one leg on a sofa, bouncing up and down with a punch line. Obie enjoyed himself so much it looked like he might need oxygen to get through some of the good parts. At one point he got the hiccups, which made the stories even better. The two of them could have been a comedy team, Great Gorge and Gracie, or something like that.

Obie was rolling.

When things calmed down a bit, with Obie holding his breath to cure his hiccups, and Petey wiping the tears from her eyes, I cut in.

"Did Dream cast around a lot? I mean, make dates with girls he'd never met before?"

Obie's face clouded.

"What do you mean, Duf? He met new girls every day."

"But how long did he have to know them before—"

"You're kidding, Uncle Duffy," Petey said.

"No, I'm not. You mean to tell me that there's fences, security guards, unlisted phone numbers, bodyguards and every barrier you can imagine between the fans and the stars, but if a pretty young lady wants to get close, she walks right in? No background check?"

Obie shrugged, "Sometimes they weren't even all that pretty."

"Dream entertained girls he'd met only a few hours earlier?"

"Minutes, sometimes," Obie said.

"No wonder . . ." I said, looking off and feeling like some kind of hayseed.

"We're talking about dating, not murder," Petey said.

"In Dream's case, where's the difference now?" I said, perhaps too quickly.

"Low blow," said Obie.

"Wait a minute," I said. "I didn't mean it like that. I was out of line there. What I mean is that it seems to me a guy in Dream's position, when he gets in the mood, has to be careful."

"He was always in the mood," said Obie. "I had all I could do to direct traffic. But you knew that, Duf. It's like that in the big leagues. Not just the Annies, but the steadies, the travelers, the respectable girls with their mothers, even the ones who just want to bake chocolate-chip cookies. I just hoped to God that they were healthy."

"How about ones with husbands or boyfriends?" I said. "Did Dream go that route?"

"You heard the rumors," Obie said.

"Can't miss them," I lied.

"They're just that," Obie said. "Look, I leaned on Dream on that score. The ballclub liked to trot him out for the big fund raisers and the corporate shows. He had to go and he went.

"You wouldn't believe the come-ons. Young, old, it didn't matter. Middle of some reception, maybe a thousand people standing around, and women would slip their numbers into his pocket. Wives of guys worth millions. Just want to touch the Dream, maybe do more than touch."

"Stuff rumors are made of," I said.

"It was all nothing, pure crap in big portions. Not Rohe's wife or Sheckard's honey. None of 'em! I leaned on him on that, Duffy. He had all he could handle without going into that kind of snake pit."

Obie was sweating now. I made a mental note of the general manager's wife and a girlfriend of the Cubs' center fielder. More names, more sticky questions.

"There had to be no love lost between Dream and Sheckard," Petey said.

"None. Not a whit," Obie said. "And who could

blame Deano? In Wrigley a center fielder can make or break a pitcher. That pissant little Sheckard cost Dream a no-hitter and two wins last year. You can look it up."

"So Dream flirted with his filly?" I said.

"No way on God's green earth," said Obie. "Well, maybe he *flirted* with her."

He looked down and began picking at the few kernels still in his bowl. He was silent; we all were. He shifted his weight and the bowl fell to the floor, the kernels disappearing into the pile of the carpeting.

"This place is a tragedy," he said.

"What will happen now?" Petey said. "This place? To you?"

Obie flinched. I caught it and memorized it. The speculation was an obvious one: how much of this opulence now belonged to him. Then he passed me a look of fatigue.

"It's all lawyers," he said with a dismissing wave of his hand. "Dream didn't have a will. It was the last thing he thought he needed. Who would have thought such a thing? So it's all probate. Lawyers, lawyers, lawyers."

He slouched off to one side, like an ocean tanker about to capsize.

"The worst of it all," he continued, "apart from the fact that he's gone, that remarkable human being, that great athlete, is the pain that all this is now over with." He spread his hands out wide to indicate our surroundings. "All of it. Just a brief fantasy time. Kids go to Disneyland; I worked for Dean Weaver. Nothing like it will ever happen again. Not to me.

"Captain Whale, that's what Deano used to call me. But without him and that life we lived—and you don't have to say it, Duffy—well, it's time to start a new book."

I strained to hear him, he blubbered so low.

"What's all that supposed to mean?" I asked.

"The extreme," he said.

Then he bared his teeth, and with his choppers clenched, he said, "I'm going to have these wired shut."

"No!" exclaimed Petey.

"Feed myself through a straw," he said, talking normally again. "It's either that or take out a half-mile of intestines, and I couldn't stomach that."

"How much you aim to shed?" I said.

"Start with a hundred and a quarter and work down," he said.

"You'll be a new man," said Petey.

Obie smiled at her, a smile with a hundred lines to it.

"No, I won't," he said softly.

We had made reservations to stay at a hotel, but Obie wouldn't hear of it. He set us up in two of the four guest bedrooms, but not before we all had dinner in town. A seafood joint, so I had the surf 'n' turf, which is as fishy as I can get. Petey chewed on a plate of squid. She had acquired all the current tastes.

Obie, well, Obie ate as if it were his last supper. Which it may have been. He ordered grouper, sea bass, and a hunk of swordfish. He ordered a plate of hush puppies, the creamed spinach, a bowl of bouillabaisse. He ate and giggled and perspired, finishing off with not one but two bowls of something called cappuccino ice cream.

The food kept him loose, and as he ate he recited a virtual dossier concerning Dream's doings and the people he did them with. He had made up a list of people who had reason not to like Weaver. It consisted of a few former dates with broken hearts or slashed egos and a few young ladies in the same condition because Dream had *not* dated them—"I swear, they get more hostile when you don't take them out than if you dump them." There were a few jealous boyfriends, and, finally, Obie admitted to a few spouses. Even with Obie's screening, some married ones snuck by.

"Back at the house," he added, "I'll show you a box of nasty letters. Nasty!"

When I asked him if Dream made enemies for activities other than those social, enemies with bull necks and nicknames, Obie suddenly stopped stuffing swordfish into his mouth.

"Who told you that? That's bullshit. Nothin' to it!" he snapped.

Then he continued to consume, chewing harder, it seemed to me, than before.

Only seconds later he went on to detail the action around the league: which teams were loose after hours, which managers scotched the action, and which ones turned their backs. He suggested at least six more potential Hall-of-Famers with Dream's inclinations. Four of the six, interestingly enough, were also pitchers.

It was the information I had come for. I did not take notes, and I didn't need to. You don't write sports for forty-five years without acquiring a memory for these things. Don't take me on in a sports trivia contest unless you want your ears plastered. Should the coroner cut open my noggin, he'll find a pile of rosters and consecutive copies of *The Sporting News*.

Which only means that Obie's information gave me something to go on.

Then I caught him, laying it in between his last hush puppy and his first bowl of ice cream: "Who did it, Obie?"

He looked at me oddly, half lost in thought, half in calories. He had been closer to Dean Weaver than any mortal, and knew the kind of person who would want to kill him. Or so I thought.

"Remember that line from *St. Valentine's Day Massacre*? When Bugsy Moran heard about the bodies lined up against the wall. 'Only Capone kills like that,' Moran said. Yeah, well, as far as Dream was concerned, whoever murdered him hated him, 'cuz only hate kills like that. I gotta say it: he made enemies on account of what he became. They were two: women and other players.

"Look no further than that, Duffy. Find the jealousy, the revenge, the spite. Then you'll find your killer," he said.

"Who?" I repeated. "Give me a name."

His expression changed, his system calmed somewhat by the massive infusion of provender, and his face became as blank as the one on the fish he had just downed. In that moment there was not a sound in the restaurant, and he mouthed the words like a priest: "I don't have a name."

It was a poignant yet pathetic moment, one tinged with mystery and sadness, and Obie stared vacantly at the table. Yet even with his touch for the dramatic, his downcast eyes and fading inflection, I didn't buy it. It wasn't enough. Obie was too sharp, too attuned to take the pose of an aggrieved widower. The gap between what he was saying and holding back was big enough for even him to walk through.

I sucked on an after-dinner mint and said nothing.

Sometime later the check came, something I thought might arrive with trumpets and a bow around it. Obie offered to pay for his own meal, but I wouldn't hear of it. The carte blanche of the commissioner's office knew no bounds.

I was tired, and as soon as we got back to the house I went to bed. Obie and Petey made halfhearted resolutions to do the same. I thought I knocked off in a hurry, the bed being comfortable and the day more busy than any since I had quit the column. But at some point during the night I was awakened by what sounded like laughter. Giggling, to be more specific. Two kinds: Obie's and Petey's. I lifted my head off the pillow and listened closely. Again I heard it. As if I were supposed to.

The next morning I awoke to a perfect quiet. It took nearly an hour before Obie and Petey came out of their rooms for air. Neither of them said anything about the giggle-fest of the night before.

Obie went about preparing breakfast, but we didn't want much. I noticed that he did not eat anything.

As I gathered my things he gave me a sheaf of letters—the ones, in light of what had happened, that were threatening enough to look into—and a small black notebook.

"Just about every name and number you'll need is

in there," he said, then added, "People would kill for that book."

"Maybe they did," I said.

Petey came on us, smelling good and looking fresher than anyone has a right to look. She dropped her oversized bag to the floor and put her arms around Obie.

"I had a great time," she gushed. "Can I come back?"

"I wish you would," Obie said.

I looked sideways at him; he had spoken with his teeth clenched.

"Bring eight of your friends. With bosoms. You know I love the bosoms," he said, still not parting his jaws.

Petey's face asked the question.

"Just getting in practice," he said, twisting his fingers in front of his teeth.

Twisting tight the wires.

"You're serious about it?" Petey said.

Jaws locked, he said, "Definitely."

A cab honked in front. Petey gave Obie a big kiss, and we walked out past the massive oak door.

"God love ya both," Obie Blintstein said, and threw us a kiss, his mouth now wide open.

8

Jimmy & Bonehead

The next day, back in Chicago, Petey and I pored over the letters given us by Obie Blintstein. They were full of angry sobs and pained peals, gasps of frustration and scorn, fawning adoration and undying promises. They were also rife with pointed threats—"If I can't have you, nobody can . . ." "I'll kill you and kill myself, slowly, so we can share each other's dying breaths . . ." You get the idea. A few you've-broken-my-heart-so-I'll-cut-up-yours, some you'll-never-hurt-anyone-again, and one I'm-gonna-smash-your-balls-sucker.

Obie had penciled helpful, explanatory notes on some of the more inflammatory letters. Repeaters, he called them. He also pointed out the ones that troubled even him. A few had come from men, apparently husbands or lovers who suspected Dream of hanky-panky with their beloveds.

Petey was fascinated by the material. She pored over those pages as though they were the lost diaries of Warren Beatty.

"Such misplaced passion," she said, her eyes never leaving the Corinthian scrawls—i's with heart-shaped dots—on scented pink, blue, and peach-colored pages.

"Enough to kill for?"

" 'Hell hath no fury like a woman scorned,' " Petey quoth.

" 'Heaven hath no rage like love to hatred turned . . .' That's the first half of that line," I said.

"Really?"

"So who wrote it?"

"Shakespeare?"

"Common mistake. It was William Congreve. The Neil Simon of his day. A good century after Shakespeare."

"You're remarkable," Petey said.

Dream's little address and phone number book was equally obscure: a bevy of names and numbers, area codes and zip codes, which meant little to me even though Obie had also supplied a few identifying notes here and there. I tried to cross-reference these names with those of the letter writers. A few matched. I knew I'd have to get back to Obie when and if I got serious about contacting any of these characters.

"I didn't know people kept things like this anymore," Petey said, tripping the pages with a wet finger.

"When the action gets heavy, it's probably the only way to keep track," I said out of pure hypothesis.

"I can really use this," she said.

"You can?"

"Can't I?"

I looked at her and growled. She was tugging my chain and I knew it.

"What do you have in mind?"

"Sleuthing," she said. "Real gumshoe work."

"How so?"

"Easy. I could go undercover, make a few contacts," she said. A look of pure smugness washed over her face.

"Obie Blintstein suggest this?"

"Ixnay. Obie never said a word," Petey insisted. "But I confess, I got the idea rapping with him last night. I mean, there he was laughing and having a few sodas and baring his soul. Just telling me everything."

"He was in mourning. You took advantage."

"I *didn't*. Guys are like that, Unk: They get around a cute face and they just start to blab. You can be a perfect stranger, but if you've got the looks, normally intelligent men make total fools of themselves in front of you. Candice Bergen said that."

"Who'd she play for, and what makes you think you could use something like that to our advantage?"

"It's so obvious! With what Obie told me, my strategy is the only way. Get down in the pits. Arm-wrestle."

"Not on your life."

"That's what you said about me helping out in the first place, and you changed your mind on that."

"That did not mean undercover work in what I would consider a pernicious environment."

"Oh, for Christ's sake, Unk."

"Don't cuss. It's out of the goddamn question."

She bunched her eyebrows, clenched her teeth, and fumed. A superstar pout was on the way. She was as cute when she was frustrated as otherwise. I waited for her counter. It didn't come.

"Besides, there's no way you could pull it off," I suggested.

"Obie'd help. That black book there too," she said.

"Not a chance, little lady."

"I'm not a lady," she said.

"As long as I'm around you are."

She got up and walked away. She was mad and I didn't care. If this is what a father feels like nowadays, I felt like a father. I didn't much like it; but dammit, I was making the rules.

Blintstein's references to some of Weaver's teammates, not to mention General Manager George Rohe's wife, sent me out on a familiar trail. When an old columnist is faced with the big white yonder, be it a blank page or a vacant larder of ideas, he goes to his legs. He talks to people. He scrapes and pries and noses around.

I knew the cops had interviewed or otherwise accounted for everybody, because Jimmy Slagle had given me a list of every person on the field or anywhere near the murder scene. Minus the several thousand fans, of course, who, by virtue of the unlocked tunnel access door, could have physically done the deed. It was improbable, as far as I was concerned, but, I had to admit, not impossible. But I had not talked with the players myself. That was a lapse, I decided, because I had made a career out of talking with the players. I circled the name of center fielder Jimmy Sheckard on Slagle's list.

Sheckard was a waterbug of a center fielder, a little guy from rural Pennsylvania who could skitter over the grass as well as anybody. He played center in Wrigley as well as Bobby Dernier did in '84, hit line drives from both sides of the plate, and did the job. He would never make the Hall, but he would help a few others get in just by the way he contributed.

On top of that, Jimmy liked me, and that showed character. It took only a phone call to get him to swing by the neighborhood for a half hour of a verbal pepper game before he had to show up at the ballpark. Sheckard was prompt, appearing in the light of the doorway of a corner all-night eatery on Broadway just south of Addison. It was one of those places that serves breakfast around the clock, which was a good idea since on this street there was no telling if someone was just getting up or going down. Sheckard, you could tell from the scowl on his face, didn't like it. A lot of today's ballplayers don't seem to feel comfortable in any place that doesn't look like it belongs in a shopping mall.

"Duffy, my wheels safe out there?" he asked.

"Unless you're parked in front of a hydrant," I said, knowing he probably was.

He sat down. A pair of sunglasses hung from a red string around his neck. In my day only librarians and farsighted school teachers wore those things.

"So, Duffy," he started in. "This ain't on no record, is it? You know the cops been all over us. 'Specially me, on account of Weaver and I weren't sweethearts."

"Wasn't that bad between you two, was it?"

"I don't wanna knock the dead, but I don't feel like bullshittin' you either."

"What you say to me stays here. No cops. No columns," I said.

It was good enough for him.

"So, okay," he said. "You know I didn't like the guy. And that's rare 'cuz I can get along with anybody. But

Weaver decided he was Mr. Universe. A head bigger
than the team, hell, the whole franchise. You knew him,
Duffy. Got so he thought he was untouchable, and when
somebody did ding him, it wasn't his fault. Christ,
'member after that Astros game where he comes right
out and burns my ass for costing him a no-hitter? Yeah,
that's right, bucko, when Puhl just crushes the thing,
right at me, dead-center, the hardest damn ball to catch
in baseball, ask anyone—I mean, Willie Mays woulda
been handcuffed by that shot—and I'm an asshole because it goes over my head. Hits the base of the wall on a
line, but he don't mention that.

"What he did was chickenshit, and I told him that.
You go public with your beefs and it shows you don't
have any respect for the guys around you.

"Did he ever mention the times I saved his ass—
when his stuff wasn't that good—by breaking my ass to
cut off a double or diving on the carpets? No way. When
he got a shutout it was all Dream, Dream, Dream.
Didn't need nobody in back of him at all."

"Cripes, Jimmy, I wish I had brought up something
you had an opinion on," I said.

He smiled. It was a grudging smile, but a smile
nevertheless. He drank a glass of orange juice.

"Hope they sterilized the glass," he said, looking
around at some of the leather and lace gentlemen in the
joint. I had coffee.

"You know my horseshit, Duffy. It's ball talk.
Dream and I kept our distance. We're pros, so that isn't
so hard to do and still produce. And it didn't mean I
wanted to see him get capped either. I'm stupid, but
I'm no idiot. He was the best ride to a World Series ring I
ever had. The whole team, for that matter. You don't
think one of us had anything to do with it, do you,
Duffy?"

"No, I don't. I mean that. But everything helps to
put a frame around this thing. So tell me, what is there
to the stuff about him and other guys' girlfriends?"

"Like mine, right?" Sheckard said. "Well, it was
bullshit, that's what. With his ego and all his chickies,
there were all the stories. Guys on the team used to

make them up just to piss him off. Like he was supposed to be screwin' Rohe's ol' lady. If you ain't heard that one you been dead for a while.

"You gotta understand, Duffy, that most of the other guys didn't like Dream much better than I did. He was goddamn great—I'm glad I didn't have to dig in against him—but a lot of us thought he was a full-time asshole."

"So there was nothing to it with your fiancée?"

"Well, yeah, I guess. Carla and I had some problems about a year or so ago and we called off the engagement. Right about that time there was this charity thing. Carla got ripped on Fuzzy Navels and started throwing herself at Weaver. It made the gossip columns the next day. I coulda killed her. But that's where it started, and that's where it ended, as sure as I'm sittin' here," he said.

"So his reputation as a Lothario was bona fide, as far as you were concerned?"

"A what?"

"A great lover."

"Oh. So yeah . . . no! I mean. I seen better. With the broads, you know? In this league you gotta have more than a high hard one. Between you and me, Duffy, I don't think Dream got on that well with women. With that ego, how could you? He had all he could handle, but who doesn't, if that's what you're looking for. But as far as I was concerned he was never looking for anything with class. Until Carla came after him.

"But forget the pussy. It makes no difference unless it translates on the field. Is a guy for the team or for himself? Is he there to cut you or build you up? Is he gonna break his tail when you're four runs down or is he gonna lay down? Is he going for the average, or is he gonna throw his body on the line when it counts?

"Look, the team isn't one big happy family. It never was. Not even with Dream being unbeatable. No team is. It's like any other business: some people you like, some you can't stand. Some you see off the field, some you don't. Only the guys who think they're the whole ball game, The Franchise, are the ones everybody pretty much avoids."

I pressed on. "So no jealousy? Not with you or the other guys as far as women were concerned?"

"Aaaah, it pissed us off once in a while. You know, with some guys no matter where you are on the road, or how late it is, they always have to score. Keep proving they can do it. That was Dream. You ever see that Warren Beatty movie *Shampoo*? Like that guy."

He yawned and stretched a leg outside the booth.

"But look, Duffy, as far as I'm concerned . . . well, maybe I shouldn't say anything about this . . ."

"You already have."

"Yeah, well, as far as I'm concerned, the stink side of Weaver, besides his bullshit and his ego, was Obie Blintstein," he said.

"Obie?"

"Yeah, and all the guys who'd pick up the phone to him and bet on the ponies, boxing, dogs, football—you name it. It was pretty common knowledge around the league. Blintstein was the book. Better 'n Vegas. Shit, Merkle about moved in with the fat boy, he was playin' so heavy. He'd check his watch and lay off some odds between innings, for chrissakes! They don't call him 'Bonehead' for nothing," Sheckard said.

"C'mon, Jimmy. I knew Freddie played the ponies . . ."

"And anything else that runs. I heard he lost his ass. Guys wondered if he was gonna have a good set of knees after a while."

"Who knew this?"

"Everybody. From the ball girl to Rohe. But I don't think anybody woulda said so to the cops after the Dream thing. No way. Two reasons: Bonehead's a good skipper—the guys'll play for him—and they don't see it as a big problem that he plays the ponies too much. That's the first reason; and the second is too many guys know they dropped a little something on Obie now and then themselves. Can of worms, if you hear what I'm saying."

"How about collections?" I said. "Obie ever give anybody a problem with that?"

"I'll tell you what he did. I never heard of no one have the arm put on him. Nobody. But every once in a while, maybe when the team was coming in from a road trip or getting on a bus somewhere, all of a sudden Obie would be there. All friendly and slaphappy, and standing next to him, not saying a word, was this big motherfucker. Big! Like André the Giant, the wrestler. A monster, I'm not kiddin'. And the guy just stood there rubbing his hands together while Obie's tellin' everybody to have a happy fuckin' day.

"How do you like that?" he asked.

"I don't."

"Didn't think you would and I gotta split. Time to go to the shop," Sheckard said.

"I appreciate it, Jimmy," I said.

"You better. We got a gag thing on us like you wouldn't believe," he said as he got to his feet.

"Rohe comes in a few days ago and tells us now that the cops are gone we don't talk to nobody. No media, no TV, no telephone calls. He wasn't suggesting, he was *telling*. And you thought the club was going to fall all over itself with memorials and armbands and all that shit. Well, not from ol' George. He just says to keep our mouths shut real tight. 'Play the game, don't play cops and robbers,' he said.

"The Game. That's what life is all about, right, Duffy?" Jimmy said. Then he creased me with a look that would have shriveled an umpire.

I liked Sheckard, liked his instincts, his values. He knew the feel of the warning track, the carom off the bricks, and the importance of the cutoff man. He was also a good ballplayer.

Not wanting to let this thing wither, I waited until Jimmy had driven off, and then I grabbed a cab over to the ballpark. There was time to see Freddie Merkle before he went out onto the field and started jawing with reporters about his middle relievers.

I found him in his underwear and in his office talking to his pitching coach. Since Weaver's demise, Merkle had been doing a lot of talking to his pitching coach. The Phillies were in town and loaded with a bunch of swingers who salivated over videotapes of Mike Schmidt's wallops over the screen and up Kenmore Avenue. Keeping them in the ballpark would be no trifling chore.

Freddie Merkle was no Frank Chance, no peerless leader, but he could run nine guys on the field. He'd been around, put Boston into the playoffs twice, and had a grasp on this club. Merkle was a player's coach, a scrapper. Not the type of guy to ream the cadets for no reason or run off to Wisconsin in the middle of a pennant fight like Durocher did in '69.

Of course, being a Cubs skipper was a test for any man, or god for that matter. It's been said that the Cubs recycle managers like aluminum cans, and I can attest to that. I've dealt with a raft of them: Gerbils, Banty Roosters, Lips, Good Kids, Fordham Flashes, Smilers, and Jolly Chollys. In fact, it was Charlie "Jolly Cholly" Grimm who stood on that perilous bridge back in 1935 when I started out. He was real jolly that year because his ballclub won him one hundred ballgames. Then came Gabby Hartnett, Jimmy Wilson, and Jolly Cholly again. Grimm's Cubs won pennants in '35 and again in '45, and it's too bad he wasn't around in '55. You had to love Cholly for his banjo playing and his blithe spirit, though I saw the kind man eat his insides out over the years.

Lo, there may exist no wider spectrum of mankind, from the sacred to the profane, spitters to mincers, than that which has occupied the manager's office in Wrigley Field. I've lobbed queries and fielded retorts, winced at bile and ducked at barbs from Frankie Frisch, Phil Cavarretta, Smiling Stan Hack, Silent Bob Scheffing, and Good Kid Lou Boudreau. I was dumbfounded in 1961 by the rotating College of Coaches—Vedie Himsl, Harry Craft, Elvin Tappe, and Lou Klein—all of whom lost more than they won. With the use of colored cue cards, Bill Veeck once let the box-seat fans manage a game for his St. Louis Browns. He did it for a gag; the Cubs, with their rent-a-skipper, were serious. "We cannot do much worse under a new system than we did under the old," said P. K. Wrigley. And they didn't. No better, to be sure, but no worse.

I thought Bob Kennedy was on to something in '63, and I knew Durocher was going to blow it in '69. And there was Whitey Lockman—"The blond leading the bland," wrote Eddie Gold—Herman Franks, Joey Amalfitano, Jim Marshall, Preston Gomez, and, of course, that Lee Elia guy from Philadelphia, and Jimmy Frey, who finally put something together in '84 and then left his ace pitcher in so long in San Diego that he blew the pennant.

Frey had some horses, and therein lay the difference. Cub managers through many years, for all the scorn and raspberries you can heap on their ample midsections, never had much to work with. Not the live arms of L.A. that made Walter Alston look so wise. Not the Musials, Brocks, and Gibsons who shone in St. Louis. Not the "boys of summer" in Brooklyn, not Stengel's Yankees of the '50s and '60s, or the Big Red Machine of Cincinnati—and any fan can go on with great assemblages of stellar players not clad in Cubs blue. Ever since '45, with crews that were waiting till next year before this year had even started, Cub skippers have been in deep, treacherous waters. Every one of them took the helm, spouted bravado and bunk masquerading as wisdom and strategy, and, with a few May-to-June detours at the top of the waters, ultimately steered the boat into an iceberg and sank like a stone. "Nearer My God to Thee."

So I am a kindly, understanding soul when I enter that office, knowing the gloom, the despair, the dark night of the soul that lives within those walls like a dark fungus. For his part, Freddie Merkle fit the mold like an old Wrigley Doublemint gum wrapper. A spitting image of Don Zimmer when Popeye was smiling, Merkle was a guy I always got along with. Whether or not his Bruins were going to break even was another question. On Merkle's desk was a pile of corn chips and

Cheez Whiz and some kind of little green peppers you could smell a block away. He called it nachos; I called it heartburn.

"I shouldn't eat the damn things but I'm hooked on 'em, Duffy," he said. "Here, have some."

He wiped his fingers on his blue Cub undershirt. His ample stomach hung over the elastic of his white mid-thigh briefs. He was barefoot and minus the chaw of tobacco whose effluent often spilled down the cleft of his chin and played havoc with his diction. I declined his offer with a wave of my hand.

"So okay, don't eat my food. Piss all over my hospitality." It was Merkle's way of making me feel at home.

"Mexicans feed that stuff to their goats," I said.

"To hell with 'em then."

He nodded at his pitching coach and closed the door behind him. Then he eased himself back behind his desk.

"That was a hell of a piece you did on the kid. Just a hell of a piece."

" 'Preciate it, Fred. Sometimes they write themselves."

"These young pricks around today can't touch ya, Duffy. Can't carry your jock."

"Don't tell them that, Fred. Just make 'em mad."

"So I hear you're hangin' around again. How 'bout that." He was letting me know he knew.

"Word gets around . . ."

"You forget, Duf, we know a lot of the same people."

Indeed we did.

"And if anybody could put this thing together, you could, Duffy. I don't read books, but I'd read yours," he said.

"How's the club hanging together through all this?"

"Aw, they're awright. It's me that's all tore up inside. I miss that kid, Duffy. I miss goin' out to the mound in the seventh inning and havin' him tell me he can still throw the ball through a wall. That big head of his, God, it rubbed off. You know how it is, your best guy is throwin' and it makes everybody play better. Makes ya manage better too."

I nodded. "As Casey used to say, 'I couldn't of done it without my players.'"

"You got it," he said.

"So after all that's been said and done, Freddie, you got any feel for what happened that day?" I asked.

"Who dunnit, ya mean?"

"The whole thing."

"I got horseshit. From what I hear the cops got horseshit. Everybody's got horseshit," he said. "I also got a lot of innings to pitch that I never used to worry about."

"I talked to Obie," I said.

"Huh?"

"Blintstein."

"Ah, for cryin' out loud," he said.

He swung his arm across the top of his desk and swept the empty plate and anything else in the way into the wastebasket.

"For cryin' out loud. What'd he say? Forget it, I know what he said. Ah, dammit to hell. Whattaya want from me, Duffy?" Merkle said, his voice descending from a bitch to a moan.

"Tell me what's out there. Blintstein and his bookmaking, I mean. The kind of guys he dealt with. Is there a connection?"

"Oh, I hope to Christ not! Look, I had this problem, you know that. I had my excesses. I know better than anybody. But if I thought what I was doin' had anything to do with the kid's murder, I couldn't face myself," he said.

Perspiration broke out on his brow. He got up and paced the office as if it were the dugout and the boys were blowing a lead.

"Now, right here let's set the record straight: I never, *never* bet on The Game. I swear on my mother's memory. Don't try to do to me what they did to Pete Rose, Duffy. Don't even *suggest* it. Why, you know I was rocked by that whole mess with Charley Hustle. All us guys were. We seen Pete play the greyhounds in St.

Pete all those years in spring training 'cuz we were right behind him at the window. And we all heard about Shoeless Joe when we was comin' up. I personally don't think he even knew what he was doin', poor sonuvabitch.

"You can't scratch a guy in this game and not find a gambler beneath his skin. Hell, you gotta be! Just takin' a skipper's job is a gamble, and a pretty goddamn bad one on account of the fact that your boys can stink up the place and you can't get rid of 'em, but as soon as we start emotin' any odor at all our ass is gone out the window like a pot of piss. Gone. Pink fuckin' slip. Day-old bread. Whatever you wanna call it. And you can quote me on that.

"But don't include me in on some bum rap. No sir, I never bet this game. And I'd rip the throat out of any guy who would."

He was hot. The words caromed off the walls like pop-ups off a fungo. The guys in the clubhouse stopped whatever they were doing and wondered what kind of mustard Merkle was gassing me with. Had I been taking notes I'd be six lines behind, telling Bonehead to slow down and cool off. In this case, I just let him vent.

He let up, the steam cleared, and he lowered his voice.

"I gave it up, Duffy. All the vigorish, all the action. I really did. I haven't played the nags or anything for weeks now. I don't even check the odds anymore, and that used to be the first thing I turned to in the sports section. Even before I read about me. Believe me on this. It's comin' from my gut.

"Blintstein don't bother me no more," he went on. "I cleared my sheet with him. Christ, I dropped a bundle. Now I'm out. I'm clean as a choirboy. And that's how I'm stayin'. You gotta believe me on this, Duffy. I level with you because I know if this thing went public I'd be in the toilet. My job wouldn't last out the week. And no other club in their right mind would touch me. I'm not shittin' you, Duffy. I sit up nights on this thing, not countin' sheep either. Just repeatin' over and over what a dumb bastard I've been. Just a dumb bastard. And I hope to God it never gets outta this room."

I sat there and felt the man's agony, and also his remorse. I believed him. He'd lived up to his moniker—Bonehead!—and in those moments he was a broken one.

I left well enough alone.

9

George and George

Being in the vicinity, I decided to take a whack at two birds with one stone, so I used a clubhouse phone to call upstairs to the office of George Rohe, the Cubs' G.M. I had to touch base with the man, for whatever good it might do me. It was easier than I thought, given the fact that I had not always had the rosiest of professional relationships with Rohe. My emeritus status alone would have been enough for him to say that he had no time for me. But he did nothing of the sort. Not the G.M. directly, but his congenial and occasionally obsequious assistant, a fellow named George Whiteman—the two Georges, by George—invited me right on up. You would have thought the commissioner himself had come calling, or, and this dawned on me later, that they were expecting me.

"Mr. Rohe said he would like nothing better than to talk some shop with Duffy House," Whiteman told me. "His private box during the game?"

"I'll be there in time to sing the Anthem," I said.

"Bring an appetite. Mr. Rohe's menu is not to be missed," Whiteman said.

I idled awhile in the dugouts and behind the backstop, barbering and keeping my ears open. Not much time had passed since the murder, yet things seemed pretty much back to normal. Security was tighter, and doors and gates were tightly locked, but business went on as usual. Only the obligatory black bicep bands served as a reminder of Weaver's demise, and a few fans even commented that they added a nice commemorative touch to the Bruins' blouses. The added fabric did not impede pepper games or infield practice. Grounders were charged, slumps were fretted over and worked out of. Baseball is like that, a dogged, methodical routine that has to be drilled constantly lest the knack be lost, with only brief pause, if any at all, for human tragedy. Why, the nation has been engaged in world wars and our pastime has played on.

In no time the crowd was thick, the vendors were hawking, and game time approached. I made my way up to the mezzanine of new skyboxes—a place, I must admit, I have purposely avoided since their construction in 1989. Sure, I know all about the economics of the game and how important these privileged chambers are to the coffers of the franchise, but I don't like them any more than the grandstand sitter whose view of a fly ball, be it a pop-up or a clout, is rudely interrupted by the overhang. It's one thing to have some jamoke block your view because he has a weak bladder, it's another thing to have somebody pay a ransom to do it all the time.

Hell, I don't like the very idea of boxes. There's something wrong with the existence of pampered chambers in the middle of a ballyard, of cable television, air conditioning, and chocolate-chip cheesecake served from carts by waiters . . . and I like cheesecake. I don't like the glass in front of them that keeps out the elements; I didn't approve when the boys in the press box pulled the windows closed during those frigid spring and fall games, and I . . . ah, horseshit, I could go on, but I won't because Bill Veeck made the point in his first book and did so a lot more eloquently than I ever could.

But the G.M. had extended the invitation, and I knocked on the door. It was opened by George Whiteman. He was a burly guy in his early thirties, thin of hair and thick of neck. He extended a hand that reminded me of Moose Moryn's and shook mine as if it were wet. He was wearing a short sleeved shirt with a Cub logo on the breast and a pair of black running shoes. There was a Mick Kelleher intensity about the guy, sort of like a utility infielder on the bubble during the last days of spring training, which Mick, who played a good fifteen years, of course, always was.

"Come on in, Mr. House," he said.

He ushered me into what can only be called imperial digs. Carpeting, leather sofas and wingback chairs, lamps, mahogany tray tables, and nicely framed Cubs memorabilia on the walls. It was the kind of skybox fit for Winston Churchill. I half expected to peer outside and see cricket.

Whiteman noticed my gawking, spread his arms, and beamed as if the place were his.

"Class, isn't it?" he said.

"Hmm," I explained.

But I made him feel good by looking around, taking in the television screens, the sound system, the kitchen facilities, and even, by God, a private bath and shower.

"What time do we sail?" I said.

Whiteman laughed, a little too loud and a little too late maybe, but it came from the belly.

"Still sharp as a tack, Mr. House," he said.

Through the glass partition, sitting in an armchair and cradling one of two telephones by his side, I saw President and General Manager George Rohe. But he did not immediately take my glance, for seated on the divan, reading what looked to be a quarterly report of the Corporation which presently owned the franchise and these here opulent confines, was a beauty. She was not a day under fifty but with lovely, flawlessly tanned skin, thick blond hair, flashing, uncapped teeth, and enough surgical enhancements to keep all other undisciplined body parts tightly in place. She was a classic, a cross between Marlene Dietrich and Dinah Shore, with a touch of Melina Mercouri thrown in for spice. She was Lila Rohe, the G.M.'s missus.

She looked up at me, smiled, and extended her baubled hand.

"Hello, Duffy," she said.

I'll throw Lauren Bacall in there too, because her pipes put out a voice that was like gravel on the road.

"Lila, it's been too long," I said, taking her digits and feeling the current.

For a brief instant, with George on the phone and Lila radiating from the sofa, I thought back to when times were different for these two.

When Rohe was named G.M., I had checked in with the usual profile. I wrote about all the baseball jobs he'd had and what he'd done in them. I pulled out percentages and trades and quotes and hot-stove league aphorisms. I fed the goat, which is how Norman Mailer once described the voracious sports-reading public.

Yet what I wrote was only part of what I had learned about George Rohe. As I was working on the piece, calling around and checking the stats, I came across a skeleton. Lila Rohe was not Rohe's first wife. Not even close. Years earlier, while in the low minor leagues, Rohe had fooled around with a divorcée long enough to get her pregnant. The girl's name was Tinker, I remember. You cannot be a Cub fan for as long as I've been and forget a name like that.

Anyway, the girl already had a kid at the time, a little boy by an unknown father, so when Rohe married the woman he adopted the boy. The marriage lasted only a few years, until their own child, who was also a boy, got out of diapers. Rohe's son was no problem, but the stepson came a cropper. As a teenager, the stories went, he started knocking off gasoline stations. By the time Rohe came to the Cubs, I was told the kid was a hardened con doing time for manslaughter in some state penitentiary.

But the world never read about it because I never wrote it. I don't even remember who tipped me off to the story, only that I checked it out. I always do. That's the way I was taught. If your mother says she loves you, check it out. That's what the old cigar-chewing night editors in the city room used to say when I was a cub. So I checked it out and found chapter and verse: the woman's name and the stepkid, the places and dates.

Then I sat on it. I did not believe then and do not

believe now that it had a damn thing to do with Rohe's
new job. He was hired to run a baseball club, not a
reform school. Hell, I'm no altar boy. I'm not about to
blame a guy for the misdeeds of a stepson. Maybe I
tucked away the story to use one day as a little leverage
when Rohe pissed me off. I don't know. I only know that
I never used it. I never asked Lila about it either—the
situation never arose. But I never forgot about the story
either.

"What brings you down?" Lila asked.

"I was wondering that of you," I said, resisting the
double meaning, noticing her purse by her side and that
she seemed dressed more for the boardroom than the
ballpark. I sat down across from her on the sofa and
caught a wisp of her perfume.

"Oh, now that these boxes are here you can't keep
me *away*," she gushed, then raised a palm at the ex-
panses outside. "This is my own little ballpark, with real
players out the window and plenty of champagne on
ice."

"Just so you don't reverse the two," I said.

"Smarty," she said.

Rohe slapped a hand over the receiver and cut in.

"Can't get her outta here," he said, and winked.

"I may not be an expert on baseball, but I know
people," Lila said. "Ask George if I didn't help bring
Brucey Sutter out of the pack."

I nodded painfully, knowing that Freddie Martin's
instruction in the art of the split-fingered fastball had a
little bit to do with it.

"How about Dean Jamie Weaver?" I asked.

"Oh, he was a *natural*. A thoroughbred. I didn't
have anything to do with him. I just told George to be
patient in those early years. I know a gem when I see
one," she said.

"Can I get anybody anything?" said Whiteman.

"What's your pleasure, Duffy?" Lila said.

"Good pitching and good defense," I said.

"Stop it. You sound like George."

"I do?"

Whiteman laughed again.

"Whatever's wet and cold," I said, trying to be good.

"Oh, don't say that. George stocks six kinds of imported beer and a respectable wine list," Lila said.

"Give me an Old Style," I said.

"I'll have to run out for that," Whiteman said.

He had to be joking, but after he handed Lila a glass of pink bubbly, he was out the door. He returned a few minutes later with two cups of beer, one of which he then poured into a frosted mug from the icebox. All these gyrations made the beer's head a nightmare, and it soon degenerated into the thin layer of soapsuds so common to ballpark brews, but I toasted his efforts nevertheless. Whiteman was a gofer's gofer.

By that time Rohe was off the phone, no doubt having just made a Sutcliffe-Frazier-Hassey for Carter-Hall trade that would bring the pennant to Wrigley. More than likely he was haggling with his stockbroker.

"Duffy, always good to see you," he said, and leaned over with a handshake. The leather of his chair sighed. "Whattaya think of this little shanty?"

"A far cry from the Pink Poodle," I said, referring to the venerable Wrigley Field front office lounge.

"Problem is, now that the accommodations are first class, I got plenty of company."

Lila smiled through her teeth.

"Hey, I'm pullin' your leg," he went on. "Lila and I put our heads together right here more than anyone knows. She sees a side to a player that you and I'll overlook. The old forest-for-the-trees thing.

"Now with you and Lile both here, I figure I got two pretty fair baseball brains at arm's length."

I gave him a nod. He was working overtime on the butter routine, and I wasn't sure for whom.

"Doesn't this cut into your schedule?" I asked Lila.

"Oh, c'mon, Duffy. Place me *not* with those girls who do lunch. That's yesterday's mousse. George says he'd rather have me here with him running the team. So this is where I am."

"Is that right?" I said, envisioning Eleanor Roosevelt and Rosalyn Carter, but not, somehow, Lila Rohe.

Just then Wayne Messmer launched into the Anthem. I stood up, switched hands with my beer, and put my palm over my heart. It's an old, quaint, and sometimes embarrassing habit. It served, however, to momentarily chide the Rohes, who stiffly and, I fear, uncharacteristically made it to their feet by "what so proudly we hail."

"So. A book thing, Duffy? Or what? Kahn, Angell, Bosworth—I read all those birds," Rohe said. He drank black coffee from a thin, gold-rimmed china cup which he refilled from a Cub thermos.

"They've all put out feelers, you know. You're the first one I've—dammit, Orville, bust the plate! I keep telling Freddie, 'Get the guys ahead in the count, for godssakes!' You know, it's the leverage thing. Go one-and-two on a guy instead of two-and-one, two-and-oh, three-and-one, and I don't care who he is, he's a different hitter. You look at that Hershiser kid—count, count, count. Never gets behind. Always has the hitters in the hole and thinking 'What's he comin' in with? What's he doing?' and when you get 'em thinkin', you got 'em. Ah, shit, see what I mean?"

A Phillie had laced a double in the hole off Cub flinger Orville Overall on a three-and-one count, and I saw what he meant. Pretty standard stuff, to be sure, but inarguable.

"'Course, ol' Grover Cleveland Alexander didn't want 'em to think. Pitched fast and said, 'What do you want me to do? Let the sons of bitches stand up there and think on my time?' " I said.

"He was before my time," Rohe said.

Just then the crowd roared when Overall knocked the next guy down.

"Can't accuse Orville of being too fine," I said.

"Orv's a gamer," said Rohe. "Comes at you. That's why I got him. If he busts 'em early, he's on my team."

The crowd cheered a swinging strikeout.

"Right there! Look at the count. Got the son-of-a-bitch on a one-two pitch. One-two. Had 'im rockin' on his heels and guessin'. The count thing all over again, Duffy."

My eye caught Lila. She had finished with the quarterly report and had what looked like her datebook in front of her. She wasn't paying any attention to us and our intellectual banter, much less the ball game.

"You know, the Weaver thing threw me," Rohe said.

I perked.

"I can't describe it—the wind was just knocked out of me. I got the call in my office and I went numb. Like the Kennedy thing. You could have told me I had cancer and I'd have taken it better. How do you replace that kind of arm? Where do you make up the innings? The kid was a gamer—Stick it, Joe!—just came at you over and over again. I got on him as much as anybody—you *got* to with that kind of talent—but I never had anything but respect for the kid. Like Jimmy Frey used to say about Sutcliffe, the guy just 'threw the hell out of the ball.' That's why you had to love him, even with all his bullshit.

"I don't care what anybody says, I loved that kid," he finished.

It was a hell of a quote and, had I been scribing, I would have used it all. He said it staring at the field, never turning his eyes to his coffee cup or to me. Baseball men are like that, I should add. I've had some of my best confabs with them and never made eye contact, never was able to search the baby blues for truth or treachery. It's like a manager coming out to the mound to yank his pitcher. He'll look at the ball, he'll kick the slab, he'll turn and scowl at the umpire, he'll squawk at his catcher whose mug is behind the mask, but he'll seldom look his pitcher, the kid who just got clocked, never look him in the eye and say, "You stunk up the place and I'm jerking you."

My own eyes roved and I again took in Lila, who seemed unmoved by her husband's sudden burst of sentiment. Nary a cold stare, a loving glance, or a supportive nod bothered her countenance. She remained implacable, and soft on the eyes.

Just then George Whiteman, who had been up and down like a batboy ever since I got there, waved in a waiter. He was a young black kid with an earring, a bow tie, and a silver tray loaded with raw vegetables, seafood, and petits fours of cream cheese, celery, and fish too small for nets. Not your average vendor and not your average ballpark fare.

"Tasties," Lila perked.

Rohe poured himself more coffee instead, then lit a cigarette. It didn't look like he enjoyed either one. I looked for something to chew on on the platter, found a couple of healthy shrimp, and yearned for a hot dog.

"How will you make up the innings?" I said.

"The bastards are picking me to death. The other G.M.s know I need top drawer, and they're offering me birdshit. And they want the meat of my lineup. I got no control—I wish to hell I could dip into the farms and tell 'em to go screw themselves. But this team is too close to come up short—we were picked to take it with Weaver, you *know* that. I can't see us curling up—Good bang, Jimmy!—and dyin', and I can't see me selling the store just to patch up my hole in a hurry. But you wait, Duffy —and you can put this in the bank—I'm gonna surprise 'em. I can't say just what, but it'll be a banger, a real banger."

I leaned over and placed my empty mug on the tray table only to have a full one put in its place by George Whiteman. I was reaching for my next question when Rohe continued.

"That's where it is, Duffy, a control thing. I got no control over the mess. Can't call the shots like I could before this mess. Hell, I can't even control the clubhouse. Coppers say they got to get in and talk to everybody whenever they want. Come in and talk to my players, my coaches, my whole organization here— Send him, Freddie, for godssakes!—and I can't do a damn thing about it. I know we had a murder here, but I got a franchise to run. These detectives—and it's a different one every time, like some fan club—tell me I got no choice but to cooperate.

"And to top it off, from what I see they don't got shit! They don't know who killed the kid—Yes! Lean on that slider!—or why or how in hell the bastard got in the tunnel to do it. Isn't that a crock? That's what bothers me more than anything. I had a monumental security breakdown here and nobody in hell can tell me how in hell it happened. But they sure as hell can tell me it's none of my business and don't tell them how to run an investigation."

"Can I get you anything, Mr. House?" Georg Whiteman said.

The hell out of here, I wanted to say, but only good-naturedly raised my palms.

"If you want my opinion on the thing, Duffy"—the freight train was rolling, so I nodded and let it come—"they shouldn't go any further than Weaver himself if they want to crack the thing. The apple don't fall too far from the tree, I always say. Look at the deadbeats and the leeches around the kid. Start with the overweight houseboy of his, and you'll find things that don't smell right and never did. Nowadays you wanna play funny, it ain't like the old days when you'd go out on the town and get your ashes hauled or tie one on and forget about it. Nowadays it's drugs and cocaine and gambling and all the low-rent that comes along with it. And these coppers are talking to my players? Barking up the clubhouse door when they know damn well what Weaver was up to!

"And I'll tell you another thing," he went on. "I got the lid screwed on that clubhouse so tight the players have to open a window to fart. Nobody comes around that place who don't belong, 'cept for the damn flatfoots, of course. Wives, floozies, cousins, moms and dads—and none of those 'friends,' as they're always called. Nobody not on my list or they have to deal with me. That's one thing—The count, dammit, Orv!—that's changed around here, so help me."

Just then the Phillies were retired and Rohe got up to drain some of the coffee out of his system. I turned to take in the rest of the inhabitants of the executive suite. What I saw momentarily took me aback. Lila was sitting with her gorgeous gams crossed, her gaze fixed somewhat vacantly onto the field, and her right palm extended. Into it, one, maybe two at a time, were placed roasted peanuts. Each had just been shucked and skinned by George Whiteman. It was a mechanical but curious routine, the peanut being lifted and dropped into her mouth where it was slowly, almost lovingly masticated, the palm returning to receive another from the chunky, efficient digits of George Whiteman. Yet while I watched, neither of them seemed to think the two operations out of the ordinary.

"Anything you need, I'm your man, Mr. House," Whiteman suddenly said.

Lila smiled, slightly lifted her eyebrows, and worked on another peanut.

"Munchies," she said.

I stayed for a few more innings. Rohe had pretty much said his piece. We talked the game in front of us and nothing more. He did not try to keep me when I thanked him for his hospitality and time and said I had to be going. Lila, in fact, seemed relieved. Whiteman jumped up to get the door for me.

"Good to have you, Mr. House," he said.

"Good to have been had," I said, and quickly buffered it with a chuckle.

Whiteman took the buffer.

I later learned that my audience with Rohe was significant. For all of his nonstop, unsolicited patter with me, Rohe wasn't talking to anyone else. Not in the media, and barely at all to league officials or detectives. Not that he often had. Rohe liked to address groups, usually captive clusters of sportswriters that he himself had assembled after he'd made a move. Even then he controlled the questions and kept the answers short.

Funny, but I knew that it had not always been that way. I did a profile of Rohe way back when he was just coming into the managerial ranks. Then he was open and quite candid, even likeable. Today, lo these many years and developments later, he had erected the stone walls, the pretenses, and the bluster.

I was not back home but a few minutes when the phone rang at me.

"Duffy?"

"You got him," I said.

"Chambliss."

"Heard of him," I said.

"I don't know what you're doing out there but you got competition," the commissioner said.

"How's that?"

"George Rohe has his own investigation going."

"Is that so?"

"You didn't know?"

"I hear a lot of things," I said, covering.

"Well, it got to this office in a hurry," Chambliss said.

"Maybe George had something to do with that."

"His guy's supposed to be a pro."

"They always are," I said, trying to sound blithe and unruffled.

I was nothing of the sort.

10

Steinfeldt and Howard

I was still drifting some on this thing. There was action out there. A killer was running the base paths, I was sure of it, but I couldn't get the ball out of my mitt. My initial contacts were promising, but I still didn't know the operatives, the suspects, the terms, or the identity of the player to be named later. I decided to hit the phones and shake the bushes. There were a dozen scribes I could have called. Sportswriters are incurable gossips, rumormongers with rabbit ears. If there was anything to be heard or known, they'd be on it. I started to dial Red Carney but went another route, surprising even myself.

I called Harry Steinfeldt. He was a veteran eyeshade, a grizzled old snapper who used sticks of linotype for paperweights and still shouted "Copy!" when he was finished with a story. Because he still breathed, he was still on the beat. His was hoodlums, the Capone guys and their latter-day mimics. He had been dogging them as long as I had been sniffing jocks. Where I kept track of runs, hits, and errors, Steinfeldt just kept track of hits—the felonious kind. He had a running file of every gangland murder since Dion O'Banion arranged his last bouquet. Before you even asked, Steinfeldt would tell you that the only ink jockey who knew Capone and his mugs better than he did was Jake Lingle. And everybody knows what happened to Lingle.

Steinfeldt did not want any part of the phone. He said he would meet me for a bite at a joint. He could sniff my expense account a mile away. I let him pick the spot, and he chose Gene and Georgetti's, a little Near North steakhouse tucked behind the Merchandise Mart and underneath the El tracks. With those kinds of shadows you wouldn't think anyone would be able to find the place. Think again. With steaks as thick as a catcher's mitt and as tender as a rosin bag, everybody from Sparky Anderson to Frank Sinatra dogged the joint.

"I'll bring a friend," Steinfeldt said, mysteriously.

His friend was a beefy guy who reminded you of Hank Sauer if Hank had gone to Notre Dame. He wore a white shirt and tie under a blue suit that did not cope well with his shoulders. He was every bit of forty years old but in good shape. Went by the name of Del Howard. The two of them nodded me over to the far corner, a booth, Harry cracked, usually reserved for some heavyweight hod-carrier union bosses with last names ending in vowels. Harry liked to point out such details. Howard smiled and rubbed a pair of meaty hands together. Howard was FBI.

Sportswriters don't often rub elbows with J. Edgar Hoover's protégés, and Harry Steinfeldt knew that. Harry also knew that anybody looking under rocks in the Dream Weaver murder would be interested in gambling. Harry was a fan, more of one than he cared to admit, and he kept a keen ear turned toward the ballpark. What it had picked up for some time were the rumors of betting action connected with Weaver, specifically through Obie Blintstein.

Now I'm not your seasoned Mob-watcher, but even I know that in Chicago the name of the organized crime game is gambling. Cash cow, as big to the Mafia boys as bootleg liquor was to Capone. Oh, the kneecrackers dabble in a few other vices—stolen auto parts, or "chop shops," the term Steinfeldt put on them, pornography, juice loans, and union racketeering—but they live and die, with heavy emphasis on the latter, on gambling. People, respectable ones who sit at desks and must dial nine to get an outside line, put money on games. They put all kinds of money on every kind of game, and the Outfit, with its army of bookies and wire rooms, is happily there to handle it. Should one of their hoods screw up, should he welsh on his payoffs to the bosses or make an unauthorized foray into someone else's turf, he ends up in a trunk with his throat slit and a two-dollar betting slip in his cold hand. It happens often and a lot in every major city and especially in Chicago, where the tabloid papers and the TV stations still lavish long, leering, St. Valentine's Day–style looks at it. After a big Mob guy expired in his sleep a while back, Mike Royko, the local kid columnist who can turn a phrase or two, said the bum "died of unnatural causes." It was a line he stole, I'm sure, from Harry Steinfeldt.

And, of course, wherever the mob goes, the FBI boys, if they haven't got the poor sap bugged already, follow closely behind. Guys like Del Howard here.

"Del's always wanted to meet ya," Steinfeldt said. "I sure as shit don't know why."

Howard shook my hand.

"I'm honored, Mr. House. I've read you all my life. You always told it like it was."

"That was Cosell, not me. I tap-danced and ad-libbed," I said.

"Listen to this maloche," Steinfeldt said.

"Your piece on Ernie Banks's last game: 'Others swung bats. Awkward, heavy, pine-tarred cudgels. Banks flicked a tapered, varnished piece of ash as if it were a rod and he a fly fisherman.' I have it framed in my office," Howard said.

I listened with reverence.

"Buy this young man anything he wants," I said.

A waiter wearing a white apron that drooped nearly to his shoes came over armed with a basket of bread and three glasses of water with tin butter plates balancing on the rims. He spilled the water, upset the basket, dunked a pat of butter, and queried "Coke-tail?" all in one motion.

Howard had a beer, Steinfeldt a double Johnnie Walker Red, and I passed.

"So you're sniffin' around on the Weaver thing," Steinfeldt said, wasting no time with small talk.

"Just talking to people so far," I said.

Howard cleared his thick throat. Dean Weaver was dead, he informed me, and while the Bureau was interested in his demise, they did not investigate murders. His tone suddenly dropped an octave to somewhere between official and noncommittal.

"But we had been aware of his activities prior to his death," he went on.

"So what *was* he up to?" I asked.

"Book," said Steinfeldt.

"We had credible information to that effect. Our people put him in the company of Brovia and Cortazzo," Howard said.

"Clams and Teets," explained Steinfeldt.

"Both report to Chiozza," Howard added.

"Needle Nose," Steinfeldt clarified.

I waved my butter knife in the air to signal a time-out.

"Somebody talk English, for cryin' out loud," I said.

Howard went on.

"Weaver was a tease. He liked to hang with the boys in Vegas and Tampa, dog races, restaurants, a little golf. Throw some money around. His pilot fish was Blintstein."

"Obie?"

"Yes."

"Blintstein. Former Chicago guy you know, from Grand Avenue, Pupo's old neighborhood. He ain't no angel," Steinfeldt explained.

"Blintstein carried action. Considerable numbers at times. Liked football. But it was Weaver who bet heavy," Howard said.

"Dream himself?" I said.

"They held some big markers on him," Steinfeldt said.

"We know he didn't bet often, but he bet big. He covered his losses. Didn't owe anybody anything. No problem with any muscle," Howard said.

"So Weaver was a bettor," I said, savoring the fact. "Not baseball, I hope."

"Not that we know of," said Howard.

"Blintstein's too smart for that," said Steinfeldt.

"So where did the problem come up?" I asked.

"Weaver made big money so he covered himself. He didn't have problems as much as he made problems," Howard began.

I waited.

"A couple months ago he—through Blintstein—changed people. Just up and told their bookie he was out. That was Cortazzo, Chiozza's boy. That didn't go over too well."

"They probably got the word from out west to get him back on the rolls," Steinfeldt said.

"We don't know that," said Howard. He saw my pained, confused expression once again and explained. "We have no reason to believe that Pupo got involved."

That name I knew. Dom "Big Tuna" Pupo was the kingfish of the Chicago mob. Out west was either some western Chicago suburb, where a lot of the Outfit guys lived, or Palm Springs. I knew that much.

"We *are* sure that Cortazzo paid Weaver several visits here and in other cities," Howard said.

"On the day he was killed?" I said.

"We don't know that," he replied.

By this time the waiter had returned. Howard and I had ordered steak sandwiches slathered with Thousand Island dressing—which tastes better than it sounds. Steinfeldt had asked for something called a garbage salad, which wasn't on the menu but should have been. His garbage came crammed with everything from black olives and anchovies to tomatoes, shrimp, and chunks of Greek goat cheese. The sandwiches followed shortly, and we had at them like savages, especially Howard.

"So was this beef the Boys had against Weaver enough to murder him?" I asked with my mouth full.

"We can't be sure," mumbled Howard.

"Discipline's breaking down nowadays," said Steinfeldt, smearing salad oil on his chin as he spoke.

"It's a problem. You got these apes who need a calculator to add two plus two and the bosses can't control 'em."

"This isn't my bailiwick, but my man at the track used to say that dead men pay no debts," I said.

Howard nodded and bled his beer dry.

"Let's just say it'd take a big problem to have somebody like Weaver hit. They'd sooner take out the mope Dream switched his action to."

"Who was that?" I said.

"We don't know that. Our people don't know."

"What did Obie say?"

"Nothing. He's been uncooperative."

"Whatta surprise!" Steinfeldt mocked.

Howard mopped his plate clean and accepted a fresh bottle of beer.

Steinfeldt motioned for the floor, his mouth full.

"It ain't what you're thinkin', Duffy. The boys and markers and all that. Obie Blintstein's problems are his problems. They might put a cigarette out in his eye, but they don't whack his ballplayer. You don't butcher the cash cow.

"Bank this, Duffy: Weaver's hit don't fit with the way things are done. The Boys take guys for rides. They whack 'em in empty parking lots. They line 'em up in warehouses. They hang 'em by meathooks in rendering plants. They plant 'em in cornfields in Indiana. But for cryin' out loud, they don't take 'em out to the ball game!"

He wasn't finished.

"In that tunnel by the dugout? Give me a break, that's State and Madison! If you ask me for my modest but learned opinion and from what I hear about all the horizontal action that guy Weaver got, some broad had him wiped."

Howard raised his considerable brows.

"Figure it: whoever did it had to know his way around the ballpark," he said. "That was some nifty footwork."

"Nifty and pretty stupid," Steinfeldt cut in. "Just too much exposure, for chrissakes. That's why I think it was some broad just dumb enough to try and lucky enough to get away with it.

"Reminds ya of the Waitkus thing at the Edgewater, huh, Duffy?" he went on. "I was the first one in that room. The sheets were still warm. Lot of people don't know that."

"I was standing right next to you, Harry," I reminded him.

"Oh yeah," he said, and smiled like a weasel.

We waved over the coffee and waved off dessert.

"So you fellas aren't officially in the thick of this thing?" I asked Howard.

"That's correct, Mr. House. We're watching. It being the Cubs and all. Damn shame to lose an arm that good," he replied.

"He tried to score once too often, that's all," Steinfeldt grumbled.

"Reminding us all of an old line about Joe DiMaggio," I said. " 'No man can be a success in two national pastimes.' "

Steinfeldt smiled over his coffee.

"Jimmy Cannon?" he asked.

"Oscar Levant," I said.

"Who's that?" Howard asked, immediately eroding my regard for him.

The check arrived seconds later. With quick hands I'd seen only in great infields, it was shoved over to me. I covered it like a pro, and in no time we were standing outside the joint picking our teeth.

Howard palmed me his card.

"Anything I can do, Mr. House, just call," he said.

I nodded, inwardly marveling at the manners of the Bureau.

"Tell me, over the years with the Cubs, who'd you like best?" he asked.

The question of a true fan. He waited like a child anticipating a treat. I resisted the temptation to say Lou Brock.

"You had to love Ernie," I said, "but you could build a ballclub around Gabby Hartnett."

"Knew it," Howard said.

* * *

When I got back to the apartment, Petey was waiting for me. She knew I had been doing some legwork and she was worried that she was missing out. I could tell. She was antsy.

"Some guy named Moran called from San Diego. He said it was deadline," she said.

I moved on it. Pat Moran was family, a former colleague, a damned good rewrite man who had retired to the copy desk of the *San Diego Bee*. But he hadn't retired his old Chicago newspaper skills, and when the Weaver thing broke, Pat hopped on Obie Blintstein for a West Coast angle. His Chicago blarney got him an ear with Obie, and after buttering the fat man with a few old neighborhood memories, Obie, who wasn't talking to anybody in the working press, opened up to him and Moran got a hell of a local story.

The number got me right to him at the paper.

"Just put it out over the wire, Duffy. Obie Blintstein's dead," Moran said.

"Judas priest!" I hissed.

My head spun, I regrouped, and I motioned Petey to pick up the phone in the bedroom.

"Give it to me, Pat."

"I figured you'd wanna know. Blintstein told me you came out here for an interview. Confidential stuff, eh, Duffy? Mr. Big Investigator and you don't even ring up your old bunch."

"Your line was busy."

"Yeah, yeah. So you owe me one."

"What's the story?"

"Dammedest thing. I heard the police report and I about fell off my stool. I hustled out to see for myself. He was a Chicago guy what did me a favor and I owed it to him," Moran said.

"Seems he went and got his mouth tied up to lose weight. Wires," Moran continued.

"Jesus H.—he went through with that?!" I was incredulous.

"Yeah. Guess his doctor said he was a walking time

bomb with all that extra suet. If you ask me, it was grief. Big-league, Stanley Cup grief. Guy knew his steady date with two-inch New York strip steaks was about up with Weaver gone.

"So he goes over to this doctor on Santa Luna Drive, some quack artist who sells him on a quick fix. Wires his jaws shut, gives him a box of straws, and tells him to drink fruit juice.

"Criminy, can you imagine Obie Blintstein on a liquid diet? Need one of those old-time water towers they used for steam engines just to keep him fed. But never mind. He got the juices and went and bought gallon cans of protein supplement and crap from health stores. It was all over the kitchen.

"Of course, it didn't take long before he snuck in a few malted milks. That's what killed him."

"A milk shake?"

"No, a malted milk. It's thicker," Pat said.

"*C'mon,* Pat."

"Yeah, Duffy, this is gospel. They found him sitting in his living room surrounded by a lot of booze and a malted milk from Margie's—a little joint makes home-made ice cream up on the Hill—in front of him. He'd downed half of it when he blew lunch."

"Huh?"

"The official term is 'aspirate.' He vomited, then inhaled the liquid, and choked to death. All because of those damn wires. Couldn't get his mouth open to breathe. Least that's what the story is on it as of now. 'Course, a copper told me he wouldn't be surprised if some coke was involved. Seems it always is."

"What a rotten way to go," I said.

"Oh, he was a mess," Moran added.

"Autopsy?"

"Yup. Won't that be a tour!"

I collected my thoughts, trying to arrange the images of Obie and autopsies and malted milk. I thought I heard Petey's breathing on the extension.

"That means those birds were close, dammit," I said.

"Huh?"

"You know, Pat, the Mob-watchers like Steinfeldt blew a lot of smoke about Blintstein and the gambling mess. Said the hoods *lived* with the guy."

"Whacking a pooch with a milk shake ain't exactly their style," Moran said.

"Hell, Pat, nothing in this case has been their style, whatever that is. But we got a dead ballplayer and now his backup man is dead of the most suspicious damn causes I ever heard of, and I'm starting to think it wasn't no coincidence and maybe this is a tangled damn mess that smells of a lot of people I don't much like."

"Talk English, Duffy, for cryin' out loud."

"Ah, I'm burned up and now I don't know which way to squirm."

"Murdering is like that. Not the neat nine innings you're used to," Moran said.

He was right, a sharp old mick who never should have left town. But I'd had enough. I had to ring off and figure out where to go to from here. I had two deaths on my box score now, maybe two murders, for all I knew, and the game was getting damn complicated.

"You know, a guy like Obie Blintstein," I said, "I could understand choking on a chunk of steak or a pork chop. File that under poetic justice. But not on a lousy milk shake."

"Malted milk," Moran said, ever copyediting. "But you're right. It's not fitting."

"When's the funeral?"

"Tomorrow. Open casket."

"Wires off?" I said.

"I hope to Christ or I'll climb in the box and cut 'em myself," Moran said.

Petey took it hard. Very hard. In fact, she cried her eyes out. She wanted to get on the next plane to San Diego.

"He was such a grand guy, Unk," she wailed. "And so sad! Think of how desperate you have to be to wire your mouth shut."

That was a threshold I had not crossed, so I kept my

mouth shut. Petey dropped onto the sofa and pounded her knees. She was young and not used to shocking news. I had taken Pearl Harbor, JFK's assassination, and Kenny Hubbs, so my veneer was a little thicker.

She was pretty serious about going to Obie's funeral. I told her to send flowers instead.

11

Cookie

I waited for them, but they never came. Petey's schemes, that is, the plans I knew she had pedaling pell-mell through her head like Phil Cavaretta going from first to third on a sacrifice bunt.

In the days that followed Obie Blintstein's demise, she did not rekindle the issue of becoming a mole. After recovering from that shock, she just sprayed pleasant small talk like a singles hitter, lobbed a few questions, second thoughts, conjectures, and noncommittal banter about the whole kettle of fish, and went about her business. But something had changed. Something was up. I can smell a rally before the first pitch. But I didn't say as much.

One day Petey announced that if I did not need her, she wanted to go out and look for a pair of shoes. She had on a pair of jeans and perfectly fine sneakers, a beer T-shirt, her hair pulled back and tied with a piece of terry cloth. The new shoes line was pretty ordinary, and I was surprised she tried it on me. From what I could see, her shoe tree consisted of a couple pairs of overpriced Reeboks and those soft leather boots. She needed another pair of each about as badly as I did.

But I nodded and waved her to the door. I waited a few minutes and followed. In the lobby I stopped at Biz Wagemaker's post. He had the *Sun-Times* open to the box scores, and next to it was a black-and-white TV no bigger than a lunch pail.

"How are you today, Henry?" I asked.

"In the late innings but I'm still alive," he said.

"What are the chances today?" I asked.

"Wind's blowin' out and the Cubs"—he pronounced it "coobs," as if it were a diminutive, slightly foreign entity—"got that sorearm lefty goin'," he said, and shook his head as if to say no thank you. His voice was thin, and his hair was white, but he still took his baseball seriously. Then he threw back his head and launched laughter that echoed off the marble.

"See my niece just now?"

"Couldn't miss her. She give me the good word. Now tell me, Duffy, where she get henna hair like that?"

"The family's full of beauties, Biz."

"Could that be so?"

Then he laughed again.

"You see which way she went?"

"North. Up the Drive."

Biz was right. She had a couple blocks on me, so I had to hustle. But even if she lost me, I had an idea where she was going. North to Addison and then west. She was walking at a good clip, and it was all I could do to stay with her.

It was a clear day, a sky full of powder-puff clouds and Biz's southerly wind, which wasn't much of a wind at all. In no time the walk made my legs groan, my lungs ache, and my heart race. I sucked air like Harry Chiti running out a triple. As far as Harrys go, Harry Truman used to do this kind of thing every morning before work. That was almost enough to lose him my vote for fear he'd make it a federal law. But he didn't have to worry; I voted for Harry then and I'd do it again now.

Five more blocks west on Addison, away from the musky smell of the lake, across Broadway and all that nonsense that passes for something called New Town, over to Halsted and the Town Hall police station, where I spent many a night trying to find out about the latest trouble Hack Wilson had gotten himself into. Hack used to tell me, "I never played drunk. Hung over, yes, but never drunk." He also said that on some of those gray afternoons it wasn't unusual for him to see three base-balls coming from the pitcher's hand. How did he know which one to swing at? "The middle one was usually the real one." Joe McCarthy once put a worm in a bottle of whiskey to show Wilson what it did to the creature. Said Hack, "It just goes to show that if you drink whiskey you won't get worms."

I continued west past a school playground and a row of Chicago three-flats, graystones that up until a few years ago were inhabited by a bunch of gang punks with spray paint, but now are being bought up for un-godly sums by people who drive German cars. I walked beneath the tracks of the Howard Street El, whose rid-ers, thanks to a tradition started by old Will Veeck, know if the Cubs have won or lost by the color of the flag ahoist on a center field pole. Finally, I came into plain view of that shrine known as Wrigley Field.

By this time I'd gained considerable ground on Petey, who had slowed and seemed content to let Cub fans carrying knapsacks and thermoses and ball gloves pass her on the right and the left. She prized these fans, knowing how steadfast they were, as tenacious as Wrig-ley Field's ivy, I too often wrote.

They were fans who had coined the word "long-suffering," fans who had fed on the crumbs and picked clean the meager bones thrown them by that dismal club in the bleak years since they won the pennant in '45. Dozens of tear-down and rebuilding years, the Col-lege of Coaches, and P. K. Wrigley watching on televi-sion from Lake Geneva, Wisconsin.

Then came 1969 and hope eternal: Durocher, Banks, Santo, and Williams on a team that led all the way until September when "swoon" was too gradual a term. Then came fifteen years of pouting and punching bags until '84 and the playoffs with San Diego. That ground ball under Leon Durham's glove, a mitt soaked, we learned later, with Gatorade, and heartbreak was mingled with the misery.

Petey knew all that and more. She also knew that Cub fans were kids, off from school and watching base-ball in the daytime, under the sky, on real grass. She walked past the souvenir vendors on the sidewalks, the open air corner bars, the parking lot hawks waving customers into spaces the size of bacon strips, the hot dog joints and that goofy appliance store with the stuffed gorilla out front. She passed peanut salesmen and ticket scalpers, the rabid evangelists, and T-shirt vendors.

Then the ballyard itself, the white stucco and decorative stone, and, until they put an electronic and inane message board along with it, the venerable, scarlet WRIGLEY FIELD shingle above the gates at Clark and Addison, the queues at the turnstiles, the ticket booths. The day's traffic was busy but not hectic, no shoving, no barricades to control the lines. It would be a good crowd but not a mob.

Under cover of the fans, I could stay on Petey's heels without her noticing me. She bought an unreserved grandstand ticket. I followed, not buying but flashing my card, a lifetime pass courtesy of Cub management upon my retirement. Since I had spent the better part of my life writing about the team and still had not convinced people to abandon all hope, the brass decided to punish me by allowing me to watch some more for free.

Petey roamed, first buying a hot pretzel, then strolling about the stands in the aisle separating the box seats from the rest of civilization. My pass allowed me to sit on a folding chair on a catwalk suspended in a godawful space between the lower and upper decks, but as the same old Will Veeck, whose daddy was once president of the Cubs and who ran the stands first as a vendor and then as groundskeeper, once said, the game looks better from the cheap seats. After several minutes of this, of Petey walking and gawking from one end of the park to the other, I decided to hop up to my isolated perch if for no other reason than to watch her without having to hoof it.

I lost sight of her, of course, getting up to the catwalk, but found her again in a few minutes. She was still lolling, but now she seemed intent on looking into and about the stands, as if to locate a friend. She did this even after the game began, during a Philly rally, a Cub double play, and a frozen rope foul ball that knocked an Old Style clean out of a vendor's clutches.

Innings passed and she had still not taken a seat, and I began to wonder. She seemed oblivious to the game, which wasn't like her. Some years earlier I'd taken her to the park and she'd watched like a scientist, absorbing the whole thing, studying every move, asking more questions than even I could answer. Today she could just as well have been at a tractor pull for all she seemed to notice.

Then, in the flurry of a two-and-two hit-and-run pitch where the Cub hitter actually poked the ball through the spot the second baseman had vacated to cover the bag, I almost missed it, and her. Where she had been strolling lazily, she had suddenly stopped and was talking to a short, thin, dark guy near an exit tunnel just behind the Cub dugout. I did not get a good look at him, nor could I see where he came from. He wore a rumpled white sailor's hat with the rim pulled down, skin-tight shorts, and tennis shoes. But he didn't look like he knew a clay court from a clay pigeon.

For some reason he looked familiar to me, but I couldn't figure out why Petey would be interested in him. He was Latin, or thereabouts, a runty version of Adolfo Phillips. The kind of guy you meet on street corners for all the wrong reasons. He seemed very interested in Petey, and Petey seemed very interested in him. I was interested in both of them, and doing my damnedest to try to figure out where I'd seen this guy before. As Petey talked he nodded, oozing charm and invite, as smooth as Manny Trillo covering the bag.

Then they turned and walked down the steps, out of sight, but not before I saw him put his arm on her shoulder.

I hopped out of my seat like a nervous uncle. Half the alphabet away from that section, I stumbled down the stairs and beneath the stands, moving in and out of fans like a drunk in search of a bathroom. When I got around to that side of the ballpark there was no sign of either of them, not in the ballpark saloons or hot dog stands. I checked back in the grandstands. To no avail. I pedaled like an idiot down the concrete steps and into the lower concourse. I looked both ways, craning my neck, cursing under my breath, when I heard the shout.

"Hey, Mr. House!"

The voice was familiar, too familiar, and I turned and looked smack into the earnest mug of George Whiteman.

"Good to see you again. Everything's okay, isn't it?" he said.

"Yeah, so how are ya, George?" I said. "Lost track of my niece and I'm trying to spot her."

No sooner had I said it than I couldn't for the life of me figure out why I told him the truth.

"Not a youngster, is she? I could have security put a blanket out for her," he said.

"No, she's no youngster. We just got our signals crossed, I guess."

"Ah, that's good. I hate to see people not enjoying themselves at the ballpark. Especially you, Mr. House. And I know Mr. and Mrs. Rohe enjoyed your little visit the other day."

"It was mutual, to be sure," I said.

"Good, good. Where you sitting? You okay? I always have a few open seats . . ."

"No, no, you've done too much for me already, George," I said. "See if you can do something for that team of yours."

"Boy, ain't that the truth. We get hitting, and no pitching. We get pitching, and the hitters take a pill. I gotta run now, Mr. House. You know where to find me. Anything, anything at all," he said, and patted my shoulder.

Then he was off, no doubt on an errand of some inconsequence. In the meantime, I'd been ditched, dammit. Petey was long, and I mean long, gone. Ignoring the soprano swell of cheers above me—which might mean the Cubs were creating a bona fide rally but more than likely signified a pop-up so impressive that the puerile eyes of the crowd believed it was destined for the bleachers—I left the ballpark.

I took one last trip around the premises. Going

north up Clark, I checked the doughnut shop and Mc-Donald's. At Waveland I turned east, past the car wash and the players' parking lot. The boys in the firehouse across the street lifted their cups to me. I kept walking, beneath the left-field bleacher wall and the cyclone fence stuffed with beer cups to spell "CUBS" and past the ball shaggers slouched on parked cars along Kenmore Avenue. A decent poke to left would clear everything, and these guys were ready to swarm after it like pigeons on bread. Behind them gleamed the house and apartment building windows that had been shattered through the years by such feared sluggers as King Kong Kingman, Andy Pafko, and the immortal Barry Foote.

At Sheffield I checked Murphy's, and observed a moment of silence for Murphy and the saloon that once was here. Still no Petey and friend. I trooped south along Sheffield and the right-field wall, wondering if ever there lived a mortal who swung an ash as viciously and errantly as Swish Nicholson. I walked around the Phillies' team bus, then crossed the street and poked my head inside the Sports Corner saloon at Addison. Again nothing.

Hailing a cab back to the apartment—I'd done more walking and running than any of the current crop of overpaid Cubs would do in one afternoon—I decided to go about my business. I napped for an hour and woke in time to hear Red Carney wrap up the game. Over a bowl of chicken noodle soup I listened as Red compared a Cub relief pitcher who had come on to save the game in the eighth, to Lindy McDaniel, a tribute I thought premature even by Red's standards. And McDaniel, Red went on, was one of the most underrated relievers of all time, a tribute Red had borrowed from yours truly.

Be that as it may, Petey came in just before seven. She looked like her usual self, pinked by the sun, hair mussed happily by the wind, and yet not a thing out of place.

"Shoes fit?" I asked.

"Huh?"

"The new pair you went after."

"Oh, them. Couldn't find what I wanted. Ended up around Diversey Harbor watching old black guys fish."

"Cubs win?" I said.

I got not even a sidelong glance.

"They in town?" she said.

Which was the wrong answer.

I waited for a better one. It never came, and I decided not to press. Her answers contained too much tap dancing, and I suddenly got a feeling for what she might be up to.

I heard no more from her that night. She stayed in, as content as a bunny. She put on a pair of little earphones connected to a little tape deck clipped on her little waist, liberated a couple stalks of celery, and lit into a book. I left her to her reading, or plotting, I don't know which. I was bushed from all the mileage and, despite the nap, fell asleep a little earlier than usual.

The following morning Petey slept a little later than usual, but when she came into the kitchen for some V-8 juice she was scrubbed and ready. Red hair in the light of day—she looked better than Red Schoendienst and RustyStaub in their primes.

"And a good morning to ya, Uncle Duffy," she said.

Coming from anybody else it would have been baloney. From Petey I bought it.

"You too," I said.

She flipped through the *Sun-Times* and cut a banana into a mountain on top of her Rice Krispies.

With an eyeful of one and a mouthful of the other, she mumbled, "Have you changed your mind?"

"No, ma'am. I'd take Lindy McDaniel over Hoyt Wilhelm any day," I said.

"Me. Behind the lines. Mata Hari," she said.

"You know what happened to her, don't you?"

"Uh—"

"Executed by the French."

"I'll stay in town," she said.

"And aboveboard," I replied.

"Then how will this investigation get off its butt?"

"Persistence. Research. Intuition," I said, impressing even myself.

"All you're doing is *talking* to people," she said, putting the italics on "talking" as if it were a crime.

"It worked for Nero Wolfe."

"Who's that?" she asked.

"For shame," I chided.

"Oh, I *know* who that is. But this isn't a pulp mystery by a deceased writer, this is vérité," she said.

"Let's not profane writers, living or dead," I replied.

"Sorry. But time's a-wasting."

"To put it into your language, ixnay," I said.

Thus ended another game of pepper.

A little later Petey said she had to check in at law school that day. Around noon she was on her way. Again I followed her. I know a scheme when I smell one.

The route was the same. The Cubs were in town for ten days of an extended home stand. Only this time Petey did not stroll. She walked briskly over to Wrigley, bought a ticket, and proceeded to the first-base side and a spot in the stands behind the visitors' dugout, now occupied by the Pirates, where she was joined by her new Latin acquaintance.

At the same time I went furtively over to the Cubs' dugout and whistled over Jimmy Sheckard. The muchacho, Sheckard told me, was a guy named Cookie. He was about to tell me more when he was suddenly beckoned into the batting cage. I frowned and looked across the diamond to the spot in the seats where Petey and this Cookie were huddled. Today he reminded me less of Adolfo Phillips than of Roberto Duran. The two of them chatted briefly, then walked casually toward the Pirates' bullpen in right field. It was still a good while before the 1:20 start, that now-eerie time when Dream Weaver had met his 3–2 pitch. The teams were alternating batting and fielding practice, and the players bantered with each other, the coaches, and even a few fans. A line of pitchers ponied through laps, reminding me of Mickey Lolich, the old potbellied Detroit lefty, who once told me, "The only thing running and exercising can do for you is make you healthy."

Petey and friend lingered for about ten minutes, then backtracked around home plate until they got to the Cubs' bullpen. This time they stood at the railing. A few players sauntered over. They seemed very friendly with Petey as well as with the Latin mystery man. It all looked pretty innocent if you didn't know what you were looking at. I wasn't sure I did. Before I knew it, a local talent had sung the National Anthem and the game was on. Petey and Cookie had box seats.

Petey came home that night at seven o'clock. She said she had already eaten. Again I asked, and she said she did not know if the Cubs had won or lost. I took her word for it.

That night the first of the phone calls came in. I picked up, offered a hearty greeting, and listened as a definitely male voice stuttered and stumbled. At my second utterance the intruder hung up. Another call came a minute later: the same moron, I presumed, yet this time emitting no sound at all before the hang-up.

Petey got the next one, and the next, and both apparently were for her. In all, six calls came in just under an hour. I got the fifth one, in which a basso profundo asked for a "Miss Biggers." Gratified by the unexpected show of manners, I answered likewise. Petey had suddenly become a very popular girl.

She was also out the door. Though it was after the hour of the nightly news, she suddenly appeared in a fresh set of clothes, a jangle of bracelets, and a whirl-wind of scent.

"See ya at breakfast, Unk," she said, and gave me a kiss on the side of the head.

"Watch yourself," I said.

"You bet," she said, as if fulfilling the assignment would be effortless.

As soon as she left, I phoned the desk. DeWayne, the night man, was on duty and, as usual, was on top of things.

"DeWayne, give me a line on whatever picks up my niece," I told him.

"Gotcha," said DeWayne.

He phoned minutes later.

"Big boy. 'Bout six-two, two-ten. Dead ringer for that third Cub starter with no smoke."

"Pfiester."

"Got him. Went off in one a them short Caddies."

So I had presumed right. She was her uncle's niece. The urge to dig was too much for her.

A little more digging of my own told me that she had made contact with Cookie Sopas, a park fixture whose role in life was to facilitate meetings between players, both home and visiting, and interested female fans. It was an arrangement as old as the sport. As far as anyone knew, Cookie was innocuous, a mañana, without a care and—thankfully—a rap sheet. He was one of those eager flotsam that seem to pop up in parks, carnivals, fests, and arenas like mushrooms after a rain. The good news was that it had taken Petey no time to find him. She had keen antennae; she was good. The bad news was how quickly Cookie took to Petey.

I stewed over it for the rest of the night, to where I got sick of arguing with myself. So what if she was spending a few lazy summer days at the ballyard and meeting a few ballplayers? It was a perfectly American thing for an American girl to do. That was my most charitable assessment. Having scratched the underbelly of Dream Weaver's trysts, I made other assessments that had no charity about them.

Whatever happened, Petey was indeed up for breakfast the next morning. She was cheery as a robin, noisy and hungry, and she uttered not word one about the previous evening. At noon she went to the ballpark.

That night, after another flurry of phone calls, she had another date. I got on the house phone.

"Who you got, DeWayne?"

"Pitching change."

"Another arm?"

"So to speak. Boy with that dink slider."

"Orville Overall?"

"That be the one."

She was working her way through the starting rotation. I decided I had to stop her before she got into the middle relievers. And do it that night, or the next morning, whichever came first.

12

Pfiester and Overall

It was 3:10 ante meridiem when her key aligned the tumblers. She was a night hawk all right, as quick at this hour as she was at noon, and when she saw me conscious she swooped.

"Great, Unk, I'm glad you're up!" she gushed.

"I am?" I said.

"Great line," she said, losing me.

"I've found out some dynamite stuff on the case," she went on.

She landed with one leg beneath her tail on a footstool, facing me as I sat like an old grump in his pajamas and bathrobe and overstuffed chair.

"Prick up your ears! You'll never guess who Dream was seeing!"

"The general manager's wife. Name's Lila," I said.

My words lanced her, like bad news and heartbreak. Hers was the face of a relief pitcher who just threw a ninth-inning pinch-hit home run on an 0–2 count.

"You knew?" she said, her voice a whisper.

"And I didn't have to hook up with Cookie Sopas, the park pimp, or dally with half the Cubs pitching staff to hear that one."

"You know about Cookie too?"

Her tone had fallen from that of Lois Lane to Bambi.

"I thought we had an understanding," I said.

"I just dated a couple guys. Harmless stuff."

"After what happened to Weaver and Blintstein, nothing's harmless."

"Obie? Is there something new on Obie?"

"I didn't say that. As far as I know he expired on a milk shake—"

"Malted."

"Whatever. But his timing stunk. And your covert activities have a similar bouquet."

"It can work, Unk. These hunks told me a lot of stuff. Names, places—stuff I know they wouldn't tell you or the cops."

"I'm all ears," I said.

With that Petey set out on a recap of her trysts with Pfiester and Overall, the Cub flingers who'd worked in Dream Weaver's shadow for the last few years. Both on and off the field, as Petey was to learn.

"Jack—Pfiester, okay?—he makes the big come-on. Drove up in a black Cimarron, a Cadillac, with black leather interior, if you can believe it, the kind guys used to borrow from their dads—except Pfiester owns this one. Pretty sleek, I'll give him that, not your land yacht model 'cuz Cimarrons are more like Bimmers—BMWs. But it was a Cadillac just the same and that's so déclassé for a young guy, except Jack didn't seem to know it.

"Trouble with these guys is that they've got major dollars and never learned how to spend 'em. They hang with all those agents and restaurant guys who drive those pigs so they think they should have one too.

"But Jack was pretty smooth. Little too much gold jewelry, but he was okay. Kinda cute, good bod. He's got this little crooked grin when he's amused that you'd swear he copied from Tom Cruise or something. I can just see him standing in front of a mirror, playing *Top Gun* on the video about a thousand times to get the smirk just right. At least that's how it hit me.

"So as soon as he hears I'm from Cincinnati and relatively new in Chicago he gets an attitude, as if I'm some coal miner's daughter or something and he's the big-city Mr. Suave. I didn't tell him I knew he was from a little horseturd town in Oklahoma. You gotta let guys have their pretensions for a while, otherwise you piss them off and they get grumpy and the next thing you know you're paying your own way. It's happened, trust me, Unk.

"So he takes me around the places all the Bear players own. Ditka's, et cetera. Definitely frantic—lots of women with capped teeth and layers of make-up and outfits that cost them a mint but look really stupid and will be out of style the day after tomorrow. Half of them you want to go up to and say, 'Darling, look in the mirror. It isn't working.' But who has the time?

"Anyway, Jack really got off on driving up front and stopping dead, right in a traffic lane—he didn't care. Then some Iranian car jockey who pretended to know him—but you know he didn't—came running up and Jack'd slap ten bucks at him and saunter on in. I'm talking show time.

"It was all I could do to stay with him, even though he played the Mr. Macho Man with his hand on my arm. Soon as we'd get inside he'd look around for someone to recognize him. I gotta say, it didn't take long. Those places play to the jocks, and Jack was in his element. We walked into Harry Caray's, and you'd a thought he'd just won a Series game. They all sucked up to him— women, guys, didn't matter—and me too, in that I was the DF—designated floozy—for the evening. They were all winkers. I got winks from guys I wouldn't hold an elevator door for.

"Trouble with all those places is that they're too loud and crowded to even hold a conversation. So I didn't get much out of Pfiester until later, in the car and his place, you know. I won't go into just how we managed that, but trust me, Unk, it was nothing the kid couldn't handle.

"I'll tell you this: Pfiester hated Weaver's guts. More than the jealousy thing, if you ask me, even though that's a big part of it. You got to have an ego to play, and these guys all have one as big as a house. Trouble was, Weaver just wiped them in the talent department and he never let them forget it. If somebody pissed him off, he loved to go out that night and see if he could get the guy's date. Really! Just intensely played up to the chick and worked on her to see if she'd leave with him. Sometimes he'd even lay bets with other guys on how long it'd take him. And enough of these chicks had no class—none, bimbettes—so that he actually got away with it.

"Jack said he treated his own women like hookers and cleaning ladies. Just cruised, used, and abused. When he got sick of one of them, his favorite trick was to get on Lake Shore Drive and really get her chafed, you know, screaming-tear-the-hair-out irate and then say, 'If you don't like it, babe, get out.' And the girl would be so hosed that she'd insist on getting out and he'd pull into one of those little turn-ins the cops use to give a guy a ticket and open the door. Right there on the Drive. Then he'd peel away laughing himself silly.

"Great guy, huh? So Jack said he knew a lot of chicks who just hated the guy. Wanted to break his neck. What I found interesting was that he said some of them had boyfriends or relatives who could get the job done, you catch my drift? 'In this town somebody always knows somebody,' he said. He thinks some guy did it as a favor to some chick. He's sure of it. I said, 'Get out, Weaver was too big for someone with half a lobe to seriously consider such a thing.' And he says, 'There's your trouble, a lot of these guys don't own half a lobe.' I didn't press him but I know I could get names out of him if I tried.

"And then he swears, Unk—I mean, he said he could give me chapter and verse on this—that Weaver and George Rohe's wife had a thing goin' on. So help me. Unsolicited. I didn't talk him into it. But I don't want to get into that all over again.

"Now Orville, my beau of this enchanted evening, was another thing altogether. Hard to believe these two guys play the same sport. Pfiester's all pose and veneer, and Orville's from Georgia and just crazy. Jack Pfiester shows up in a Caddie; Orville, he shows up in a Jeep. No top, just a roll bar between us and the wild blue yonder. Pfiester's got on a couple hundred bucks' worth of designer clothes and Overall's wearing jeans and a Grateful Dead T-shirt.

"Reminded me of the Bird, 'member? Mark Fidrych? Same overbite and curly hair and just as loony. Whatever happened to him? Rotator cuff? Anyway, Orville—'Call me Orv or call me Orville, jes' don't call me late for dinner.' I swear he said that!—he got major amusement out of cutting through gas station driveways and 7-Eleven lots just to avoid red lights. Laughin', said cops pull him over all the time and then let him go when they see who it is. Yeah, and who wants to take on Beetlejuice?

"But Orville's a good time and he's making me laugh. I can go a lot of rounds with guys who make me laugh, Unk. First thing he does is ask me if I know the rookie statues. Of course, I don't, so he beats it over to Lincoln Park and the statue of Ulysses S. Grant on horseback. He says rookies from visiting teams have to paint the horse's balls on their first trip to town. Bright enough so they can be seen from the team bus on the way to the ballpark the next day. I was impressed. Orville said he'd painted the balls on more statues than he can remember, and I didn't argue with him.

"Next he heads over to his favorite bar. Get this, the place is called The Big Nasty. I swear it was *Animal House* revisited. Out of control with kids spraying Silly String—this gooky string out of an aerosol can—and downing Jell-O shots. That's grain alcohol and Jell-O. J-E-L-L-O. A big hit on campus. The place is for kids physically out of college but mentally still in the frat house.

"Orville walks in like this place is made for him. I was cracking up. This guy wouldn't be able to find the john in college and he knows it. He told me his mother used to call cottage cheese 'college' cheese. That convulsed him. I said, 'I guess you had to be there,' and he didn't know what I was talking about.

"So I figure with the Silly String and the Jell-O shots that Orville is good for laughs and nothing else. I had to beg him not to take me to the Checkerboard Lounge, some R&B joint on the South Side, he says. I said I was definitely not ready for that, so he floors me and takes me to a place called Andy's instead. Little street bar behind Harry Caray's with live jazz. Honest to goodness. Even had beef jerky for sale on the counter. I loved the place.

"And Orville sits in a booth, gears down several RPMs, and gets frank about Weaver. Talk about a night-and-day opposite of Pfiester. Orville said the Dream never bothered him. He didn't try to take him on in the ego department. 'Anybody who brings me playoff money is my good buddy,' he said.

"What he said that interested me was that Dream had too much excess baggage for him. Too many deals, too many people around him. None of the players hung with him, it was like he had his own social zone. He said that was Obie's doing, that every time the team went on the road there was a new guy waiting for Dream, squiring him around. Guys in big cars with retinues, Orville said, except he didn't say 'retinues.' 'Restaurant guys' is how he said it. He said Dream was tied into a bunch of deals with these guys through Obie. Some of them went bad and people lost money, he said. Left some guy high and dry on some kind of franchise deal. Another time they were into the home water purifier business that went down the tubes.

"I asked him about Obie taking odds, and he said that was like saying—oh, how'd he put it?—like saying 'does snuff get stuck between your teeth?' or something like that. Everybody knew it, and most everybody stayed clear of it. Most, not all, as we already know.

"So I asked him who killed Dream. Just came right out. And he said he could throw a stick at a half dozen guys who looked the part. Down in Arizona during spring training he saw one of them pin Obie by the collar against a wall. Said the guy lifted Obie right off his feet, which is no little trick, and ripped into him. Orville said he didn't know what it was all about but it didn't look good. 'One of those restaurant boys,' he kept saying.

"And I'll tell you, Unk, he left me with the impression he knew more. He plays that country crazy boy bit to the max, but Orville Overall is a smart guy. Goofy smart. I can work on him. I know he can give me leads in all directions—"

With that she exhaled and yawned. It was a remarkable show of frailty from such a young specimen. I jumped in.

"So many leads and so little time. Weaver's notorious affair with George Rohe's wife. Obie's gambling. A bunch of bad business deals and guys who look like they own restaurants. A saga of intrigue very well told. But hold on, Pedro. This is getting too exciting for me." I yawned.

She slapped my leg. Hard.

"C'mon, Unk. Give me a break."

"Tell me why. Here it is a few innings shy of daybreak and we're rehashing clichés picked up from a couple of sorearms whose combined fastballs couldn't equal that of the deceased. I know you're not in law school yet, but surely you've heard of hearsay. For cryin' out loud, young lady, don't you realize that these guys are professional bullshitters?"

I was coming down hard on her. I was tired.

"I can sort through the jive. I've got the best teacher," she said softly.

I put my gnarled mitts on her knees.

"There's a killer out there, Pete. Somebody good enough to stitch a million-dollar ballplayer in broad daylight in the middle of a big-league park. And you're running around with his teammates trying to wring them for everything they know. How long before that gets around? How long do you think you can poke that wonderful nose of yours into this business without it being hacked off?

"So in the interest of prudence and cowardice, we work together on this. No more solo, sub rosa, hot dog stuff. Finis. Thirty. Or I'll send you back to the bushes, to Cincinnati for the summer."

She sniffed. I countersunk the point.

"Don't think I lack confidence in you and that brain of yours. Chrissakes, it probably did laps around those poor guys. That's not the point. What *is* is that the good uncle and caretaker in me says you got to watch your pretty little behind."

I cupped her head in my hands, her eyes locked onto mine and shone like green tips of neon, and suddenly she broke into a magnificent smile. How I loved this kid.

What was she pulling on me?

13

Sally

It didn't matter, I went to bed feeling lousy. Staying up half the night put me out of sync and out of routine. The digestive system was in turmoil and promised ill times to come: the commercials call it "out of sorts." The next morning, or what was left of it, dawned full of sunshine and clean air—the city's weather being on some kind of a roll—and I got out of bed feeling just as lousy as when I crawled into it. It reminded me of some dugout philosophy from Gil McDougald, the sturdy Yankee infielder: "It's easy to have a good day when you feel good, and easy to have a horseshit day when you feel horseshit. The question is, when you feel horseshit, can you still have a good day?"

Just what *was* I doing? I was talking to people I knew—Sheckard, Merkle, Harry Steinfeldt, the G-man Howard—and I was running down some of the names on the list Jimmy Slagle had given me. I was trying to coordinate the letters and phone numbers Obie Blintstein had provided. I was calling on contacts— sportswriters, general managers, scouts, agents, restaurateurs, clubhouse boys—spot men still inside the game who might know something hard enough to strike a match on.

What I had learned was that Weaver had had his share of dealings with questionable characters outside of baseball. Suspicious people seem to hang around big money, a fact that made it quite possible that Dream had been indirectly involved in illegitimate activities he knew nothing about. Del Howard had promised to keep me informed about anything he came across in his bailiwick—interstate violations, money laundering, that sort of thing.

As far as I could see, there didn't seem to be any kind of drug trail to unravel here, and for that I was grateful. On the other hand, Obie Blintstein, who had been charged with keeping Weaver straight with respect to drugs and women, was himself tainted. His gambling action was so thick he should have worn an eyeshade. I was disappointed. I considered Obie a friend and confidant. That didn't give me the right to define his morality, but this gambling business—which was common knowledge in the clubhouse, for crying out loud—cast a long shadow on what Obie had told me. And now he was dead, and I couldn't consult or confront him.

I was still haunted by the inside character of this crime. Right there in the ballpark, in the middle of the day, twenty minutes before game time, and *nobody* I had talked to in the Cub organization—from the front office down to the players—had seen anything or even sensed anything was wrong.

All in all, I had learned a lot but not really uncovered much. Theories, rumors, a lot of if-you-ask-me's, but nothing thicker than your average freshly spat puddle of tobacco juice. I was beginning to feel like the proverbial rosin bag: fondled, squeezed, tossed up and bounced in the palm and the back of the hand, useful and downright concentrated on for a few seconds, then tossed into the grass.

Petey, on the other, unrosined, hand, was a different matter. As I was to learn from her in detail somewhat later, she was sobered but not deterred by my toothless ultimatum that night. Indeed, from what ensued she must have thought my words were tantamount to a Leo Durocher pep talk.

What she had not told me that night was that she had learned of the existence of a young lady who knew as much about the private life of Dean Weaver as anybody warmer than Obie Blintstein. She was an insider, an enduring yet very private companion of Dream, one with whom he had shared many a bivouac but with whom he was seldom seen in public. She was a mysterious young lady, bordering on the mercurial, a presence so evanescent that not even Jimmy Slagle and his fellow detectives had drawn a bead on her. Petey, however, was to see her as vividly as Nestor Chylak saw a slider on the black.

Petey had pried this lead out of Pfiester, who let it slip that the lass's name was Sally. She had first engaged the Cubs and Weaver in her capacity as a flight insurance clerk in one of those islands at O'Hare. Ah, fate. Ah, the wandering ballplayer. Pfiester knew—or would divulge—nothing more, not the company logo, the terms, or the premium. It was up to Petey to do some old-fashioned rooting, à la pigs seeking truffles.

To do this, she fired up my oft-dormant stick-shift, fading maroon 1979 Volvo 162. A boxy, deceptively frisky roadster with 90,000 soft miles on it, the Scandinavian scurrier slumbered in the recesses of the building's parking garage. Our arrangement meant that Petey got an ignition key; she was an honorable young lady, and I trusted her with something as basic as a machine. That afternoon she guided it onto the Outer Drive heading north and west to the airport.

From a current insurance island mistress Petey learned that the female in question was named Sally Hofman. She had quit the white-knuckle business months earlier and become a pork belly trader at the Mercantile Exchange. And she had retreated from that mindless arena to something more cerebral, becoming a receptionist for a neurosurgeon. While there, she worked evenings as a Nautilus instructor at a downtown health club. When the neurosurgeon died of a previously undiagnosed aneurysm, she became a secretary in a law office. Finally, she had quit the law firm to clerk in a pawnshop on North Clark Street.

It was a raveled odyssey that would have taken an ordinary mind countless hours to undo, a tour that might easily have filled three make-work chapters in a garden-variety procedural. But Petey had no ordinary mind and required no such bland accounting. In a whirlwind afternoon of brick work, she deciphered Sally Hofman's code: peril before swine, brains to brawn, ad hoc to in hock.

As Petey recounted it to me later, the first thing she saw was three golden balls over the door, then cases full of watches and jewelry and walls hanging with electric guitars—thirty cents on the dollar—and there was the peripatetic Sally Hofman. She was a pressed, severe young lady, with a demeanor not unlike the cut of her punk-white hair, which was clipped shorter than that of a lot of starting pitchers I know. Oh, she was pretty, no more than twenty-four years old, fair skin and dark, darting eyes, a beauty reminiscent of Ida Lupino, provided Miss Lupino had a haircut like Whitey Herzog. The haircut alone set her apart from the usual tinsel hanging on ballplayers' arms, girls with hair like collies and teeth like cocker spaniels.

Petey saw all this and proceeded cagily as she browsed the pawnshop with genuine curiosity. These emporiums have always existed and always will, yet members of Petey's generation think they are relics of the days when gypsies came to town in horse-drawn wagons. It was midafternoon and business was light. Miss Hofman came out from behind the counter and exchanged small talk with Petey. They got on well.

In the course of chatting, Petey spotted the bauble. It was no bigger than a thumbnail, hanging from a thread-thin gold chain around Sally Hofman's neck, picking up the sunlight and coming into view in the cradle of her collarbone. Petey studied it until she was sure: it was an official All-Star game pin. This one was a *T* set inside a gold oval, the '85 classic in Minnesota.

The pin was not a common souvenir, but one of a very limited set the league makes available to players, the press, and certain associated individuals at each midsummer affair. It is part of an old and treasured tradition, a keepsake designed to reflect the year and place of the occasion, and tastefully but not gaudily produced. Any one of them is special, a collector's piece rare and valuable. I have a few myself.

Petey knew all this because Obie Blintstein had enlightened her. He had pointed out Dream's pins, and he lovingly displayed those he had collected for himself. Seeing one hanging against Sally Hofman's alabaster neck was a clear sign to Petey that she had found what she was looking for.

"I love that," Petey finally said, her eyes on the pin.

"Hmm," Sally said, absently fingering it.

She did not elaborate.

"Did Obie give it to you?" Petey said, then held her breath.

Hofman suddenly inhaled; her expression tightened.

"You know Obie?" she then asked softly.

"Knew," said Petey.

The chord was struck, and Sally Hofman opened to Petey like a lost manuscript. She did not need much coaxing or convincing. The very fact that Petey had found her, something she attributed to Obie Blintstein, was good enough for Sally Hofman. She started right in, a tapped vein of background.

"Well," she began. "I was the trophy Dean could not win. Oh, we dated. I was his lover. I was his big sister. I was his maid, his shrink, and his confidante. I spent more time with him than anyone knows.

"But he could not parade me. No way. No party doll here. I wouldn't go with him to his hangouts and his admiration society meetings. I wouldn't go down to spring training, and I wouldn't sit in the ballpark with the wives and girlfriends. I wouldn't fall for him, and I wouldn't get jealous enough to try to put a rein on him. It drove him nuts. And it drove me nuts too."

It came out like a carefully crafted cadenza. Halfway through, however, Sally Hofman, whose hard shell was thinner than she knew, began to tremble.

"Now he's gone. They're both gone—Obie too. He was so great. I think I loved him more than Dream—know what I mean? He was my Jewish father. Now I know how princesses are made. It's no mystery."

That brought a smile, then a sob. Bright sun streamed through the front window of the shop, mercifully unpatronized at this moment. Having found an empathetic ear, Miss Hofman was not about to stop. She went on about how she and Weaver had met, how she navigated through his fame and his money, the bravado of the team, and the incessant worship of the fans. She waxed eloquent on how she too had been swept up in it, how initially intoxicating it was to be with Weaver in public when he was instantly recognized and feted. How infectious that was, as if she too were somehow worthy, somehow elevated in the eyes of the public.

That passed sooner than she had thought possible, she said. But she stayed with him. Mostly because he kept coming back. No matter how many new women or new kicks or new highs came along, he came back like a lost puppy, she said.

"A lot of Saturdays he'd show up at my door at seven in the morning. Lean on the doorbell, force me out of bed. Unshaved, hair all matted, reeking of bodily juices—his own and somebody else's, obviously having slept little or not at all. What a dream, huh? He'd shower and shave and then we'd sit and eat Frosted Flakes and watch cartoons together. 'Rocky and Bullwinkle,' that was his favorite. He'd do all the voices. 'Watch me pull a rabbit out of the hat, Rock.' *'A-gain!'* "

She spoke matter-of-factly, inflecting only the cartoon voices, losing herself in the memory.

"Then there was Obie," she said wistfully, taking a while to get started again.

"He was a keeper. Just one of those people you tell yourself you'll never lose contact with," she said.

"Oh, did we cook! Did we eat! Chicken fried steaks and steamed lobster, lasagna, tacos à la Obie—God, you felt like you were going to explode," she said, laughing and choking.

By this time Petey felt her throat tighten.

"Oh, it's good to talk to someone who knows," Sally added.

Once she had cleared the deck of all of that, Petey set in.

"So what do you think happened?"

At that, Sally Hofman's eyes dried.

"There were so many sharks. You can't imagine," she said.

And she proceeded to detail business contacts, agents, hangers-on, fans, other players—all the points in Dream Weaver's wide and populous universe. He ran with a circle of questionable restaurateurs in Florida. He rubbed elbows with a half-dozen guys who claimed they were his partners in some venture or holding. He had a clique of real estate developers and business entrepreneurs buzzing around him. He once was thick with a lawyer who had been disbarred in three states and who had put him into several businesses, either as a visible partner or a silent investor. He owned racehorses in Kentucky with a breeder who was once a prime suspect in the disappearance of a wealthy candy heiress.

The ledger went on and on, and Sally Hofman knew every entry. These were leeches and parasites, some less benign than others, but the kinds of individuals who would have everything to lose, not gain, with the demise of the host organism.

"It was *Obie* who had problems," Sally said with added punctuation. "Imagine, here's the guy who kept Dream clean. Oh, you better believe it. Drugs, booze—to an extent, at least—and women. He was the guard dog, the filter, the tester. You couldn't get to Dream without going through Obie.

"So who was running book? You guessed it. Obie took bets. He had action all over the league. You could gamble on anything with him—anything except baseball, of course. He knew better than that. But he'd give you odds on any game in any other sport, on the next Miss America, or on what they'd find inside the *Titanic*.

"And I know for a fact that some first-class assholes came after him for it. Outfit guys. You know, creeps with open collars and no necks who just sit and glare at you. They don't want anyone cutting in on their action. Obie just laughed at them. He was Dream's guy, and you couldn't touch him. He never said that, but that's the message he put out," she said.

Petey's mind was clicking with the possibilities. Suddenly Dream Weaver was no longer the callow, innocent golden boy; Obie Blintstein was more than just the overstuffed, giggling gourmet. All roles were redefined. The stew was meatier; the murder in Wrigley Field rife with new players.

She asked Hofman which Cubs were Obie's best clients, but Sally said she did not know.

"Do you think somebody got Dream because they couldn't get Obie?" Petey asked.

"I doubt it, but I don't know that either. I don't know who killed Dream. I only know that there were bad guys who didn't like Obie."

"You don't sound like the jealous lover," Petey said.

"I don't believe in jealousy. You make your bed and sleep in it. Dream slept in mine. And elsewhere," she said.

"So I heard," said Petey.

"It's all true. He was incredible. As far as Dream was concerned, where there was smoke there was fire. His."

"Even the general manager's wife?"

"I've never told anyone this, but yeah, Rohe's wife. Honest to God. There's a case where the rumor has been around so long everybody figures it's a lie. Like all the politicians around here who are supposed to be so gay that everybody takes it as fact except nobody, not even the mortal enemies of these guys, has been able to mess them over with it. So I left it alone. The big stars always have stories hanging around them.

"But with Lila Rohe there was something to it. She went after him with an appetite. And what Lila wants, Lila gets. Dream said it was *her* idea right from the start," Sally said.

"Did Obie know?"

"I'm sure not. He would have *shat*."

Hofman cackled, and Petey laughed with her. Petey's mirth, however, was an act. Having been singed on the Dream-and-the-Mrs.-General-Manager item before, Petey didn't buy a word of it. In fact, it put a ring of baloney around everything Hofman had said.

"What have you told the police?" Petey said.

"The cops? Are you kidding? They haven't come calling and it's fine with me. You start talking to them and the next thing you know you're a suspect," Sally said. "That's their style, you know."

"How do you know I'm not a cop?" Petey said.

"Easy," she said. "You appreciated Obie."

Petey said she let it go at that, having given Sally Hofman our number, saying, almost in passing, that she was determined to find out who killed Dream Weaver.

"That's fine, I guess," Sally Hofman sighed. "But Dream and Obie are gone. Two big, wonderful flames suddenly put out. Like John Lennon. You miss them so much you just don't care at all about the person who did it."

"That's a nice sentiment," said Petey. Then she added, "But I care."

Hofman shrugged. Then she lifted an eyebrow.

"You're not a cop, are you?" she asked.

14

Howard M. Key

Charged with her new sheaf of leads, Petey did two more things. She returned to the apartment, and while I was off barbering with a friend of Red Carney who said he had a golden piece of information on the case, but which turned out to be a vision of nonsense from a suburban psychic, Petey called up Pat Moran, my friend at the *San Diego Bee*. She bandied my name so convincingly that even Pat bought it, and then she asked him for a big favor. Moran said he would do what he could.

The next day she ran off to the ballpark—which she told me afterwards rather than before—nabbed Cookie Sopas, and fixed herself up with a visiting ballplayer. His name was Johnny Kling, and he was a peach of a catcher for the Montreal Expos, the team that enjoyed the dubious honor for so many years of consuming more Skoal and sunflower seeds than any other club in the National League. Such are the nuggets you mine when you've spent as much time in visiting clubhouses as I have.

Kling was one of those new-wave catchers, a remarkable departure from the old backstops. In the days of Hartnett and Ernie Lombardi, a catcher was a human brick wall, a maw, a gruff, slew-footed mountain of gristle with tree-trunk arms and ham-hock hands riddled with knuckles so often broken that they looked like gnarled stumps—and maybe a few missing front teeth. Catchers' togs were called the "tools of ignorance," and as Rocky Marciano's mother said when her son chose boxing over baseball: "I didn't raise my kid to be a catcher."

What a catcher did was run through the signals until the pitcher was satisfied, and then flop in the dirt in front of a slider as readily as he would dig into a plate of potato salad. He wore a cup the size of a pith helmet and took foul tips off the same—as well as off knees, toes, fists, and Adam's apple—with a grunt and a curse. Catchers had names like Chiti, Cannizzaro, McCullough, Cochrane, and Burgess. In the real old days a catcher would wedge a chew in his cheek and expectorate a stream of tobacco juice on the back of an opposing coach or manager as he loped by. The best of them could fire frozen ropes to second base and hit for the long ball.

Except for the shotgun peg, Johnny Kling was none of the above. He was wiry and fleet, weighing in at about 175 and looking more like a second baseman than a catcher. He was quick and cocky, with a low crouch, his right hand safely tucked behind his back as Randy Hundley devised and Johnny Bench patented, a mitt with its rim painted fluorescent orange, and his body girded with so many modern pads and flanges that a foul ball had no chance of grazing his bones. Kling was also, of all things in the spectrum of catchers, a base stealer, a go-go gnat who caused all kinds of problems when he got on base.

Off the field, Johnny Kling was just as quick, a fast-track guy with an eye for tight cars, loose women, and odds. He was also a sucker bet, a player who loved to gamble, which made him one of Obie Blintstein's biggest fish. He liked Petey the moment Cookie Sopas gave him the nod, and a postgame rendezvous was arranged for the next day. Petey was quietly ecstatic, convinced that she had a line on a whole new layer of intrigue in the private worlds of Dream Weaver and Obie Blintstein.

She kept all this under her carrot top, however, and let on little more with me other than to inquire about where we were going next and how soon. I wasn't sure.

I had some irons in the fire and some principals in the Cub organization itself that I wanted to talk to. She, for reasons hardly obvious to me, did not seem to mind.

That night she got a call from Pat Moran in San Diego. He told her that he had made further contact with the police detective working on Obie's death on the outside chance that it was not accidental. He had made a detailed inventory of Obie effects and told Moran that as far as he could find, Obie's did not have any All-Star game pins in his possession at the time of his death. Dream's were accounted for, all encased in glass, but there was no sign of any others.

Petey thanked him profusely, and she thought of how beautifully Sally Hofman's pendant had caught the afternoon light.

So Petey was on a roll. The next day she went off to the ball game and her date with Johnny Kling. It was a 3:05 game, one of those abominations the Cubs' front office devised to accommodate the expense-account fans and terrorize the players. Yes, it was nice that gaggles of lawyers and commodity traders could bolt the office at midafternoon and see a ball game. No, it was not nice that the late starting time provided the infamous shadow, the specter that, due to the position of the playing field, crept ominously across the infield at around 5 P.M. and plunged the batter into shade while bathing the pitcher in sunlight. Even the new lights couldn't do much against the shadow.

It is bad enough to face a 90-mph fastball the size of an arachnid in equitable conditions; it is a horror to do it in the disadvantage of the shadow. Lo, such was the origin of that slight smile on Lee Smith's face those many years when he was called upon to "bring it" under such circumstances. It was a wonder no one got killed. The players railed about 3:05 games; management, bolstered by full houses, never budged.

Petey sat in a seat comped by Johnny Kling and watched the Expos slap the Cubs 4–3. The Expos scored all four runs in the first inning, which is a foolproof way of defeating the shadow. The game ended at just after 6 o'clock, and Petey stretched out and watched Wrigley

Field empty. It was a golden, dusty time of day, with the sun setting behind the grandstand to the west. A few members of the grounds crew attended to the bases, the mound, and the batting area. One by one, the metal numbers of the scoreboard were pulled in. A red flag— Cubs lose—was hoisted on the pole for the benefit of fans passing by on El trains.

What had been, only a few moments ago, a field of motion and tension, an arena of flashing cleats, *thwocks,* and pistol shots from bats and gloves, whistles and chirps and a roar as a ball became a blur between pin-striped young men, was now just a calm, breeze-swept pasture with paths of red clay. The ivy rustled along the outfield wall. Windblown beer cups careened drunkenly along the aisles.

Petey sighed and gazed dreamily about. Real baseball fans love these moments, love a ballyard at dusk, and they drape their legs over the empty seats in front of them and envision themselves rounding the bases, these or others on fields far away. It is the summer's favorite reverie.

There is a story told of one day sometime after the Corporation had purchased the Cubs in 1981 from Bill Wrigley. After a game, when the fans had left and the stadium was abandoned, several Corporation executives came down from their perches and ran onto the field. They shed their brand of pinstripes, loosened their yellow ties, grabbed gloves and bats, and proceeded to run around the bases, toe the rubber, catch fungos, and take whacks at soft lobs. They chattered and yipped.

Such were Petey's visions for a few languorous minutes before she got up and ambled to the concourse below. There, just beneath the tarp-covered catwalk on which visiting teams clatter from the dugout to their clubhouse and just across from a balcony where visiting players often stand before the game and ogle the crowd, Petey presented her credentials to a security guard at the door leading to the tunnel. He let her inside.

She was directed to an area just below the steps

leading up to the visitors' clubhouse. It was at the mouth of the cavelike tunnel and storage area running beneath the box seats from dugout to dugout. A few battered folding chairs had been set up for spouses and friends such as Petey as they awaited their respective players. Two such young ladies, one black and expensively dressed in a leather dress, nylons, heels, and much jewelry, and a white woman wearing an Expo jacket and tolerating a toddler on her knee, were already seated. They sat silently, with dull looks that led Petey to believe they had endured similar waits in similar places many, many times before. And, she thought, they probably knew who she was supposed to be as well.

Along with the company, the area was dank and chilly. No matter what the weather outside, it was always cool in the ballpark's bowels. The place had all the charm of a groundskeeper's shack, which essentially it was, and Petey, in her trademark jeans and a thin short-sleeved sweater, began to shiver.

She sat only momentarily before her curiosity moved her to wander about. On tiptoe to avoid soaking her running shoes in the random puddles, she nosed deeper into the dimly lit cavern. There was little to sniff among the piles of sand, bags of chalk, thick watering hoses, wheelbarrows, rakes, shovels, tampers, rollers, the whole range of field maintenance materials haphazardly stored there. Yet she was genuinely interested in the underbelly of a ballpark.

It was eerie, like the dank sewers of Victor Hugo's Paris. Though a few fans still lingered in the ballpark, and its concourses still echoed with the timeless *pop!* of stomped popcorn containers, Petey felt totally alone. She heard only the dripping water, the scrape of her own feet on the muddy floor, an occasional groan of a forklift outside. She could almost see her breath. She touched the salty, white-dust efflorescence on the concrete overhead.

For Petey this was something like looking into someone's medicine cabinet, except that she was well aware of the significance of this place: the path and various access points to the tunnel were germane to the murder investigation. So absorbed was she in contemplating it all that she never thought to check for rodents —either the four- or two-legged variety.

She was only a dozen or so yards into the tunnel when the still air was concussed by a gunshot, a crack that reverberated through the cave and smacked off the wall behind Petey's shoulder. Petey jumped, instinctively spinning around toward the origin of the report, her eardrums buffeted by the sound. In an instant she saw a flash of light and she winced at another *crack*, this one followed, it seemed, by a rush of air.

She screamed, then flattened herself against the wall and screamed even harder. A light bulb down the tunnel exploded, plunging that area into darkness. The two women on the folding chairs also screamed, the baby cried out, and suddenly the tunnel was chaos.

The women's shrill cries brought the security guard from outside along with a phalanx of clubhouse attendants and partially clad Montreal Expos from the locker room above. They clamored down the steps, tripping on one another and shouting to learn what was going on.

"Down there!" Petey shrieked, pointing into the blackness.

"Somebody down there!" she repeated, learning firsthand how inarticulate one can be in moments of high drama.

The guard charged past her, his pith helmet flying off his head, into the newly dark abyss of the tunnel, unaware that he was running into the range of a man with a gun. The posse of players and attendants followed; one of them, wielding a Louisville Slugger, paused briefly at the stunned Petey, then rushed eagerly but blindly past her. The chasers scrambled headlong, shouting, splashing in the puddles, stubbing toes and twisting ankles on the lawn and sprinkling equipment strewn about in the tunnel. The toddler was now bawling uncontrollably.

Suddenly there was another popping sound, now distant and muted, followed by more shouts, scuffling, and what sounded like equipment being overturned.

Whatever degree of hell the underworld of Wrigley Field might have been heretofore, it was now breaking loose.

Petey, shaking and feeling her heart beating in her throat, numbly followed the parade. She was scared stiff, just now realizing, even in the midst of the frenzy, that she had been shot at. A real gun, an explosion, a gouge cut out of the concrete stadium wall like a divot from a freshly mown fairway by a piece of lead imbued with equal disregard for human flesh and bone.

Then she tripped, sprawling headfirst on the wet, muddy concrete like Charlie Grimm trying to take the extra base. She scraped her hands and bruised her right knee, and she had mud all over her. Hurt and groaning, she got up and continued on toward the melee.

She had not been alone in falling. After smashing the light bulb, the perpetrator, or "perp," as the police would call him, had turned and sprinted down the tunnel toward the west exit. He was still on the first-base side of the crescent-shaped cave when he hooked a foot on a hose and fell ass over heels. That lapse allowed his pursuers to gain on him, and their commotion brought attention from the opposite end of the tunnel.

Suddenly the shooter was caught in a squeeze play. Security personnel, two umpires, and a Cub batboy came at him from the third-base end of the tunnel, while the lead guard and the Expos closed in from first. It was not your classic rundown, but close enough. The assailant dove behind a stack of boxes full of giveaway "hot seat" cushions, then sprinted for what he thought was an exit door but was really a cardboard "Hey-Hey" display left over from the Jack Brickhouse days.

He fumbled and struggled amid surplus giveaways, cartons of Cubs umbrellas, Cubs travel kits, Cubs painters hats, Cubs wristbands, Cubs windbreakers, and Cubs bats, beanies, and key chains, all with the famous logo and your participating sponsor. He banged a hip on a broken-down condiment wagon, cursed, then knocked over a bevy of empty soda tanks which fell like bowling pins and clanged like chimes in a carillon. All in all, he was as stealthy in flight as he was adroit in his marksmanship.

In his confusion he wisely chose not to use his gat anymore. Instead, he was pounced on by his pursuers, who then turned attackers, and transformed the dark pocket of the tunnel almost directly behind home plate into a full-scale ruckus. Chief among the punchers were the two umpires, who, not carrying their usual burden of having to keep the peace, were uncommonly ferocious. They strained to get in their licks.

They wrestled the gunman to the floor in a scene reminiscent of the apprehension of Jack Ruby. His gun, a particularly lethal 9-mm automatic that police and bad guys alike have lately come to favor, skittered on the floor. Naturally, it was picked up by the Cub batboy before a player could trip over it and be awarded a base for interference. This batboy, not the same poor adolescent who was the first to come upon the murdered Dream Weaver, fondled the gun with more curiosity than he had ever shown a weapon belonging to Andre Dawson or Ryne Sandberg.

"We got 'im!" came the cry.

" 'Im," a wiry mug in his twenties, was pulled to his feet. He was muddy and bleeding, sporting a burgeoning shiner administered by one of the umps under his left eye, a welt on his neck, and two broken ribs. He looked like Don Zimmer after a bench-clearing brawl. He was jostled and pulled by clutches of security guards, who momentarily showed him off, like a catcher displaying the ball to the umpire.

"Hey, it's Key!" said the Cub batboy.

His words drew some curious looks and a glance from the perpetrator himself, but no one picked up on them. At that, a guard told the batboy to hand him the gun, and the keepers of security, as if they were escorting a drunk from the park, pushed their collar toward the security office.

Suddenly the guard who had led the chase from the start stopped and turned back to the crowd.

"Hey, where's the girl?" he shouted.

Petey was right there, excited and milling like the others. The players parted, and she followed the guards.

As they moved off and the scene settled, one of the Expos asked the question on everybody's lips: "Think that's the guy who corked Deano?"

Fortunately for Petey's hide, she called me from the ballpark as soon as she could. Had I learned any other way, another gasket would have blown. I do not have an endless supply.

"Uncle Duf, come down here!" she gushed into the phone. "You wouldn't believe what happened."

She called from a security office where she was being questioned by a roster of Chicago police detectives, including the inimitable Jimmy Slagle. They were on her like camera buffs at a nudist colony. She loved the attention and chatted gleefully, momentarily forgetting that she had stood up Johnny Kling. Actually, Petey had little to say, and, with the instincts of a good sleuth, she told them less. She had had a date with Kling. Fixed up by a guy in the ballpark who knew the players. A postgame drink and dinner, two consenting single people of legal age. She offered nothing more.

As for the incident, though frightening and inexplicable, she only knew what everybody else knew. She had taken a few steps away from the waiting area and suddenly somebody had started popping at her with a gun. In the darkness of the tunnel she did not know who it was; in the light of his arrest, she did not know why. She had never seen the suspect before.

This last statement was completely truthful. As to the why of the matter, which she was to divulge later, Petey had sundry opinions.

I arrived via cab at Wrigley and managed to huff my way past park guards—who had suddenly become efficient—over to the main security office. Nearby were a TV camera crew and a suit-and-tie on-camera reporter who gave me a dirty look as I gained entrance to a place he apparently had been shooed from. I moved quickly. I wanted no part of those video birds.

Inside was Petey. She sat there like a celebrity, her legs crossed and her foot jiggling, her white-rimmed sunglasses perched in her rust-colored hair like a Hollywood script girl. Detectives and club officials were leaning on her, almost literally.

Petey got up and gave me a hug, then stood back and spread her arms. She had cleaned off the marks of her fall, though I could see the strawberry on her knee.

"Unscathed!" she said.

I could see that this thing had all the makings of a lark, and I didn't like it. Whatever fear Petey had experienced in the initial ambush had faded in the glow of all this attention.

"What's going on?" I said.

"That's what we'd like to know," said Jimmy Slagle.

To continue the conversation, Slagle suggested that we change venue. Some fifteen minutes later, now after the supper hour, the bunch of us had moved from the chaos of the ballpark to the fluorescent wattage of the Belmont police station. Only a few rooms away was the perpetrator. Petey and I were talking. The arrestee, on the advice of an attorney who had come in on an oil slick, was mum.

"His name is Howard M. Key. People know him as 'Key.' And he's well known."

So began Jimmy Slagle.

"He's a hanger-on, a mooch. One of those chicken-choking types who gravitate toward ball players and big shots. And not for autographs neither. Key's a supplier. You name it, he can get it. Girls, tickets, meals, tapes, cassettes, and, of course, the big C. 'Just say nose,' and all that stuff."

Petey and I sat at a long Formica-topped table. A couple other dicks stood by, comfortable to let Slagle talk while they ogled Petey.

Slagle went on with his monologue.

"Key's got a sheet for possession. Been arrested more times than Jack Brickhouse said 'Hey, hey.' But no convictions for dealing. That means his lawyers plea

bargain their asses off for him. He's unemployed with
no visible means of support and drives a hand-waxed
Audi Five thousand. Wears the Rolex and the clothes
and pays tabs at the sports bars with C-notes that look
like they were printed yesterday."

"So what's a guy like that doing around the clubhouse?" I asked, starting to steam.

"Good point, Mr. Duf," said Slagle. "The Cubs people tell us he was persona no good—on top of shit list A
—ever since the drug fusses hit them other teams back
when."

"But somehow he got inside the tunnel."

"The pooch has his ways. And his friends."

"How about the gun?"

"It didn't ice Weaver, if that's what you're wondering. Could have nicely ventilated your niece here
though," he said.

He produced a police envelope and let a large
black weapon slide out of it onto the tabletop. It was a
handgun the size of Clint Eastwood.

"We found another one under the seat of his Audi."

"Complete with this attachment." He fondled the
barrel. "It's a silencer as nicely tooled as you'll find
anywhere this side of the Outfit. But it didn't do Weaver
either."

The gun smelled, or something did.

"So we struck out there, but the inning's still alive.
Which brings us to the question of why Howie M. Key
would take pistol practice at a nice girl from Cincinnati?"

"Who says he did?" Petey finally said.

She had the floor, and ran with it.

"He was down there. Who knows why? There's a
lot of merchandise there, some of it even stealable.
Maybe he's into old popcorn machines and giveaway
seat cushions. Then again, you said the guy has a history
of nose deals with players. To get near them, he has to
get the security guards to wink. He gets by them with a
gun, not your typical ballpark souvenir. I happen to
wander close by. In that light he probably saw me about
as well as I saw him, which wasn't well at all. He may

have thought I was on to him. Maybe he didn't think at all. He panicked."

"Sounds okay. You're a smart cookie," said Slagle.

"What's your theory, Detective?" I interjected, sensing an attitude I did not like.

"Well, let's just say that in this business, Duffy, you usually find people get shot at for a reason," he declared.

"And that people are sometimes in the wrong place at the wrong time," Petey interjected.

"That too," said Slagle, motioning the two silent detectives to leave the room. Jimmy Slagle pulled a chair in front of Petey and sat backwards in it, his two arms resting on the back. It was a classic pose, one as familiar to modern America as a manager with one cleat on a dugout step. Slagle assumed it well. He was the Gene Mauch of homicide detectives. He glared at Petey.

"Now I'll tell you what really don't smell good," Slagle said. "We got this twisty-looking niece of an ex-sports columnist, the same columnist, I might add, who's way out of his league sniffing out a murder case, thanks to the commissioner of baseball. All of a sudden this niece gets shot at by a guy with a rap sheet only a fart's breath away from the scene of the actual crime. I used to like your stuff, Duffy, but this time it's too damn purple for my reading taste."

"Well spoken, Jimmy, but you're full of shit," I said.

With that we went for the door, Petey's elbow firmly in my grasp. I was mad as hell. At Jimmy Slagle, at Petey. I was burned up about this whole can of worms, this kettle of fish, this tunnel of rats.

We got ninety feet away from the front door when I saw them, the same pack of TV and radio hounds that ambushes the winning pitcher or the home run hitter. Not only that, but among them was John ("Bulldog") Drummond, an old hand who knew every face in town, including mine. Bulldog and the others were lurking at the station in hopes of giving the ten o'clock audience a look at the Wrigley Field shooter.

Or his intended victim. I deduced that in a hurry,

stopped dead in the base path before Drummond could get me in a rundown, and swung Petey in a U-turn toward the opposite exit. Another step, a second's look at the young redheaded doll on my arm, and they would have jumped on us. And we could have kissed our own private investigation good night. With the help of a janitor we squeezed out the loading dock and headed for a far bus stop.

As we scurried away, I decided I needed a healthy bowl of soup, a robust cup of coffee, and a vigorous talk with Petey. We were crossing Western Avenue at Belmont when it suddenly hit me—not something big and vehicular, but a memory. I had not trod this corner in years, yet years ago I had crossed it hundreds of times. The locale was etched upon the hearts of Chicago kids like me as deeply as the feel of the Wrigley Field bleachers. In my haste and the attendant fuss of the police station it had not sunk in. Now the digression was a welcome one.

The cop shop stands on the site of Riverview, one of the best doggone amusement parks ever built. I'd haunted the place as a kid, losing my cookies on the dreaded Rotor, developing neck muscles like leaf springs in defiance of the fiendish Whip, riding the Bobs as if I were taming a frothing bronc.

As I was dropping my old man's nickels, kids like young Will Veeck—who had two good legs at the time— were picking them up. Literally. Veeck used to work the Cage, a mad ride that flipped you upside down and shook you up for a while. The idea was to scare you silly, let the blood rush to your head, and keep your feet above your head long enough to dislodge the loose change from your pockets. It fell down into a four-inch bed of sawdust through which helpers like young Veeck would later sift and split the take with the operator.

As a young man I'd also pitched considerable woo here, back when the Tunnel of Love smelt of roses instead of stinkvine. Now the barkers and the lights and the smells and the sawdust were gone. In their place are an asphalt amusement park in the form of a police station and a shopping center, two hollow but essential edifices in modern-day America.

"If you strain oh-so-hard you can hear the echoes of a million kids screaming with joy," I said to Petey. The memory had temporarily suspended my pique.

We crossed Western and walked into Bubba's All-Nighter, an emporium that plays on the erratic schedules and bad stomachs of the Belmont coppers. The place was deserted except for the fry cook and two customers, a black woman sitting at a table thumbing through a suburban real estate guide, and an off-duty bus driver with his nose in the racing form.

I took a chance on the cream of broccoli; Petey abandoned caution and ordered a hamburger with grilled onions.

"We almost blew the ball game back there," I said.

"You handled them beautifully, Unk," Petey replied.

"Smarten up, for Pete's sake! Pun intended," I growled.

"C'mon, I played dumb in there," she said.

"Smarten up, play dumb—who's on first?" I was ready to wring her neck.

I crushed a packet of Saltines in my bare hands. It was controlled but impressive fury, like Dave Kingman throwing a batting helmet.

"What were you doing down in the tunnel in the first place? Johnny Kling, for crying out loud! A catcher! What in the name of Willard Hershberger does he have to do with all this? And what are you holding back? Just what new stuff do you know? And I thought we had an agreement about free-lancing?"

My rapid fire was interrupted by the food: my soup, a green sea in a crock pottery bowl, her hamburger, a gelatinous briquet crawling with angry onions and sitting on a glossy bun. French fries as solid as Lincoln logs ringed her plate.

Petey lit into the mess like a famished adolescent. It was safer, she knew, than taking on me and my foaming at the mouth.

"I thought we had a deal the other night. You stop

the funny stuff or it's back to Cincinnati with you," I said, then slurped some cream of broccoli, which wasn't half bad.

"I plead innocent," she mumbled. "I heard Kling was a good time, so I made a date. I also heard he gets around—used to run with Weaver in Montreal—so maybe he knows something. Since the Expos don't come back to town until September, I figured it was worth a shot."

"And you got two of them. About head high, I hear."

"Good line! That'd be your lead, wouldn't it?"

"Oh, Petey," I moaned like a manager watching his starter get consistently behind in the count. "You could have been hurt down there. Real bad. I don't like to think about that. I like you. I love you. I also love your mother, and she'd die if anything happened to you. Ever consider that?"

"I'm sorry," she said.

"Were you scared?"

"I didn't even know what happened, it happened so fast."

"The fright comes later, or so I'm told," I said.

She pushed a french fry around the plate.

"What say we put a stopper on the tandem thing?" I said. "Say good night, Nick and Nora. Call it a nice try at being battery mates."

"God, no! Uncle Duffy," she said quickly. "We're close, so close. I know I can squeeze—"

"Close to blowing the whole thing," I interrupted.

Yes, I interrupted. My big mouth, I realized later, kept Petey from coming clean right there. And she would have if I had kept on with the notion of retiring her from the probe.

"If your face had made the papers I'd have no choice," I went on. "As it is now, more people will be calling you than vice versa. Imagine what the phone is doing back at the apartment."

It was my best grump. It worked insofar as she felt genuinely chastised. It may even have caused her to be a little more careful, but it did not open the floodgates.

That is, I still knew nothing of Miss Sally Hofman or of Petey's true hunches as to why Howard M. Key shot at her. She kept that on the back burner, fielded my bluster and vinegar, and kept the details to herself. She was a savvy, driven little bloodhound with leads to sniff out. She couldn't wait for the next day to come. The two shots in the tunnel had scared her—she would not like her dreams that night—and yet, they had totally invigorated her.

"Okay, from now on I'm Tonto and you're Kimosabe," she said.

"I'm Tinker, you're Evers," I said.

"And we leave nothing to Chance," she said.

I spilled soup all over my shirt.

* * *

WRIGLEY GUNMAN SEIZED!!!

DANGER IN THE DEPTHS: WHAT NEW EVIL LURKS IN THE BOWELS OF THE BALLPARK?

OUT *BEHIND* HOME! UMPS HELP NAB SHOOTER

SECURITY CHECK: ANOTHER UNSAVORY CHARACTER PENETRATES CUBS' INNER SANCTUM

Those were some of the headlines blaring from the tabloids thrown out of newspaper trucks in the early morning hours after the incident. Complete with photos of the suspect and his captors, mention of the presumed target—a redhead we have come to know and love—and drawings of the previously unknown netherworld of the ballpark. It was Weaver redux, or as Yogi would say, "Déjà vu all over again." Thankfully, without the attendant bloodshed.

I was right about the phone calls. Back at the building I told Biz Wagemaker not to give any reporters or TV crews more than the day's box scores. Inside the apartment the phone was an uninterrupted siren. The only newsies I talked to were my old editors, who seemed amazed that I refused to don my old eyeshade and tap out a dozen timeless graphs on the whole thing for a one-time payment of $250. Next came the team beat guys who'd been browbeaten by their editors to get to me. I told them Petey knew nothing more than what she had told the police. Then I bluffed and added that she was too scared to talk about it. Shaking like a pinch hitter about to face Lee Smith in his salad days. As I said it, Petey sat a few feet away gesturing and swooning and mugging like Theda Bara in the silents.

Then came the phone call I was afraid of.

"Duffy?"

"You got him," I said.

"Chambliss."

"Heard of him," I said.

"Dammit! Knock it off!" the commissioner said. The vocal assault rasped over the wires bad enough to make you want to switch long distance companies.

"What the hell is going on out there!?" he bellowed, before I could counter.

"Dammit," he continued. "I put you to work because things are going to hell in a handcart, and in no time Weaver's man Friday dies out west and now, of all the cockamamy deals, the papers are screaming that somebody named Patty Biggers—your *niece*, my secretary tells me—gets shot at inside the ballpark!"

"Petey. Short for Petrinella," I said.

"I don't give a shit! I want to know what's going on and I want to hear it from your mouth. Or do I have to hop a plane and personally kick ass and take names?" Chambliss was smoking.

I filled him in. He calmed down and bought it. He didn't like it, but there would be no ass-kicking or name-taking. He said he was glad Petey didn't get hurt.

Then, in a tone of voice like that of a suspicious hotel clerk, he said, "Your niece, eh?"

15

Graceland

The next morning Petey was out of the box like Billy Williams dragging a bunt. I had been up half the night fighting my belly, so I was asleep when she left.

My gastric discontent was telling me something about patronizing late-night greasy spoons. I'm a day-ball man, and I shouldn't tamper with tradition. Facing the dawn, I felt like Hack Wilson in his binge days. "Gin was his tonic," wagged Al Drooz. Nobody threw lemons at me when I got out of bed, as they did at poor Hack when he botched that fly ball in the seventh inning of the fourth game of the '29 Series; but nobody pealed trumpets either. As I poured my V-8 juice I thought about the cottonmouths old Hack must have endured. "Wilson was a highball hitter on the field, and off it," wrote Warren Brown. An easy, unkind cut.

By 8 A.M. Petey was gone without a trace or a note. I couldn't even guess what she was up to now, but if I could, I would have known that she and my Volvo were retracing the path to Sally Hofman, the pawnshop maiden. She did not have to go far, for she had learned that Hofman lived close by in a renovated three-flat just north of Wrigley Field and just west of venerable, noble Graceland Cemetery.

Graceland's well-appointed grounds cover several square blocks within walking distance of the ballyard. On game days, dozens of fan buses disgorge their riders and then park along Graceland's burgundy-colored brick walls. Though the barbed wire atop its walls appears foreboding, the cemetery has always been a favorite Chicago place of mine, often exhibiting more life and as many memories as the ballpark itself. Unfortunately, few passengers on the buses idling beyond its gates possess even an inkling of the greatness lying therein.

The same was true for Petey as she sat nearby in my flivver's front seat and munched on nouveau stakeout fare: hot tea and a croissant. As she munched and sipped, Petey was unaware that she too was being birddogged. Idling just down the street was an unmarked but obviously police-occupied sedan. The occupants were Jimmy Slagle and a companion. In his inexhaustible wisdom, Slagle decided to put a tail on Petey. He did this for two reasons: he did not believe Petey was as pure as the driven snow in this whole pepper game, and he was desperate for even a shred of a lead.

In a few minutes Sally Hofman appeared wearing $100-a-pair jogging shoes, a silver spandex leotard so tight it made traffic veer, a sleeveless Cubs T-shirt tied in a knot at her midriff, and a set of tiny headphones of the style Petey is fond of tucked over that inimitable white brushcut of hers. Oblivious to her surroundings, Miss Hofman started jogging east toward the boneyard. Petey quietly fired up the Volvo and shadowed her. Detective Slagle shadowed Petey.

Petey watched as Hofman ran south down Clark Street along Graceland's perimeter, then actually turned inside the cemetery's entrance. It was a ghoulish but effective route. Petey, figuring that there was no rear exit to the graveyard, decided that this was her chance. She parked the car, did a few quick calisthenics, and in her jeans, T-shirt, and running shoes jogged inside the gate at Clark and Irving Park in time to see Hofman going east along one of Graceland's winding paths. Jimmy Slagle, whose exercise regimen ranked somewhere between that of Smoky Burgess and Don Zimmer, stayed in his car.

Hofman was headed toward the southeast corner of Graceland, following the winding asphalt road past austere mausoleums, obelisks, and ample headstones, in and out of the shade of regal oak and elm trees. Near the east wall she followed the road north, past smaller, less ostentatious grave markers. She jogged steadily, hardly seeing the stones, lost in her private concert. Overhead an El train clattered toward Irving Park Road, slowing for the curve like an old roller coaster, bearing its bleary-eyed riders to the Loop.

Petey pranced north, relying on a jogger's dogged penchant for a complete circuit and speculating that Hofman would be less likely to get away from her at the end of her run than now. After a while Petey slowed to a walk. She was young but hardly in jogging shape. She kept her eyes open to the east, careful not to lose sight of Hofman's path, which was difficult because of the winding roads and the massive stone bonehouses all around her. It soon became obvious to Petey that she could very easily lose Miss Hofman in the forest of granite sarcophagi, obelisks, and mausoleums.

In her youthful ignorance, Petey did not realize that she had gone into no ordinary cemetery, no field of knee-high headstones. She was surrounded by the lavish burial temples of some of the richest white Protestants in Chicago's history.

Indeed, Chicago's Graceland is the eternal home of the Cyrus McCormicks, the Potter Palmers, the Marshall Fields, and several other of the city's monied mortals. George Pullman, the old railroad car builder, whose company was hit with one of the nastiest labor strikes in the nation's history, lies here in a lead-lined mahogany casket beneath several tons of concrete and steel. Seems George and his family were afraid that disgruntled former Pullman employees might not want the boss to rest in peace.

Then there are the tombs of Louis Sullivan and Ludwig Mies van der Rohe, two pretty fair architects; Daniel Burnham, whose magnificent plan saved Chicago's lakefront and who reposes on a lovely island in Graceland's small lake; Governor John Altgeld, who pardoned the Haymarket rioters; and I could go on and on.

But my favorite plots, the ones I would have steered Petey to right off, belong not to the rich or the visionary. They belong to a pair of pioneers in the sweet science, two of the finest pugilists ever to part the ropes. One was Bob Fitzsimmons, "Ruby Robert," a feisty Irishman who ruled boxing in not one but three weight divisions. Why, as a heavyweight the man vanquished James J. Corbett! The headstone bears a picture of Fitz with his fists raised, and does him justice.

The other grave is a waist-high stone rectangle in plain view of the elevated trains on the east end of the cemetery, which, alas, does not do its occupant justice. It is that of none other than John Arthur ("Jack") Johnson, the first black heavyweight champion. A maverick to the end, Johnson is one of only two blacks—the other was a rich tailor—buried in great white Graceland. Right there next to his alabaster-skinned wife, Etta, and the world knew all the fuss that match-up raised. Poor Etta ended her own life with a bullet.

A substantial but unadorned stone marks Jack's spot—for years it was virtually unmarked!—but it has none of the style, none of the power, none of the swagger of that magnificent brawler. No granite etching outlines that lethal right hand. No Loredo Taft sculpture captures his glistening ebony brow. No timeless prose fixes his memory in our minds or recalls the days when Johnson turned the sporting world upside down like no man until Cassius Clay. But it's Jack all right.

Petey knew none of this as she stepped carefully onto the manicured grounds. She was so preoccupied with her prey that she did not even spot a nearby stone shaped like a baseball. It rests over Bill Hulbert, first owner of the Cubs and one of the organizers of the National League way back in 1876. Engraved on the ball are eight cities—Boston, Providence, Worcester, Troy, Cleveland, Buffalo, Detroit, and Chicago—the circuit's original member teams. Dead over one hundred years, the iron-willed Hulbert no doubt has turned over several times at the doings of his beloved franchise. I, for one, have written as much.

* * *

About twenty minutes later Hofman reappeared, flushed and winded but still more ambulatory than her Graceland hosts. She had run halfway around the cemetery, then doubled back and gone past the small, tranquil lake in its center. When Petey spotted her, she decided then and there to make her move. She ran diagonally across a row of headstones, sidestepping, hurtling, getting up a good charge and startling Hofman out of her runner's reverie. Hofman lurched sideways and picked up speed, giving thought to flight.

"I'll run you down, bitch!" Petey yelled.

Hofman pulled up and exhaled loudly. Her shoulders slumped. She pulled off to the side of the road like a batter who'd just lined into a double-play and came to a stop, leaning one hand against a twenty-foot-high granite headstone that read: "My Beloved Brother."

"What do you want now?" Hofman said.

A slight steam of perspiration hovered about her arms and neck. She was out of breath and she was caught. She bent over at the waist and stared at the ground in her breathlessness.

"You set me up," Petey said, standing squarely in front of Hofman.

"Get lost," Hofman said, straightening up.

Petey smirked.

"From now on, sucker, I'm in your face," she said, summoning a spirit that hearkened back to when her ancestors were repulsing the Norsemen.

"Shit," Hofman said.

"Deal with me or the San Diego police," Petey said.

"Come again?"

Petey fixed her eyes on the soft skin of Hofman's neck.

"You stole that. That All-Star pin. It's one of Obie's. The question is: was he alive when you took it?" Petey said.

Hofman visibly blanched, turning as pale as a hitter just serenaded by some 90-mph chin music. She removed her hand from the headstone and touched the necklace.

"Yes, he was alive, and I didn't take it," she said.

"Convince me," Petey said. "Convince me you had nothing to do with the death of a great guy and that you're not in the middle of this whole mess."

Hofman again exhaled, partly from exhaustion and partly from the fix she was in. She shook her hands by her side, then wiped the perspiration from her face.

"Only because of Obie," she finally said.

Petey stood and waited.

"Okay," Hofman began. She turned her head down and began, not looking at Petey, staring almost trance-like at the nearby tomb.

"I was there when Obie died. It was awful. There were three of us plus him. Two of Dream's townies, his good-time girls. Cute but dumb. Obie flew me in, like he always did. He wrote and said he had to see us all. He couldn't take it with Dream gone.

"So just like always he made us food that wouldn't quit. Mexican food, as usual. Except he couldn't eat because of those stupid wires. He couldn't even *talk*, okay? He scribbled notes on pads of paper. Spelled everything wrong. When he laughed he squealed. It was awful to see him like that. But it was good too, like old times.

"Then he gave us the pins. So we'd never forget him, he said. 'Fat chance,' I said. 'That's what I am,' he said, 'a fat chance.' That's when I started to cry. Then we hit the booze, the sweet, after-dinner stuff, and a little coke. And then Obie said he wanted a malted milk. He had one frozen and we put it in the micro. He sucked it through a straw. Oh, we were so messed up.

"That's when Obie started to bawl. He was sitting on the floor. He shook and shook. He wrapped his arms around himself, okay? He rolled back and forth. He cried so hard it hurt. I never saw anything like it. We were all crying like babies.

"Then Obie started to cough and gag. His whole body started. Coughing, choking, malted milk coming out of the sides of his mouth. It was dreadful. We tried to help him. I was beating on his back. But it didn't do any good, so what do you do? We were so bombed and he had those wires on. He was gagging and vomiting and tearing at his mouth with his hands. It was so gross. He started turning blue and his eyes bugged out. Nobody wanted to call the police or anything so we didn't do anything but scream.

"Then he fell back against the sofa. He made these gurgling sounds, those terrible, choking—oh, it was awful. Then it stopped. He stopped. He didn't move anymore. He was dead.

"That's what happened. I didn't know what to do next. I only knew I wasn't going to stick around. I told one of those chicks to call nine one one or whatever it is out there, and I got the hell out of there. I guess they disappeared like I did. Nobody wants to get involved in a scene like death."

She stopped and put her hands over her face.

Petey was motionless, caught up in her own vision of horror, seeing the pathetic Obie Blintstein in his fatal sorrow. She had silently been crying for some time, the teardrops hanging on her chin momentarily, then falling onto the green graveyard grass.

She had no idea of what to say or what to do next. She did not know whether to be furious with Sally Hofman, to view her as an accomplice in Obie's death, or to embrace her in mutual grief. So she stood and stared, like so many mourners before had done on Graceland's grounds.

Then she shook herself and regrouped.

"That stuff about mobsters coming after Obie was crap, wasn't it?" she said.

Hofman looked up at her. To Petey she seemed like a very different person from the one she had first encountered in the pawnshop. She seemed tired of the whole affair and in need of a few pints of blood.

"It was Key's idea. The paranoid jerk," she said, her color returning.

"The dealer who shot at me."

"So they say."

"You know this sleazebag well?"

"Too well. Way too well. See, Howie and Obie knew each other. They had to because they both supplied the players—add Cookie and his girls to that if you want to. Key had the blow, Obie took the bets.

"Okay, so when Dream gets shot, Key goes nuts. Not that he could have had anything to do with it—no way. He had everything to lose and nothing to gain with Dream gone 'cuz that meant Obie and his 'in' with the players was gone too. All Key ever *was* was a cheap source of coke, okay? But he is real paranoid, you know, which is how you get when you're a blizzardhead like he is.

"Anyway, he freaks and calls me up the night Dream gets killed. 'They're gonna be on my ass,' he says. 'Why?' I say. 'What'd you do?' 'Nothin',' he says, 'I don't know what went down. I just know they're gonna squeeze the fat man and he's gonna talk.' I told him to stop being so paranoid because Dream wasn't a user, but he said it didn't make no difference because Obie could blow his whole operation. I mean, that's all he's concerned about, right?

"So he says to me, 'Just be sure as hell you tell anybody who asks you about Weaver that Obie is the guy. The Mob guys hangin' around and the whole bit. I said okay, it was no big thing for me."

"But you *knew* Obie," Petey said. "And you knew Key was a scumbag who was just covering his ass, right?"

"Yeah, but I didn't think it would happen. No way I thought Key could get Obie in any trouble," Sally replied, looking down at the grass. "Besides, I had a thing with Howie."

Even though Petey could not look into Sally's eyes, she could guess what that "thing" was built on.

"So Key thought I was a cop . . ." Petey said.

"I don't know what he thought for sure. He called me up again like a day or two before you showed up at the pawnshop. He said Cookie told him there's this redhead chick he's been getting dates for, and she's askin' a lot of questions about Weaver and Obie. He says, 'I don't know if she's heat or not—she sure don't look it—or who she's workin' for. But if she comes around, lay Obie and his connections on her and get her the hell away.' So that's what I told you."

"What did you tell Key about me?" Petey asked.

"Just that you'd been to the shop, that you seemed to know Obie already, and that you were hot to find out who killed Dream. That's all."

"So you *did* set me up," Petey said.

"No way! I told Key about you, but I had no idea the moron was going to—"

"Going to try to kill me!" Petey said.

"No! Scare you off is more like it."

"Scare me? He shot at my head!" Petey said.

"Sorry. If he had, it'd have a hole in it. That I know for sure."

It was now Petey's turn to exhale in frustration.

"So what do I make of you? How much of all this do I believe?" she finally said.

"That's not my concern right now," Hofman said, edging away from Petey toward the Clark Street gate. "I had nothing to do with Dream's murder. I never did him any harm."

"And never any good either," Petey said.

With that Hofman turned and walked away, out of the gate and Petey's view, and into that of Detective Jimmy Slagle. Jimmy eyed her from brushcut to leotard. But he never connected her with Petey. Hofman walked past the cop car and home.

Petey paused to mull things, and as she did she absently noticed the bronze marker on the monument in front of her. It was Pinkerton. Allan Pinkerton. Indeed, it was the same Pinkerton who provided security during the Civil War for Abraham Lincoln and organized a network of Union spies, several of whom are buried near him. Yes, the same Pinkerton whose name in the years to follow came to stand for the best in detective work and whose talents I have come to greatly admire.

Only yards away, had she been in any mood to observe, Petey could have seen the grave of Kate Warn, a woman and one of a handful of crack Pinkerton agents who had escorted Lincoln to his inauguration ceremonies in Philadelphia in 1861. Had they the chance, Kate and Petey would have gotten along famously, I'm sure.

Instead, Petey, feeling less like a crusading op than a would-be law student on a trail gone cold, only shrugged and passed by.

16

Frank Schulte

The Key episode remained front page in the days that followed. The press tried, convicted, and all but executed Howie M. Key a dozen different ways. The sportswriters, unencumbered by the presumption of innocence, all but stoned him to death. Justice and retribution in the toy department are swift. Hanging in the air was a veritable blood lust, and the pathetic Key was the repository.

If only the bush leaguer were up to the task. Alas, no matter how deep the press and the coppers dug, they could not uproot a single fiber of evidence that put his paw on the handle of the gun that shot Dream Weaver. Howard M. Key had committed his share of crimes, and would no doubt be a footnote in the dark history of the Chicago Cubs, but he did not commit the big one.

What bothered the hell out of me was that the guy shot at Petey in the first place. If he did it because she was getting too close to his action, what *was* his action? Where'd he come from? What rock did he crawl out from under? How did he tie into this whole mess?

Right about then, George Rohe made an acquisition that not only interrupted my musings but blew Howard M. Key right off the sports pages. Not just a cozy roster switch, but something qualifying for the meatiest of diamond clichés: the blockbuster trade.

I'm talking Rogers Hornsby for Maguire, Leggett,

Jones, Seibold, Cunningham, and $125,000. I'm talking Dizzy Dean for Davis, Shoun, Stainback, and $185,000. I'm talking Grimm for Boudreau—manager to radio booth and vice versa—Brock for Broglio, Murcer for Madlock. That's what I'm talking.

Indeed, Rohe shoveled a utility infielder, a pair of Triple-A throwers, and a pile of money over to the Yankees' farm system in exchange for none other than Carl Lundgren, the scintillating but disgruntled ace of the Bronx Bombers' staff. Lundgren was almost the American League equivalent of Dream Weaver, a shock-haired Scandinavian with a Cy Young Award and an arm as lively as Ann-Margret in her New Trier days. He had won twenty-five games two years in a row but was in a snit this season because the Yanks' despotic owner, Rupert Huston, would not renegotiate his salary. Lundgren's pique was one of those modern-day player tantrums that hourly wage-earning ball fans, as well as yours truly, regard as highly as bed-wetting.

Nevertheless, the Cubs swallowed Lundgren's $2 million salary and promised more. Rohe and the heretofore parsimonious Corporation picked up the tab as if it were so much chump change. The town was amazed, and the sports world was rocked at this unpredictable move. At the press conference, Rohe was asked whether the death of Weaver, and the disappearance of his salary, was a factor in buying Lundgren.

"Yes," replied Rohe.

And he said little more. The deal smacked of one of those corporate takeovers where the sums involved are greater than the gross national products of some Third World countries but which Wall Street sharpies invariably describe as "bargains."

A day later Lundgren, his ego, his salary, and a newfound disposition as balmy as Ernie Banks about to play two, were all dressed in Cub blue. And Wrigley Field stalwarts, those fickle goofs capable of seeing the sweet side of an ax murderer if he could throw nine solid innings, were elated.

I figured it was about time for a call from Red Carney for some updated badinage on the state of The

Game. The florid Figaro of phonics did not disappoint me. When the phone rang, however, I barked at it. It was a habit left over from the past few days when the ringer never slept.

"What got into your prune juice?" Red asked.

"Don't get me started."

"Only one known antidote," he said.

"Yes?"

"Chili."

"You're on."

Just a few blocks off the Drive on Irving Park Road, about halfway between my new place and my old place and a loud foul ball away from Wrigley, stands a diner. This is the genuine article: a single row of revolving stools along a Formica counter, a skillet jockey in a T-shirt, tattoo, and white paper hat, homemade chili available morning, noon, and night, windows that steam translucent in the winter, a sign outside reading "Diner" or "Grille."

I had already planted my ample behind on a stool when Red showed. He walked in with due hoopla, being as he is now Mr. TV as well as Mr. Radio. All three customers and the grillman huzzahed as he walked in. Watching him bullshit his way through it, I almost did not notice he had a shadow.

"Scoot over, Duffy, we're a threesome," Red said.

He was as voluble as ever, the audio up a few notches, the accent on every fourth syllable. In a while he'd realize he was talking to me, we weren't in the booth, and his delivery would revert back to its familiar fits and starts.

"You know Frank Schulte here, don't ya?" Red said.

Fact is, I did not. Schulte was a stringbean of a guy, a dead ringer for Don Kessinger except that he wore a pair of Jim Brosnan bifocals and had about as much hair as Leo Durocher. He shook with a soft hand, the fingernails chewed to the quick.

"Frank here's in the front office. The books. He controls the ebb and flow of each dollar. He sharpens his pencil and performs miracles of profit and loss," Red began.

"Nonsense. I'm a bean-counter," Schulte said.

I immediately liked him.

"You still know where every nickel goes, Frank. Even the two they rub together to pay me," Red said.

"I thought the TV station paid you," I said.

"Same difference," said Red.

"That's the pity," I said, mentally ruing corporate subsidiaries.

Schulte caught my rue and nodded his head vigorously. He seemed awash with pent-up energy, out of his ledger books for the day, his fingers atwitter, and anxious to rub syllables instead of subtotals together.

Suddenly our nostrils were flared by a yawning bowl of spicy, simmering, succulent pinto bean chili placed two inches below my chin, followed quickly by two more for Red and Schulte. The grillman had not even asked, just plunged his ladle into the bubbling black-pot cauldron and poured the molten olio into waiting bowls like lava from Vesuvius. The simile is apt, believe me. With it came a side order of macaroni and cheese—which Red and I immediately dumped into our chili—extra chili powder, and enough crackers to put out a brushfire.

"How long you been with the club?" I asked Schulte.

"Two years before Rohe," came the reply.

I heard a sharp exhalation, a common response to the chili—and maybe Rohe too, I didn't know—yet a futile way to cool one's tongue. After a gulp of water he continued.

"I've always been a baseball nut, and I thought it would be exciting to keep the books for a ball team," Schulte said. "You know, like the guy who cleans up elephant shit just to be part of the circus."

I laughed. This guy was all right.

"Don't tell me you thought working for a ball club meant free seats and all the popcorn you could eat," Red said.

"Sort of," Schulte went on. "I don't mind saying I'd

rather do a W-two for Andre Dawson than Joe Jamoke. And I like it when my computer shakes when the crowd goes crazy."

"And all our friends who think we can get 'em tickets," Red said.

"But I've been a member of SABR ever since it started—"

"That's the stat junkies, right?" said Red.

"Society for American Baseball Research," Frank said.

"A crunched number for every occasion," I said, trying to conceal my reservations about the group's methods.

"Yeah, most of their stuff, like the 'Bobby Bonds Effect,' is pretty tangential. But it's fun," he said.

I had not heard a person use the word "tangential" in a spoken sentence since I last tuned in to public TV. It was refreshing.

"So what are the odds of a guy being assassinated in his home park between the dugout and the clubhouse?" I asked.

"About the same as a fly ball striking a sea gull, but it happens," Schulte said, simplifying infinity to my level. "Introduced a new category of statistics."

"Tell 'im what you told me," Red said.

" 'Bout the Japanese?"

"What? What the hell about the Japs? You didn't mention them before," Red barked, his chili jumping off his spoon.

"Inside trading. They're buying up the Corporation's stock like it was on sale at Field's. Big blocks. Public doesn't know it. Wall Street doesn't even know it, as far as I heard. But the boys on Michigan Avenue are shittin' bricks," he said.

"Wait a minute," I said. "Even I know what that means."

"What does that mean?" blustered Red.

"Means they can take over the company. You know, like all those Wall Street takeovers. The hostile ones, anyway. Accumulate enough stock, make a buyout bid for the rest, and, ah-so, Tokyo owns the whole shebang," I said, sounding like somebody whose tongue should be wagging above a stock ticker.

"Bottom line: they grab the newspaper, the stations, the Cubs—all the company's holdings," Schulte said.

"Even you, Red," I said.

"Bull-bleepin'-shit!" Red blurted.

Even the grillman howled at that.

"Couldn't really happen, could it?" Red asked.

"Could the Dodgers move to L.A.? Could P. K. Wrigley sell to Colonel McCormick?" I said.

Red pushed his chili away.

"Ah, horseshit. Ruined my meal. And that ain't even what I brought Frank here to tell you," he said more quietly.

"Oh?" I said.

Frank lifted his eyebrows. I suddenly sensed how Woodward and Bernstein felt around Deep Throat.

"Rohe," Red said.

"Our peerless general manager?" I inquired.

"That's him. Everybody's boss, from the shoeshine boy on up," Red continued. "He who came into the shop from day one and put us on notice with that 'losing attitude' speech."

" 'You could see the loser's look, even in the Wrigley Field ushers,' " I quoted, remembering Rohe's entrance as general manager and majordomo a few years back.

"Robo's consistent, I'll say that for him," Schulte came in. "He treats everybody and everything the same. If a machine's down, he calls IBM and screams at the guy. 'Get the damn thing fixed and get it fixed now!' You can hear him, I don't have to tell you."

"Tell Duffy what you told me," Red said.

"It's just a little thing us on-line guys tend to notice," Schulte said.

He spooned into a fresh helping of chili, making us wait. For a back-room stiff, this guy had a sense of timing.

He continued: "Nowhere in the wide, wide world of the sports media did anybody report how the club was going to pay the salary of Carl Lundgren, our newest piece of depreciation."

"Well, the money they saved on Weaver's salary," I assumed.

"No way," said Schulte. "Weaver's attorney wrote in some fine print which said the salary was to be paid alive or dead. It's one of those *Titanic* clauses nobody in a low-beta sport pays any attention to. Weaver's estate, and the lawyer, natch, gets every dollar promised in his contract."

"No shit," I mused, suddenly considering the vagaries of Weaver's estate.

"No shit!" Red punctuated.

"But then I get another contract on my desk. This one's an insurance policy. A job like one of those Lloyd's of London coverages actresses take out on their gams. Well, this one is legit. The Cubs bought it on Weaver. Pays out one hundred fifty percent of his contract in the event that, for any reason, our boy is no longer able to perform."

"Like iced," said Red.

"Wait a minute," I said. "This is a gimmick, right, Frank? You said the meatballs, the Hollywood cuties, buy them on a set of knockers or something. Don't tell me the policy was State Farm?"

"As good as. But separate from the club's umbrella disability coverage. A whole different carrier, and for Mr. Dean Jamie Weaver alone. I'm no Bill Veeck as far as hustles are concerned, but it's the first time I ever saw something like this," said Schulte.

"So what do you figure?" I asked.

"I draw no inferences. That's not my expertise," he said with eyebrows raised and shoulders hunched. "I dance with the numbers what brung me."

"Damn fishy to me," said Red.

"Wait another minute," I said. "What's the count here? First pitch says you got the 'Pacific Menace' buying into the organization. The Nippon Cubs and all that. Second pitch says you got the front office secretly cashing in on a suspicious insurance settlement the size of its dead superstar."

"Hasn't cashed in on it yet. These things take time, what with a murder investigation and all. But they're banking on it," said Schulte.

"Murder for insurance. I seen it on TV Sunday night," said Red.

"Give me a *break*, Red. Tell me, Frank, when was that policy bought?"

"December thirteenth, year before last."

"There you are," I said. "That's when Weaver resigned. The insurance was a cover-my-ass move by an exec nervous about the fact that he had just given away the store."

"Damn fishy to me," Red repeated.

"I like it," said Frank Schulte. "Think of the actuarial tables in that underwriting—"

With that his cheeks puffed and he fought to stifle the first of what would be many gaseous uprisings fueled by the chili. During his recitation he had eaten a tankful, and it was beginning to roil.

17

Eddie Reulbach

Frank Schulte's inside tidbits piqued my interest, and I decided to go right back to the scene of the crime and nose around. In my attempt to grasp the big picture, I had never talked to the little people, the vendors, ushers, guards, clubhouse boys, ticket-takers, and grounds crew. Not that these mortals are savants or oracles. God knows, I never consulted them when I predicted the pennant races each spring, though God and anyone with a memory also knows, there were many years I should have. Including '85, after the blown playoffs, when I had them repeating, or in '70, after '69's September swoon, when I also had them repeating, and, well, I can't go on.

So no, I wasn't interested in a grass roots poll, but I did want to shake the bushes a little. It was a Sunday, and I went to the park early once again, that quiet time around midmorning when the vendors outside the park are just setting up and the counter ladies inside are dropping the first batch of cold wieners into the cooking pots. Most fans don't realize how much preparation it takes to get the ballpark ready. Oh, it's nothing really, just 30,000 folks over for lunch and lawn darts.

Wrigley was quietly humming when I was waved inside by a familiar old face. God love them—the familiar faces, the grizzled, toothless, cabbage-eared mugs of guys and gals who have been working the ballpark for years. Program sellers, ticket takers, ushers, counter ladies, the whole crew. Not pretty, but as real as corn on the cob. Rohe and the new owners thought they could thin the ranks of these stalwarts when they first came in. They tried to convince people that ballpark personnel, along with the ball team, needed a facelift. That's like saying the village of Cooperstown needs a new summertime attraction.

They soon came to their senses. People have always loved Wrigley Field and the way they were treated there. That goes way back to the two Bills, William Wrigley and William Veeck, Sr. The former, the gum merchant, took control of the franchise in 1916 and installed the latter, a sportswriter, in the front office a couple of years later.

The story goes that Wrigley invited Veeck, who wrote under the name "Bill Bailey," and a bunch of other Chicago baseball writers to dinner. Being what they were, the scribes soon began insulting their host by harping on the organizational ineptitudes of the franchise. As a matter of fact, the team had been eclipsed by the popularity of the South Side's White Sox, one of the finest teams in baseball history. Veeck was foremost among the critics.

"Could you do any better?" Wrigley asked him.

"I certainly couldn't do any worse," Veeck replied.

Wrigley hired him on the spot. With Veeck running the club, things slowly began to change. The White Sox helped in 1919 by becoming the Black Sox, the infidels who threw the World Series and almost sold the game of baseball over to gamblers. After a wartime pennant in 1918, the Cubs had middling success into the 1920s with a motley collection of new and used players, most notably Charlie Grimm. Then Veeck signed on Joe McCarthy as manager.

McCarthy, who was to later achieve immortality as skipper of the Yankees—oh, how did we ever let him get away?—began assembling the teams of Bush, Malone, and Root; Wilson, Hartnett, Grimm, and Cuyler. In 1929 that lineup took the flag, then added three more in the next decade, and you could look it up.

What Wrigley and Veeck did most of all was create

the garden-ballpark atmosphere of Wrigley Field. They had the park, with its trademark red brick and ivy, cleaned and remodeled. Flower boxes were placed in random locations and taken care of by Veeck's son, Bill, Jr. Ladies' Day, a hugely successful promotion that spawned some of baseball's most loyal fans, became a tradition. Wrigley and Veeck believed in the quaint, altogether novel notion that the customer was boss. For the price of his ticket he had the right to a clean, comfortable, and festive ballpark. If the home team happened to win, so much the better. That standard, of course, was to be refined and raucously embellished years later by the glad-eyed Bill Veeck, Jr. It was Barnum Bill who said, "When you come away from a baseball game, you have nothing but the ephemeral idea that you had a good time." Nothing more or less, but that was enough.

Upon his death in 1932, William Wrigley passed the franchise, and his visions, on to his son Phil. P.K. was as self-effacing a gentleman as any, an heir with few airs. He seldom used the owner's box, preferring to watch the games on television at his second home in Wisconsin. When he did come to the park, he often sat in a deserted section of the grandstand. If an usher asked to see his ticket, he apologized and moved. That was P.K.

P.K.'s Cubs were a family business, and Wrigley Field was a family place. Though it was the country's need for steel in World War II that kept P.K. from erecting lights—he'd already bought the poles!—he came to appreciate the fact that day baseball not only caused less bother to the neighbors but it also put a lot of kids in the park. So when other clubs put in lights and Astroturf, electronic scoreboards, and gaudy promotions of every stripe, P.K. kept Wrigley Field pristine. In no time it became a quirk, then a curio, then a treasure, and remained that way until the summer of 1988 when . . . well, everyone has his own opinion on that.

P.K.'s shortcoming, however, was that he was never a dedicated baseball man. He was interested in the Cubs, but not hell-bent. After the great squads his father and Veeck had assembled in the 1930s passed from the scene, he presided over a franchise that was perennially—except for another wartime pennant in 1945—in the doldrums.

Still, with dogged persistence, the people came to the ballpark. They obeyed the dulcet tones of Pat Pieper, the field announcer who had been around since 1916, when he declared, "Have your pencil and scorecard ready for the correct lineup of today's game." Why, I remember when old Pat did it with a big green megaphone: the ballpark didn't have a public-address system until 1933. Fans stood at the National Anthem. They threw their straw hats onto the field on Labor Day to signify the end of the summer hat season. In later, less modest years, they doffed their shirts, the males, that is, when the sun played hot, and donned them when the shadows came. They rose and cheered players such as Ernie Banks, who shone in the face of adversity. They savored the game in sunshine, in the old-time, stoop-sitting neighborhood of Wrigley Field. Apart from the atrocities often being committed on the field, it remained a pleasant place to come to.

So I came. I moseyed around. I second-naturedly started for the clubhouse to barber with Yosh Kawano, the keeper of the den for longer than anyone can remember, or the coaches, or maybe a veteran with something on his mind. But I checked myself. The minute my face noses inside a locker room I find myself locked in the eternal discussion of the hanging curve, the hit-and-run, and other baseball verities. Any hope of a fresh talk about the subject of murder would be quashed for the day.

I turned into the men's room instead. Ballpark men's rooms, when you consider them, are marvels of function. With their long walls of stainless steel urinals and corresponding toilet stalls, they are designed for the true pit stop. Quick in, quick zip, quick pitch, quick out. All before the first batter of the coming inning has taken a swing.

Before the teeming masses and their beer-bloated bladders converge on these rooms, they are cauldrons of quiet readiness. The urinals mechanically gurgle and flush. The toilets, with seats up, look like soldiers bracing for incoming artillery. The soap and towel dispensers are full. It is all quite inspiring, if not humbling, for later the place will be mobbed with men and boys staring squint-eyed at the tiled walls. Bill Veeck used to post signs stating that the stars of the future were standing here. Occasionally the cry will go up, "While you guys are in here with your flies open, they're scoring runs out there!"

While I stood within the quiet vastness of the men's room with my fly open, I was joined by someone. The fellow walked in, turned in my direction, and, though there was a good sixty linear feet of open urinal space to occupy, he proceeded to walk over and take his position at the trough right beside me. Can't be, I immediately thought, not here in the ballpark.

"Hello, Mr. House," the guy said.

I turned.

"Reulie!" I said.

"Caught ya in the office, how 'bout that!" he said, and smiled like Dizzy Dean.

I grinned. It was Eddie Reulbach, a mug I'd encountered in this ballpark for years. Reulie was an usher, still a young man somewhere in his fifties, with a full round head and a fleeting hairline. He wore his uniform: a long-sleeved white shirt buttoned at the wrists and a drab black tie that lay on his paunch; his blue pants had a yellow stripe down the side and ended three inches above his black patent-leather shoes. As usual, he was perspiring. No matter what the weather, Reulie was always sweating—seriously, like a man who for years had been wearing a long-sleeved white shirt and tie on hot summer days.

"How ya been?" I said.

"Got a minute?" he said.

"Any time for you, Reulie," I said.

I meant it. Reulie was one of those old faces, one of those fixtures in the ballyard. He was a born usher, a loyal, courteous, unfailing usher. As a teenager he had gone to work for Andy Frain, the company that supplied ushers for sporting events all over Chicago, and

had stayed with it ever since. During the summer
Reulie worked Wrigley Field and Comiskey Park, sometimes seven days a week. He worked boxing matches
and football games at Soldier Field, hockey and basket-
ball games at the Stadium, and political conventions at
the old Coliseum.

That he made little money at it did not seem to
perturb him; I believe he still lives with his mother. He
kept that same earnest, perspiring countenance, that
nod, a pat on the back as you passed by. For Reulie,
being an usher meant crowds, games, and he, Eddie
Reulbach, no athlete, no kind of special person at all,
right in the middle of it.

Working Wrigley was his favorite assignment, and
over the years he had gained seniority and favor until
he had finally got the plum: home plate. Reulie was
assigned to a spot just behind the on-deck circle where
he kept the game's supply of baseballs. He collected
foul balls off the screen or down the line. When the
home plate ump's pouch ran low, Reulie, with his la-
bored, penguin trot, huffed out and brought him some
more.

He did it for years, capably, without a hitch or a
complaint, on numbing, forty-degree days in April
when his perspiration was limited to a band around his
neck, and on ninety-five-degree scorchers in July when
his white shirt was a sheet of sweat by the third inning.
He did it when the stands were empty and there was
nobody to bother with, and when they were jammed
and everybody wanted a favor from him.

Reulie took thrown bats on the shins and wild pegs
on the arms. The angry purple bruises that resulted
were hazards, and sometimes, when he lifted his pant-
leg to reveal a black-and-blue welt the size of a doughnut on his alabaster shin, trophies. Once a foul ball hit
him squarely on the side of his skull and knocked him
cold. When he came to, he asked for the ball, then had
the hitter sign it for him. It was, he said, the first souvenir he ever took home.

So Reulie went along year after year with a shrug, a
wipe of the brow, and an eye and ear cocked for what

had to be done next. But all his zeal and hard work behind home plate could not protect him from a pair of gorgeous legs. When the new regime came in, they decided to replace Reulie with a dame. They chose a looker, one with a set of gams as brown as almonds, put her in an outfit with a pair of shorts no bigger than a rosin bag, and told her to shake her fanny as often and as much as she wished.

Given the times and the audience, the new foul ball chaser was a big hit. Reulie was forgotten quicker than a middle reliever with a double-digit ERA. He was moved from the sunshine of home plate to the shade of the second-tier bridge leading to the press box. And there he stood, patiently checking press passes, keeping the people away from Red Carney as well as ferrying their notes over to him, lightly perspiring, nodding and greeting, doing his new job without a whine. But don't be fooled. Reulie was crushed by his demotion, wounded as surely as if the club had sent him to the minors. You could see it in his brave smile, in his eyes.

Of course, these things have a poetic way of coming full circle. After a couple years of exposure and TV fame, of commercials and interviews, of Red Carney's tongue hanging six inches out of his mouth every time the young lady delivered a new set of balls to the umpire—and yes, each occasion resurrecting that old Dizzy Dean line—the babe went for the Big Prize: she took her clothes off for a cheesecake magazine. All the sporting gents saw it. Pictures of her in uniform and smiling in Reulie's old seat in Wrigley Field placed right next to shots of her buck naked. And who said you couldn't beat fun at the old ballpark?

Well, while the TV boys and the rest of the herd clustered around the exhibitionist like schoolboys around a freshly pilfered *Playboy*, I went straight to Reulie. It was one of those columns that wrote itself. Every word was Reulie's, each one more plaintive than the next, rolling from his mouth like a foul ball cascading down the backscreen hammock. The close, of course, was Reulie's supplication for his old job, something he'd assume, he said, with a vow never to peel his togs for any lens.

If you think the front office took him up on it, you probably think Moe Drabowsky will make a comeback. Another ball darling was hired on quicker than you can say "gams," and Reulie stayed put. But he always felt a close tie with me after the column I wrote.

"There's something been botherin' me, Duffy. Just stuck in my mind ever since that day Weaver was killed," Reulie said.

We talked near the sinks, our words covered by the flushing urinals, the room still a half hour away from public invasion.

"I'll start from the beginning so's you know where I'm comin' from. Now you know I ain't no beginner around here. I seen most of the guys one time or another. The ringers they hire nowadays are mostly kids. The alderman calls—you know how it is—or the little boogers from the suburbs who are heavy with the boys upstairs.

"So before every game I sorta look around the crew to see who's there. I'm a nosy type, Duffy, that's just the way I am. You know. And that day things were all screwy. A lot of assignments were jockeyed around— not mine, jeez, they know I won't take that baloney— but a lot of coverage was changed. It didn't make no difference to most of the crew. They're just part-timers. But I'm a career guy, Duffy, and what's right is right and what's screwy is screwy.

"So when the posts are called and the names and all, I'm hearin' stuff that ain't right. Especially when they got to the tunnel spots. Those are regular guys, Duffy, you gotta have stability there. There's Charley, the fat guy with the hernia problem, and Leon, the black kid, and everybody knows Rich, see what I'm sayin'? But when they got to the tunnel assignments they come up with a name I never heard before. I jerk my head around to see who the guy is and I don't see no one! I never seen the new guy!

"But gol *darn* if I can remember the name. I

checked with the other boys and they said they sorta remember, but then they give me that look like I'm inventin' things. 'Too many foul balls done hit your head,' Leon says. Comin' from him, sure! Leon says he seen a new guy come late but he didn't pay no attention to it. You believe that! A new guy gettin' one of the top spots and Leon don't pay no attention to it?

"Now that's just fine if you're Leon. But I'm a career guy, Duffy. This ain't no vacation gig for me, and I notice when things ain't copacetic. But I don't wanna make a federal case of it and I sorta forget about it. Just once in a while I asked a few guys who been around, oh, I wouldn't go in the office with somethin' like this. Just sorta asked guys I know who'd smell a bad fish around here. So I'm thinkin', 'You're goin' buggy, Reulie, this whole thing's got you seein' things.'

"Then the dicks come around and give us the third degree. We all got the same treatment. You know, what'd-ya-see-what'd-ya-hear? So I says to one of 'em, 'Let me have a gander at the list you got.' He shows it to me. It's a sheet of all the vendors and ushers on for the game. 'Where'd you get this?' I says to him. 'Front office,' he says. So I goes over it, Duffy. I know just about all the names, at least the first names if not the last names.

"And it wasn't on there! That list was all straight on. The regulars, the kids, the usual crew. I swear the name I heard called wasn't on there—not that name called out the day Weaver got murdered. I swear it, Duffy. And I kept it to myself until I seen you were comin' around.

"You're the only man on this earth I'd go to with something like this, you know? You got a knack for it."

I heard every word and was running the scene through my mind as Reulie spoke.

"Who can get someone on the list?" I said. "Who has the clout?"

" 'Course, it's up to Mr. Brown. Fingers. You know 'im. He runs our regular crew and all the spots. But there's ten, maybe fifteen subs a game, you never know. They call 'em out of a pool they got in the office. Then, like I said, there's always some sent down from the front office. They tell Fingers to take care of 'em and Fingers puts 'em somewheres. Fingers does what he's told. That's why he's been doin' it so long. But Fingers would never put a new guy on the tunnel."

"You talk to him?"

"No, siree. After the ball girl thing, I keep my mouth shut."

"Should I talk to him?"

"He wouldn't tell ya nothin' even if he knew. Not that he'd be hidin' something, I don't think. Just he plays it close to the vest. Besides, he wasn't even makin' the assignments that day."

"He wasn't?"

"Nope. It was Whiteman. You know, Rohe's man."

"George Whiteman? He was working the ushers?"

"That's nothin' new. Whiteman fills in all over the place if Rohe wants him to. He gets on our backs when Rohe thinks there's some problem somewhere. Plays like a real nice guy but you know he could can you like that," Reulie said with a snap of his fingers.

"Let me run it back a little," I said. "You're tellin' me your captain gets his list for the day from Fingers. But your captain didn't read off the assignments, George Whiteman did. And when the cops had you look over the day's list, they said they got it not from Fingers Brown's office but from the front office. And somewhere along the line this name you heard got bumped from the cops' list. Is that right?"

"That's it, Duffy! I knew you'd get it."

"That would mean there's something rotten in Denmark," I said.

"Denmark?" Reulie inquired.

"*Hamlet*," I said.

"Hamlet?"

"It's more related than you may think, Reulie."

"Boy, Duffy, you really got me goin' now." Reulie chafed.

"Don't worry about it. Just tell me who I can go to on this. Who do you trust?"

"Here?" he asked.

"Here."

"Nobody," he said.

"So what do I do?"

At that Reulie smiled. It was a remarkable smile, now that I think back on it. It had a glint to it, a spark of intrigue and connivery I'd not thought Reulie capable of.

He held a key in front of his nose.

"It's to Fingers's office. It's the only thing I didn't give back when they took home plate away from me," he said.

"See, Fingers keeps everything," he went on. "That's the way he is. You ever have a beef with him and he goes right to his records. So I'll betcha dimes to doughnuts he's got a copy of that list Whiteman read that day. Gol darn it, I know *I'd* like to get a look at it."

I raised my eyebrows. Then I listened as Reulie told me the details of how the ballpark empties after each game. He told me of nooks and crannies untouched by clean-up crews and security checks. He told me when the lights went out, when the last vendor, the last groundskeeper, and the daytime security people left. He covered it all, then he took out a piece of paper.

"You'll need this," he said.

It was a roster of ushers.

"Where'd you get this?" I said.

"The cops. They ran one off when I tol' 'em I needed it in case I thought of something," he said.

"Holy cow, Reulie, you're serious about this thing."

"Oh, you betcha, Duffy. You know, I read over that piece you did on me again. Oh gee, I must have twenty copies of that thing. It's somethin', you know. You didn't miss a thing. You just got a knack, Duffy, in how you can get things down. So the more I'm thinkin' about this ringer the more I know you can run it down. If anybody can get to the bottom of who killed Deano, you can. You always been Number One in my book."

He gave me a slap on the back and a look like the ones Lindbergh must have gotten when he boarded the

Spirit of St. Louis. I took his key and the copy of the roster. He looked at his watch.

"Oh boy, I gotta run," Reulie said.

He was gone just as a bank of urinals flushed in unison.

18

Heidi Zimmerman

Now Petey could have limped home after her cemetery run-in with Sally Hofman like the Cubs just in from a 3–9 road trip. She did not, God love her, because she's made of tougher stuff than that. She had followed a lead and, if Sally Hofman had an ounce of credibility in her, had come up with a cold spoor of a drug dealer who would have no interest in killing Weaver, only protecting his own turf, and an exaggerated, maybe even fictional Mob connection to the gambling interests of Obie Blintstein. It was a forked path that any bloodhound worth his salt would turn up his nose at. That's horse-racing, journalism, sleuthing, and life in the shoe-leather business, and Petey had damn well better get used to it. Young as she is, there was no telling how she would cope with setbacks. Well, she coped by digging in even harder.

As she told me later, she retrieved Obie's collection of Dream's letters and Dream's little black book. From the beginning, she had been convinced that the answer to Weaver's murder lay buried somewhere among these names and numbers. She laid them out on the kitchen table and started slowly looking at each one, at postmarks, telephone numbers, and any other telltale piece of information. She did the same with the datebook. It was old-fashioned, methodical legwork, and who knows where it came from. With a kid her age, I wasn't sure whether she had read all of Sherlock Holmes or *seen* every *Columbo* rerun.

She studied the collection of pain and lust for over an hour when something caught her eye. Nothing dramatic, just a snippet of data that tripped a neuron in her quick brain. It was the familiar first three digits of a telephone number. It was a second entry, probably an office number, behind "H. Z.," one of many sets of initials in Dream's book. What Petey noticed was that the prefix was the same as that of her prospective law school, Northwestern University.

It was a long shot, but Petey took it. With a single call to a helpful university operator, she matched the initials with the name of a faculty member. They belonged to an associate professor not of the law school but of the clinical psychology department in the university's medical school. Furthermore, the professor, a sociopsychologist, just happened to be a she. Surprise.

Had that information come my way—and I'm not saying I would have even noticed—I would have spent a day trying to figure out a ploy to get inside the professor's door. Petey did not waste a minute. She just up and called the number, got the professor on the line, and asked if she could come and talk to her. What a kid, I mean, what a kid!

"Do I know you?" the professor declared.

"Obie Blintstein gave me your number," Petey demurred.

"Oh," the professor deferred.

One day I'll research the Obie Effect. The buzz elicited by the mere whisper of that name among Dream Weaver's female consorts was comparable only to what I had previously encountered upon raising the memory of Lew Fonseca among line drive hitters. Petey named her time, the professor said they could probably talk best in her office, and my partner was keen on yet another scent.

For Petey it was familiar terrain: a corridor of professors' offices, door after door filled with collages of eclectic headlines, photos, quotes, warnings, axioms, sonnets, an occasional academic schedule or notice of

office hours, and dozens of panels from "The Far Side."
"Cow tools?" Petey wondered, glancing at one of the
beloved Larson's early inscrutables.

The office she was looking for belonged to Dr.
Heidi Zimmerman. The good Ph.D. was ready and
waiting for Petey. Dash any notions that Professor Zimmerman might resemble a dowdy, chignoned school-
marm. Not more than thirty-seven, she was a beauty,
yet a cool, conservative, and totally professional one.
Her shiny black hair was shoulder length and evenly
cut, framing clear, olive skin that took only a hint of
makeup, and quick brown eyes. She wore a single pearl
in each ear. Her suit was light gray and tailored, her
blouse white with a crimson swirl of a monogram over
one pocket and a thin string tie at the collar. She was
academia and business, one part U, one part IBM.

Her appearance was a calculated—at least to Petey
—effort not to allow her natural beauty to obscure the
presence of her brain. Attractive women have that
problem, though not all take pains to address it. Heidi
Zimmerman did, for she was a bright one, as quick as
Moe Berg. She had a pair of Ph.D.'s and the tag of
"sociopsychologist." Far be it from me to argue, even
though the only shrinks I ever took stock in were Bill
Faul and Yogi.

One look at her, however, and Petey knew why
Miss Heidi's initials were in Weaver's little book. But
Petey did not let on about her source. She sat down in a
wooden chair offered her amid the organized clutter—
the books and journals, the museum prints, a stereo
tuned to National Public Radio, a container of yogurt—
of Dr. Zimmerman's office. That was all that was offered; there were no wasted words. Zimmerman herself leaned against her desk and folded her arms in front
of her. Body language, Petey thought, dabbling in Zimmerman's bailiwick. Looking at the associate professor,
she also thought that this might be a tough academia
nut to crack.

"You're the columnist's niece, right? You were involved in the shooting at Wrigley Field. The second
shooting, that is," Zimmerman said.

Petey nodded; now she was the one caught off guard.

"What do you want from me?" Zimmerman said.

She was as tough as nails, a veteran of orals and faculty politics, and furthermore she kept abreast of the latest malfeasances in the ballpark.

"Please pull your guard down, for starters," Petey said, trying to get back on track.

Zimmerman waited.

"My uncle and I have been looking into Dream Weaver's murder," Petey ventured forward. "We've got the blessing of the commissioner of baseball's office. And we *had* the cooperation of Obie Blintstein. There's nothing more to it than that. Before he died, Obie willingly gave us what he thought was relevant. He did not mention you specifically, I should point out. I spotted your number in Dream's telephone book and wondered about it."

Zimmerman exhaled, but kept her arms crossed.

"I could never really figure out if Obie Blintstein was the best kind of friend or the worst kind of sycophant," she said. "Either one, he *was* my entrée," she went on, pronouncing "either" with a long *i*, almost as if she were beginning a class lecture.

"I'm a fan. Always have been. My grandfather was a pro player. I was raised on Lou Boudreau, Vince Lloyd, and Jack Brickhouse. Hey, hey, and all that. So I came by my knowledge and passion for the Cubs naturally. And yes, I admit, I'm like every other fan: I love just being close to the genuine articles. The players. Glossy pictures, bats, autographed programs, trivia, all that good ol' baseball stuff.

"With my training, however, I became interested in the athlete as social animal. That is, here's a random member of the species elevated into a rarefied environment because of exquisite physical skills. Yet he lacks comparable social or emotional skills. A baseball player is surrounded by great wealth and its corruptions. Among other things, he sees the worst of society, and it often brings out the worst in him. In a way, at least with his quick and seemingly effortless emergence into the strata of the elite and wealthy, he is a metaphor of a society that has misplaced its values, a society of decadence.

"With that premise, I approached some of the clubs with a research project that would study player values and player relationships—team, social, sexual—the whole gamut. They weren't interested. Then I decided to try individuals. Again, nothing. Then I read your uncle's magazine piece about Dream Weaver and Obie Blintstein, and I tried another tack: I sent Obie my vitae, my prospectus, and, as an afterthought, a batch of chocolate-chip cookies. *Presto.* That's how I met Dream."

"So much for research," Petey said.

"I'm not sure how to take that," Zimmerman returned.

"Well, so far all the women I've encountered in this thing have been camp followers . . ."

"Stop right there. I wanted to meet him, I won't deny that. For some of those same reasons. Did you ever see him in the flesh? Well, Dean Jamie Weaver was a gorgeous man. On the other hand, I had ten years on him, and I have no delusions about competing *cosmetically* with women your age," Zimmerman said.

Petey, to her credit, raised her hand, called time, and stepped out of the box.

Then she responded, "I don't need the details of your relationship. That's not why I came here. What I am interested in is some kind of perspective on Weaver and women. I think he was murdered because of passion, of one kind or another. Hatred, jealousy, revenge, sorrow—I don't know what, but something strong enough to kill for. I'm just sure of it, somehow."

Petey was at her best: the legal mind probing the recesses of dark psychosis. Zimmerman paused, slowly twisting a single thin gold bracelet on her wrist. She nodded assertively.

"You're right. All the stories about gambling and drugs are padding. Certainly a woman killed him. Not me, I should footnote, but a woman did him in, or, I will concede, *had* him done in. She may not have pulled the trigger, but she was in the scheme of things."

"Tell me more," Petey said, warming to the tale.

"Not here. This place has ears," Dr. Zimmerman said.

Zimmerman's office building was part of Northwestern's downtown campus, which is close to the lake and spang in the middle of a heap of hospitals. Everywhere you turn, there are people in pale hose and white coats with stethoscopes dangling from the pockets, pushing gurneys with wan, sutured bodies clinging to life and IV bottles. It's not unlike a major-league locker room.

I have expressed with crystal clarity in my last will and testament that I am *not* to be brought to a place like this once my hulk falters. I am not to be bypassed, transplanted, CPR-ed, life-supported, or chemotherapied. Just stick a fork in and pronounce me done. My body is not a shoulder bone to be shaved or a rotator cuff to be rebuilt in the manner of Bruce Sutter or Rick Reuschel, and it never will be.

Petey and Dr. Zimmerman, with their crisp and stunning good looks, wound their way east down Huron toward Michigan Avenue, collecting uncountable gawks from male passersby. Petey followed the lead of the professor, who cut over to Chicago Avenue and Eli's, where for years the late Eli Schuman kept a good bar—and liver and onions on the menu. It was midafternoon, and Eli's was dark and quiet, catering to only a few lunch-hour stragglers and some surgeons fortifying themselves for some upcoming cuts.

Petey and Zimmerman sat in the shadows and fondled beakers of expensive water. But the professor needed little priming for her spout.

"After the preliminaries, the posturing and feeling out, I realized things with Jamie would be different than I had anticipated. Let me clarify that: I expected to encounter a rich, coddled, guarded athlete who might give me the time of day, but little else. Instead, something remarkable happened. It was as if he were waiting for someone like me to come along.

"You see, my thesis was an examination of the *sexual* athlete with no awareness of his craft. From a very early age he has been single-minded about athletics and sex. He has never reflected upon either one, just performed and performed well. And while he's taken advice and instruction on playing ball, he hasn't learned a thing about sex. Certainly, he hasn't read or studied anything about it, or even asked pertinent questions. All he knows is getting his rocks off."

She took a swig of Perrier. Petey digested the lead-off, kept her eyes fixed on Zimmerman's, and awaited the meat of the order.

"Paradoxically, as much experience as Jamie had, he really knew almost nothing about sex or about women. Sex had become another bodily function, like eating or sleeping. He was a walking antithesis of the notion that the more you do it, the better you are at it, or the more meaningful the experience becomes. Let me amend that, he *was* good at it, oh, my . . . but he was definitely a sexual illiterate. His typical girlfriend promoted his insensitivity because her only role was to worship him and gratify his sexual desires. Well, that's where I came along."

Whew, Petey thought, but again did not let on. She only made a sucking sound with her drink, a sound the irreverent soul might liken to Dream Weaver's ego shriveling in the presence of Heidi Zimmerman.

"I was certainly fascinated. I liked Jamie, and I was amazed that I did. He had a sense of humor, and a sort of hick-smart wit. Not much got past him. And he had a way of making me feel comfortable around him—a smile, a tug on the sleeve, a funny snorting noise when he thought I was amusing. I found myself fascinated by him, maybe clinically at first, but fascinated nonetheless.

"And physically, well, be still my beating libido! Between you and me, my knees actually started to shake the first time. That body! My God, he was just such a specimen. His appetite, his ferocity, I mean, well, you know what I mean."

The two of them laughed and crunched ice cubes

and threw out a few double entendres Petey said were too blue for even these grizzled ears. But Zimmerman did not digress from her treatise for long.

"What was even more remarkable—if there can be anything more remarkable—was his almost solipsistic functioning within his physical realm. He was ignorant but not unintelligent. He had simply never learned anything. He was like a panting, perfect lion. His knowledge outside of baseball, and outside of what money could buy—I mean, he *hired* people to take care of the outside world—was like one big . . ." She reached for a word: ". . . gap.

"To me he personified the mystique of the body celebrity, the sort of noble savage virtuoso surrounded by fame and wealth and all the attendant corruptions.

"Maybe he thought of me as just one more addition. I was never sure of that. I used to pick him up in my car, which is your basic professor's Honda Accord, and we would go to obscure ethnic restaurants where he wouldn't be recognized. I taught him how to eat Korean, Thai, Vietnamese, Peruvian—and he opened up to me. I believe he was kind of flattered that my interest went beyond his body. I felt like his analyst. He told me *so* much."

"Oh?" Petey elevated her eyebrows.

"Certainly," Zimmerman said. "More than just the usual stuff about his first girlfriends and his schoolboy crushes. He really let his feelings come out, his insecurities, his phobias. As he did, I could see why he lived the life he did. I understood Obie's function. I could see through the screen—a smoke screen, really—that celebrities like Jamie erect for themselves."

"Didn't you have to take a number?"

"Excuse me?"

"I had the impression that Dream didn't have enough hours in the day or night to squeeze in all the women."

"He found time for me."

"And Sally Hofman?"

Heidi's glass fell short of reaching her mouth.

"Now there's a snake! A viper! A truly duplicitous person," she said, snapping off each word.

"Was she Dream's main item?"

"In *her* dreams maybe—well, okay, he had a thing for her. She's this punk thing. The real truth: she was Obie's main item. She got around, and he liked that. I kept telling Jamie he could do better; he *was* doing better. But men have this . . . this . . . this attraction for sleaze that I'll never understand. But then, you should know all about her and her friend, the dope guy they caught outside the locker room. Jamie told me about them. I always figured her for nothing more than a supplier. Just her speed."

"Is she—Sally—a suspect in your book?" Petey said.

"No. Oddly enough, but no. She was too small-time. She had everything to gain with Dream around, and nothing with him gone. And passion—'Scratch a lover, find a foe,' as Dorothy Parker would have it—it just wasn't in her. She's hard. Hard."

"So where would you look?"

Heidi bit into the pith of her lime wedge.

"Don't think I haven't lain awake hours in the night asking that very question," she said. "Here's my hypothesis: Jamie had a way of playing with fate. Fate came in the shape of a lot of strange ladies. Obie kept the weirdest ones away, but he couldn't read them all. Jamie never realized how he toyed with these girls, how he hurt their feelings, dashed their hopes, and broke their hearts.

"You see, athletes, particularly baseball players, develop a phlegmatic demeanor. 'It's a long season,' 'Tomorrow's another day,' 'You win some and you lose some.' And they carry over that attitude to relationships. Something may burn red hot and yet they can walk away from it, just like a bases-loaded rally ended by a double play. They don't understand that the fire still rages within the other person. I mean hot, really hot.

"That was Jamie. When I think of somebody actually *murdering* him, I mean, putting a bullet into him

and stopping his breath, those fires come to mind."
Heidi looked down and squinted her eyes shut, and
Petey thought she saw real emotion coming from Heidi
for the first time, though she wasn't sure whether it was
from those fires or the lime wedge.

Petey nodded. "I've seen some of the letters. Obie
gave them to me."

"Did he?" Heidi asked, recovering. "Excellent so-
ciological data, certainly . . ."

"They don't do much for building a case, however.
The jump from a jilted lover to a professional hit job
right in the middle of the ballpark is a big one," Petey
said.

"Think vengeance. Where there are girls, there are
boyfriends. Boyfriends who are livid at the idea of their
girl flipping for Jamie. Throw in a few husbands too."

"Husbands?" Petey asked innocently.

"Oh, my yes. Jamie was indiscriminate. He shot
first and asked questions later, if he asked at all. You
must have heard about Lila."

"Lila?" Petey said.

"Rohe's wife. Mrs. General Manager."

"Oh, not that again," Petey said.

"But it's *true*."

"No."

"Yes."

"No."

"Are you finished?"

"I'm aghast."

"So was I until I learned about Lila. Rich, thin,
selfish, with the best body surgically possible. Looks like
one of those soap opera matrons, you know, the kind
who ruins her daughter's marriage by sleeping with her
son-in-law. With Lila, it was Jamie.

"For his part, Jamie never said whether or not he
was taken with her other than the fascinating fact that
she was twenty years older and he had never slept with
a woman that age. A little boy and the mother he never
enjoyed, maybe—'*Le Souffle au coeur.*' He once told me
she was a wild person in bed but he didn't elaborate—

not like he did about his other trysts. Her technique, I guess, wasn't the big attraction."

"Did her husband know?"

"Jamie said no. That she swore it was their secret. They were never seen in public together. No hotel rooms, no doormen. She went to his place, always covered her tracks, et cetera. Or so he said. So he told me.

"To which I replied that the only reason a woman like Lila does that is so she *can* tell someone. If you get it, you flaunt it."

"Even *I* heard of it," Petey said.

"Certainly. It became such a well-known rumor that everybody figured it had to be false. The big lie."

"What was Dream's reaction to it all?"

"He laughed."

"He laughed?"

"He laughed! Then he got that look in his eye. *Mano a mano* and all that."

"I'm sorry?"

"There was something about the affair that charged Jamie. He began to relish the mere idea of it. In fact, he seemed to become more passionate about being a party to the cuckolding of George Rohe than he was about Lila herself. Though he never articulated it in so many words."

"Nor could he have," Petey assured. "How long did this arrangement go on?"

"I'm not sure," Heidi said. "Jamie said it was on-again, off-again, at least with him. He was never specific. He probably took that secret to his grave."

"But Lila knows," Petey said.

"Certainly," said Zimmerman.

If Dr. Heidi Zimmerman had given her the straight skinny, my good and accepting niece was in a pickle. She was faced with having to run down the moldiest, sorriest, most threadbare lead in town. Finding Terrible Tommy O'Connor was a better bet. Getting Augie Donatelli to change a called third strike held more promise than Petey prying something cogent out of Lila

Rohe. And, remembering all too well my earlier scorn over that item, Petey probably figured she could not look forward to help from me.

With all that coursing through her youthful head, she made a move of the caliber that keeps her the direct beneficiary of my affection: she came directly to Uncle Duffy. She returned to the apartment, popped a can of ginger ale, blew the bangs from her forehead, and unloaded on me every detail, nuance, and aside contained in her conversations with Misses Hofman and Zimmerman.

"You've been taking some extra swings," I said.

"Going with the pitch," she countered.

"A major-league skill," I complimented, full of pride.

Then I told her what Reulie, the usher, put to me. I dangled the key to the security office in front of her and her eyes got wider than Hank Sauer's upon espying a hanging curve.

"We have work to do," she said, tying into a bag of overpriced chocolate-chip cookies from a Michigan Avenue bakery.

"Lila Rohe, I fear," I said.

"Or the security office?"

"Let me think about that."

I didn't like her look.

"Me, not you," I said. "You've made your share of visits to the unfriendly crevasses of Wrigley Field."

"You forget, Unk, I'm a student. Years in dormitories and sorority houses make me an expert at covert entry."

"Not anymore. Now you're a potential member of the bar, an adherent of the blindfolded lady with scales," I reminded her.

"Uncle Duf, you're a gas," Petey said.

"A quality, no; a by-product, yes," I replied.

She cracked up.

"But you won't be satisfied until we settle the Lila Rohe question once and for all, will you?" I resumed.

"Nor will you," she said.

"Well, maybe I have an angle on that."

"What's that?"

"Red Carney."

"You don't say," she said. "Red and Lila are friends?"

"Once upon a time, I'm afraid, more than that."

"Ooooh," Petey oozed.

19

Lila

The history between Lila and Red Carney was delicate territory. Red is an old friend, and I'm not the most open-minded listener when it comes to extracurricular, off-the-field, behind-closed-doors hijinks. On the other hand, what makes me squirm has never caused a gnat's worth of discomfort for Red. Catch him with his pants down, and he just waves and says life is a paper moon. Then he'll shoot you the fleshy variety. Indomitable, insufferable, indefatigable, and usually in midsentence. Over four decades he has crowed in the broadcast booth, blustered everywhere else, and people love him for it. And bring me another cold one, if you please, little lady.

Anyway, this particular item on the menu went back thirty years, to when Red was doing radio play-by-play for the Pittsburgh Pirates. To say he had a roving eye is to say Joe Pepitone liked a few beers after a game. Red's eye searched the box seats, it panned the grandstands, it spilled over onto the sidewalks and the harbors, it covered the globe.

Way back when, in Pittsburgh, it had found a port with a young blond beauty barely past jailbait who at the time happened to be married to a good-looking young pitcher on the Pirates' staff. The pitcher, a flame-throwing cross between Glenn Hobbie and Bob Rush, shall go unnamed. The blonde, of course, was Lila. But suffice it to say, Lila took more out of this young pitcher than all the bats in the National League.

Trouble on the home front flared when the kid's arm went lame and he was sent down to Triple A to work it back into shape. Lila, the daughter of a wealthy physician and a beauty who never considered herself anything but major-league, stayed in Pittsburgh. She soon found Red, or vice versa, with emphasis on the vice.

It was a gossip-column affair that might have cost Red his job had he not been so popular on the airwaves. Lila divorced the sore-armed pitcher not long afterward and, after playing the field—the diamond and the gridiron, for that matter—she moved on from Red to take up with a member of the Pittsburgh Steelers football team. The story went that Lila was in the stands one Sunday with a set of binoculars trained on the Steelers' huddle. Of course, the boys bend down and exhibit their hindquarters while planning the hut, and Lila had her binoculars trained on the assembled hams. She spotted what she later said was a choice set of buttocks and took the tailback who belonged to them. Apparently, that marriage lasted about as long as the kid's legs did, not to mention his butt, which wasn't long. A few years later Lila got back to baseball, this time the management side, and found her perfect mate in the form of George Rohe, a young, hard-charging, wheeling-dealing general manager.

Just what position—and I select the word recklessly—Red assumed through all of this I do not know. Nor did he ever tell me. Red had long been in Chicago by the time the Corporation brought Rohe in to general-manage the Cubs. Lila, older and maybe even wiser—and still Rohe's missus—eagerly came along. To the unprobing eye, she even seemed to have put a leash on herself and her libido. Little did the unprobing eye know.

* * *

It was time for me, obviously, to flap wattles with Red once again. The team, and Red along with it, had Thursday off. It was a fortunate quirk in the schedule. Normally I am not fond of quirks, but this one allowed me to grab Red at a crucial time.

"You got something new in the investigation, right?" he asked over the phone.

"Lila," I said.

That name, a single, four-letter word, and a silence went over the phone line like death conveyed.

"Dammit," Red said, which was volumes, we both knew it.

As to specifics, Red had sworn off chili for a while, so the diner was out. He had a taste for veal, and that meant Taylor Street and the Vernon Park Inn.

This joint has achieved some notoriety on account of all the gumbahs who made it a regular grazing spot. Little hole in the wall, a block off the main Taylor Street drag at Aberdeen, in the heart of what was the "Patch," the West Side Italian-Sicilian ghetto. In the early days this was Jane Addams territory, and you can just about see all the grimy-faced, knickered dead-end kids climbing the back fences and playing ball in the alleys.

That all went the way of the wrecking ball when Richard Daley decided to put his University of Illinois campus here in the 1960s. Amid a lot of howls and *bastas!*, the stoops and cold-water flats once clogged with immigrant dagos were flattened like Pompeii beneath Mt. Vesuvius. With all the jazzy campus architecture and the army of students, a return visitor from the early days wouldn't recognize the place now except for a few pockets here and there, blocks turned into culs-de-sac by some hotshot urban planner who never had to navigate or find a parking spot in them. The Vernon Park Inn sits in one, a survivor by some quirk of fate, the same nondescript facade, no sign, a place you have to know to find.

Word was that Sam Tufano, whom they called Pop O'Zeke, used to cook for Capone. He started the place, put up tripe and codfish and a good veal marsala, and the hoods, who eat as well as anybody, gave him their trade. Giancana, Buccieri, Ferriola—all the plead-the-Fifth bosses came around. Through the years, no matter how far afield the hoods got or what suburb housed them, the saying went that if you were somebody in those circles you were somebody on Taylor Street.

Tufano's son Sam, Jr., took over when the old man died and changed nothing, even though a lot of his new clientele were college kids on a budget. The Inn was cheap, dim, and good, and there was always a place in the back room for a private confab.

Petey hung on every tidbit of my impromptu history, and gawked like a tourist as I swung my scarlet Swede wagon onto Taylor Street. I'm no mob aficionado, but I know the town and have read enough of Harry Steinfeldt's underworld copy to paint a decent picture of the Outfit. It never fails to captivate. Petey devoured the data, as visitors so often do, with a relish appropriate to yarns of the 1935 Cubs.

We parked and went inside the Inn. Red was already there, sitting in front of whatever was on draft, alone and unbothered. That was another thing about the Inn: No matter who you were or thought you were, privacy was assured. Which was all the better, because Red looked like something the cat dragged in.

Petey sat down next to him, gave him a kiss, and got one back. He cradled her hand in his arm.

"Oh, my pretty lady," he crowed, regaining some of his vigor. But he still wasn't right. He had a bad shave, bloodshot eyes, and a wet scowl. People look like they feel, as far as I'm concerned, and the old bullshit and bonhomie that carried Red over his down days, including numerous skull-crushing hangovers, just wasn't there.

"I just wish *she* didn't have to hear what I know you want me to feel obliged to tell ya," he said to me.

"That's a hell of a sentence, Red," I said.

"*You* clean it up then! You're the friggin' writer," he barked. The skin was a little thin, something rubbed a little raw.

Petey went quiet.

Red pulled back.

"Okay, keep your shirt on and I'll tell you what's come up on my side of the aisle," I said.

I told him about Reulie and his suspicions of a ringer in the usher corps. I mentioned the possibility of two lists of Andy Frain ushers for the day. I threw in a few disparaging remarks about Fingers Brown and his security office. I even brought up the key Reulie had laid on me.

Red snorted.

"Arggggh, Reulie Reulbach, for cryin' out loud. Don't get me wrong, Duf, I ain't got nothin' against the guy, but I wouldn't bank a plugged nickel on him. Too much baggage, that's all, too much sour grapes."

"No question about that, Red. But listen, it's a lead, and a high hard one. And another thing: it points inside the ballpark. Inside the friendly confines. Not in San Diego or Rush Street or in some cockamamy conspiracy schemed by a damned maniac. No sir. Clark and Addison. That's where my gut and my niece say this thing is headed."

I liked that. It sounded good, like Sam Spade and Kenesaw Mountain Landis rolled into one. It was also a preface to what I wanted out of him. And he knew it. Which is why he looked like he did, which was horse-shit. But I repeat myself.

Petey chimed in.

"I ran down two of Weaver's squeezes, the ones he didn't show off in public. They each confirmed the existence of Dream's affair with Mrs. Rohe. They said it was a bad scene. They didn't know the lady, but they knew she was heavy with him."

Red came in on cue. He knew what we wanted. He looked at me, then at Petey, this time without any of the beery, avuncular good nature she had come to know. Out with it, Red. Tell us secrets; tell us no lies.

"I assume you two are hand in glove in all this?" he asked quietly.

"Petrinella truly knows more than I do. By choice and a deft hand, I must say," I said.

Red closed his eyes and exhaled, a long, tired exhalation.

"Lila, Lila, Lila . . ." he began. "Every way I read this thing I kept telling myself Lila couldn't be involved. No way. A kid gets murdered in the ballpark. That's a nightmare, for cripe's sake. Wearing Cubs blue. A blot on Gabby and Jolly Cholly and Ernie. So make a case against anybody you want, but good God Almighty, keep it from coming home. Find some maniac, like you said, Duffy, some gangster, some dope fiend, some chippie even, but don't come inside, don't taint The Franchise!"

He quaffed his beer. He'd had a good head start on us, and nobody was counting.

With foam on his lips, he added, "Not Lila."

The words hung in the air like a slow change-up.

"And I'm not covering my ass. No way! I know what I done and how deep I was into it, and that's that. I'll put it all in a book some day. I can take it and dish it. So can Lila. She's a big girl.

"I almost married her. That's something you never knew, Duffy. She and I were so tangled up in St. Louis you'da needed a bucket of cold water and a crowbar to get us apart."

Petey smiled.

"She's a powerful woman, Duffy. Smart and glamorous and all that, but most of all she's like a . . . a . . . a *force*, you know? You get so taken with her, she draws you in. You can be hundreds of miles away from her and still feel her. You can hear her and smell her, and it makes you shiver in the middle of the night. Oh my. Even after all these years."

"Good Lord, Red. I've never seen you like this," I said.

"You don't know, Duffy. So I'm tellin' ya now and you can plug it all in. All I'm saying is that I heard Lila was dawdling with Weaver. Everybody heard it. And I was the loudest guy to say it was horseshit. I had to, 'cuz I knew it was true.

"So one day I went to Lila—uh, when was it? September, last year. We had a weekend series with the

Phillies—split with 'em on that grounder hit the seam, for cryin' out loud—and I had her come clean with me. She didn't toy. We're long past that. She said it was mostly sport for her, a little dangerous, a little naughty. She liked that sort of thing. 'Red, honey,' she said, 'always keep a sweet secret.' That's the way she talks.

"But she let on that she was afraid it was more than that for Weaver. It worried her. At first it was a game for him too. But after a while, after a few contract fights, after that bad arbitration—and all them cheap shots Rohe took at Dream in the press—well, she said, the whole affair got a nasty edge to it. Like the second time a pitcher throws inside, only this time he throws *up* and in. And Dream, oh hell, he was just a kid, but he knew how to kick and deal chin music.

"But I don't wanna believe it. Tell me it's gamblers, or the Japanese—"

"Is that what Schulte, the accountant, was gettin' at the other day? Testing the waters with the Japanese buying up stock and the bit about that insurance policy?" I asked.

I was thinking out loud, trying to stay a thought ahead of Red.

"You got something there, Duffy. Maybe it was a matter of trying to convince myself it was hooey. You know, throw something against the wall and see if it sticks," he said.

"You want to stick Rohe—"

"Naw, like I said, keep it outta the ballpark!"

"—or Lila? Where's your beef, Red?"

"Look," he said, "there's nothing in that tree, so quit barkin' up it. Rohe didn't have anything to do with Lila and me. That was her bed, and she made it. I think he's a horseshit baseball man and a horseshit boss and a horseshit individual, but that's as far as it goes with me, so help me God.

"As for Lila, that woman used to tie my insides in knots. There's no telling what she does to Rohe even after all these years. And only God knows what she did to the kid."

Petey cracked a heel of Italian bread. Up to that

point she had riveted her eyes on Red, searing into him, hearing every word and reading every meaning. And her own brain was running flat out, cutting the insides of the bases, keeping the play in front of her.

"Or what Dream did to her," she said in an even, cocksure tone. "Jamie Weaver was no rookie in that league. No puppy. He did things to women. All of them."

"I don't know beans about that," Red said. "I just know that I shoulda had the guts, hell, I wish to Pete I'd had the brains in my fat head to take Weaver aside myself and tell him to get the hell out of that mess. But I didn't. Nobody did."

"Oh, but they did," Petey said.

Red looked sideways at her.

My brow lifted.

Petey fielded us both.

"Dream got the sign. From Obie, for one. And from his other girlfriends. It was loud and clear—like one finger down for the fastball. And he shook it off," she said.

All that jabbering went on before we had eaten a morsel. I was famished, and Petey was even hungrier. I chided Red for being a bad host. He called to a waiter and fixed us up with some of the Inn's best Sicilian dishes, the hot bread, veal, pasta, chicken, cod, calamari, all of it laced with garlic and drenched with pesto and tomato sauces that made us weep. We ate like conspirators.

It was Petey who got back on track.

"Where do we go from here? Who's going to shake this thing until it cracks? We're like a team making a September charge. You know, taking chances, going first to third, bunting with two strikes, suicide squeezes —the whole enchilada. Like the 'sixty-nine Mets," she enthused.

"Oh, please!" Red groaned.

"Try the 'sixty-four Cards—any race but 'sixty-nine, Petey. There's too much pain there," I said.

"Sorry," she said. "But my point stands. We've got to strangle this thing."

"Don't look at me," Red said.

"But I am," Petey said. "I want a shot at Lila, and you're my ticket."

My jaw dropped in midchew.

"Holy cow!" Red whined.

The niece was right. It was time to grab the bat at the knob, rub on some pine tar, and take a full cut. I left the restaurant that night with schemes in my head.

Petey left with a pair of tickets for a boat ride.

20

The Fromage

It was Friday, one of those damnable 3:05 starts again. The Cardinals were in town and giving us fits. It was hot and windswept, a billowing gale coming out of the southwest that made guys like Ozzie Smith think they were Mike Schmidt. (Many a pensive sportswriter has speculated what Mike Schmidt, who *owned* this park, would have done as a Cub. The wags answered— and I admit guilt—that Schmidt wouldn't have done much at all, because he wouldn't have had Cub pitching to face.) On a day like this, though, even the limp-wristed, the Lennie Merullos, the Don Kessingers, need only loft a pop fly ball, hear the shortstop call for it, then beam as a jet stream sails it into the seats. That's Wrigley Field, where scores of 26–23 are on the books, and you could look it up.

I had figured and schemed and conjured damn near a hole in my head about my next move, and the ballyard breezes were just another factor. The wind was blowing out, and I was going in. Into the security office, that is. Holy Watergate!

I dummied up with Petey. She had her own saga that night, as she told me later, and it gave me the perfect opening to pursue mine. Hers first.

Red Carney had just happened to have a pair of ducats to a charity cruise, of all things. Not your average society brie and Pouilly-Fuissé soirée at the Art Institute, in which case Red wouldn't have been anywhere near, but a lake-going benefit which just happened to be dear to the hemorrhaging heart of Lila Rohe. She had hit up Red for a pair of tickets—a double C-note apiece. He groused, but he forked over with nary a whimper. The woman was a force, I believe he had said. Of course, he still had no intention of going.

But Petey did. She implored me to come along. I said nothing doing. I'd poke my head out on the balcony and wave as the boat bobbed by. Her look went right through me. She knew what I was up to, and she knew I needed a night of solitude to do it.

I waited until after the game had begun before departing for the ballpark.

"You be careful. I'm anxious for you," she said.

I feigned innocence with ironclad resolve, which, I suppose, made me a ferrous feigner. Spend as many long days and nights in the press box as I have, and you start making up groaners like that.

"You watch your step too, young lady. The lake can get rough."

"Ship ahoy," she said.

Petey was on her own as far as her nautical ambush of Lila Rohe was concerned. But I figured there was little mischief to be feared a mile out on Lake Michigan, even with Lila on the same poop deck. Besides, there was nothing I could do as a third-base coach to stop Petey from trying to score; she'd run right through the sign. As I was to find out later, I was not the only one who decided Petey was out of harm's way that night. Jimmy Slagle, in his infinite street wisdom, saw the way she was decked out and decided to abandon his tail on her. Luckily, he did the same for me.

As Petey described it to me in detail sometime later, the affair was no Wendella quick-out-to-the-pumping-station-and-there's-the-skyline-folks shuttle, but a slow, relaxed, and well-appointed cruise. For that kind of money, it had better be. The boat was a classy 192-foot double-decker spruced up for tony lake junkets. They were a big summertime business, I found out. Get the right caterer, a handful of blithe young waiters, a swing band and a dance floor, and a half-mile away from the lights, noise, smells, and bugs of megalopolis, and people rather enjoy themselves.

Petey was all set to do so. From some mysterious rack she had pulled a slinky black dress—shoulderless, hemmed below the knee, and slit up one thigh. With a three-inch-long spangled earring falling from one ear, her russet hair whipped and stuck with a bevy of barrettes, a thin strand of pearls around her caramel-tan collarbone, a rare set of thin high heels, and holding a small leather clutch, she was a knockout. Just a gorgeous woman. No other way to put it.

She called down to Biz Wagemaker in the lobby to hail her a cab. When she appeared, Biz clutched his chest.

"Satin *doll*. We love you madly," he crooned in a passable Duke Ellington.

Petey winked and blew him a kiss.

She was down on the lakefront's Navy Pier by early evening, and she fell in with the knot of swells and bluebloods awaiting the S.S. *Fromage*. Alone, unescorted, looking as she did, Petey was lathered with male ogles and skewered on half a dozen female daggers. The average age being well over forty, give or take a goodly number of second and third wives barely half the age of the old man, this was not Petey's crowd. But she bore up, enjoying the attention like a rookie phenom at the All-Star game, lifting polite hellos and how-do-you-do's.

* * *

At just about the same time I was in the bowels of a nearly empty stadium. After the game, which the Cardinals won 11–7 by hitting four windblown homers to the Cubs' three, I went over to the umpires' quarters across from the home clubhouse, a good-sized area partitioned into an office, a dressing room, and showers. It is, as I mentioned much earlier, only a few paces away from where Weaver was shot and but a good run from where Petey was shot at.

Working the game were Doug Harvey, the venerable white-haired, tobacco-chewing crew chief whom the other arbiters call "God"; Frank Pulli, the wild Italian; the rotund and ever voluble Eric Gregg; and Bruce Froemming, the fireplug who called ball four on the last batter in Milt Pappas's try for a perfect game in '72. "If I called a pitch like that a strike, I wouldn't be able to sleep nights," Froemming had said. "Then how in hell do you sleep all those other nights when you blow those calls?" Pappas growled back.

They were all good friends and good sources through the years, and they didn't think anything of me showing up to barber a little. I sat and nibbled on their postgame buffet of cold cuts and fruit. The men in blue have always been among my confidants in this game, for they truly love it. They live an arduous, often lonely life. They travel constantly. But you will find no mortals who respect the game of baseball more, or who know it any better. Inside and out. They know who's got it and who doesn't, who's faking and who's the genuine article. And they tell great stories. Just great, rollicking, often profane but marvelous yarns. With that preface, I admit to feeling a bit of a twinge in using the umpires and their den as my cover. But it was for the greater good of the game. And they could appreciate that.

* * *

In no time the boat docked and laded the crowd of about 350 sequined, bejeweled, gowned, tuxedoed, not to mentioned tucked, lifted, and toupeed revelers. Though Petey introduced herself by her correct appellation, she supplied no other information, no affiliation, no sugar daddy. I had explicitly forbidden her to bandy my name about; Red's was to be used only at the opportune moment.

In no time the *Fromage* was navigating the lake, heading northward past the brilliant city skyline, gliding past scores of yachts, powerboats, and sailboats. It was a warm, beautiful lake night, and the band lifted cool sounds that overcame the boat's growling engines. Petey explored the decks, which were appointed with brass and mahogany, bougainvillea and ficus, ribbons and foil balloons. With each crossing of a bulkhead, she reaped lingering looks from men and frosty glances from women.

She soon became a hit with the waiters, members of the band, and a few male guests who'd managed to slither nearby. They plied her with champagne, cucumbers stuffed with tiny shrimp, and foie gras. As she filled a plate with sushi, a lacquered matron sidled up next to her and quipped, "We *do* like our fish, don't we?"

Petey smiled, pushed away, and soon made friends with Henry Hanson, a mustachioed, round piglet of a man who made a living being chums with the likes of Lila Rohe and her guests. A sort of Truman Capote of the Midwest, Hanson wore a cherubic smile and snap-brim hat, of which the latter much impressed Petey. He was also unattached and gladly served as Petey's cohort and guide since he knew everybody. In her heels, Petey was a head taller than Henry, and he loved it.

As the boat bobbed between Chicago and Milwaukee, on the now-darkening waters of Lake Michigan, Petey and Henry H. mingled and tittered. Henry had a quip, a footnote, a rumor, a medical note, and a history on anybody who was anybody on board. Petey was intrigued and entertained, and stayed close on Henry's elbow. It gave her a base, and helped to keep the wolves and defensive females at bay.

They stood at the edge of the boat's main deck as the band swung into a Cole Porter tune, and the dance floor began to fill. Henry pointed to a knot of people near the front. Petey had already noticed the traffic on the boat gravitating in that general direction.

"That's the bridge, so to speak," he said. "And that, in the ship captain's gown, complete with epaulets and anchors aweigh, looking like a refugee from the *Love Boat*, is the skipperess of this little seafaring soirée."

"None other than Lila Rohe," offered Petey.

"Aye, aye," said Henry.

* * *

As I figured they would, the umps left me to my own devices. I concocted some story about waiting for Yosh Kawano and they left for dinner downtown. I could have told them I was waiting for P. K. Wrigley and they would have left for dinner downtown. Now, according to Reulie, I had the room to myself until the night cleaning crew came in at around 8 P.M. That was no problem, Reulie had assured me. The crew was mostly Polish, a brigade of first-generation immigrants who spoke little English and would smile, nod, and clean around you if you lifted your feet.

More than that, however, Reulie did not know. I was pretty much on my own as far as navigating the nocturnal confines of the park's front offices was concerned. The cleaning crew posed less of a problem, it seemed to me, than the pair of sentries who patrolled the place 'round the clock.

Like any museum, Wrigley Field, though securely battened and wired with state-of-the-art security devices, was never left unprotected. Guards not only secured the clubhouses, the restaurants and shops, and the front office, but they kept a keen eye out for the crazies and the curious who might consider scaling the fences. It does not take a great leap of imagination to figure how many revelers would love to run the bases in the midnight hours.

The guards were also supposed to keep out people like me. Except that I was already in. I doused all but a desk light in the umpires' room. I sat and waited, hearing only occasional chatter from stragglers across the hall in the Cubs' clubhouse. A shower head dripped. It occurred to me that I had not brought along anything to pass the time with. Luckily, someone had thought of that for me. In the desk I found a copy of *Three and Two!*, the memoirs of the late Tom Gorman, an umpire's umpire. Columnist Jerry Holtzman had done the writing. I had read it years before and remembered that it read well. I remembered correctly.

"An umpire can work the plate in a pitcher's perfect game, and nobody's going to come up and shake his hand. I know. I saw it happen . . ." Gorman/Holtzman began, and I was hooked anew.

* * *

"Down periscope, Lila. It's me," Henry Hanson said as he and Petey approached the hostess of the evening's festivities.

"Welcome aboard, mate," Lila said as she leaned down and bussed Henry on his shiny forehead. "And put a lid on the ship talk."

She was solo on this affair; Rohe was landlocked with the team, or so ran conventional thought, and she was surrounded by like-heeled matrons and a few silver-haired tuxedos who looked like they had hopped on the boat from a Cutty Sark ad.

Petey took her in. She was everything Red had gushed about. Swathed in a white designer gown complete with glittering nautical appointments, she exhibited enough décolletage to make eye contact difficult. Here and there were a few unmistakably real jewels.

Petey noticed Lila's long fingers and her nails, which were pointed, and her eyes, which were exotically brown and darting and which, legend held, were slower only than her wicked tongue.

"And who is this?" Lila said, herself doing a quick mast-to-boiler-room scan of Petey.

Petey awoke from her private appraisal in midsurmise about the effect Lila must have had on Dream Weaver.

"Miss Petrinella Biggers," Henry bugled. "One of Chicago's newest and most scintillating beauties. Lover of sushi and stone crab. Soon to be a student of law at Northwestern. That's all I know so far."

"That's not much, Henry," Lila shot back, her voice cutting through the din like the Lindbergh beacon.

She fixated on Petey, having noticed her long before, and said, "And just why are you on my boat?"

* * *

By 10 P.M. I was up to Chapter Nine in the Gorman tome and had dredged up more memories than I care to admit. Bill Klem, Babe Pinelli, Chris Pelekoudas, Jocko Conlon—Gorman's career went deep, and these guys were more vivid in my memory than I had known. So intense was my concentration that I hadn't realized how quiet the ballpark had become. I also had not been interrupted by the night cleaning crew, which seemed odd.

I decided not to wait. I put away *Three and Two!* and went for the door. There were two of them, one leading into the hallway and the concourse below the third-base seats, and the other leading to the infamous storage tunnel that ran from the Cubs' clubhouse behind third base to the visitors' den behind first.

I chose the latter: dark, dank, but free of security as long as I didn't stagger over a hose or a sprinkler head or a box of souvenir Styrofoam visors. Knowing that this particular cave had a way of tripping up even the most wily, I realized it was not a sure thing. Besides, the office I wanted to penetrate was not among the administrative complex on the second floor but was tucked instead next to a vending station off the first-base concourse. The cave was a direct route.

Two sandy, noisy steps by my brogans on the dirty concrete floor and I wished I'd worn different shoes. Hell, I don't own different shoes. I kept going. The light was bad and the air a damp, foul concoction of ground seepage and spilled beer. I ignored it. This was no time for sensitivity or, though I felt like an overweight albino alligator plying the city's sewers, for introspection. I'm a scribe emeritus of a major daily newspaper, a respected sports authority, a ranking member of the Baseball Writers of America, a keeper of the legacy of Lardner, Broun, Fullerton, Red Smith, and Holtzman, I told myself, and I'm skulking through the fetid bowels of a major-league ballpark on a mission of justice. Suddenly it struck me, in as clear an epiphany as any sportswriter is likely to experience, just what Harry Caray meant when he said, "The big possum walks late."

I made it over to the first-base side undetected and headed for the steel door leading out into the concourse. This was crunch time, bottom of the ninth, do or die as far as this operation was concerned.

Not only that, but there was no telling who might be out there. There was no telling who might be in the offices. There was just no telling. All I could do was put the ball in play and face the heat. I gripped the knob and pushed the door open. It rasped against the concrete floor and I froze as the sound pealed through the concourse like the wail of a banshee.

* * *

Petey said two words to Lila: "Red Carney."

Lila lifted her eyebrows, then narrowed her eyes. "What's that overrated radio slug up to nowadays?" she said, half looking out at the crowd.

Henry Hanson whistled.

"He's still mad about you," Petey said.

Henry whistled louder.

"Henry, fill my glass and fetch some grapes," Lila said.

"Peeled?" he inquired, and reluctantly waddled off.

Lila honed in on Petey and put her voice on chill. "Don't believe everything a drunk blubbers in your ear," she said. "No matter what Red promises you."

Then she brightened, lifting her head like a marker buoy, and once again scanned the crowd. She turned to greet another guest, lightly touched the corners of her mouth, and smiled as if everything were going swimmingly.

She returned to Petey.

"Enjoying the cruise, Patricia?" she said, which was the verbal equivalent of the back of her hand.

"I want to talk about Dean," Petey said.

Lila inhaled. A trace of a blue vein appeared on the side of her slender neck, throbbed once, and disappeared. She tilted her head.

"Shit," she said, but ever so crisply, and strode off.

Petey followed, as she was meant to.

As they went off, Henry appeared with a tray of fresh champagne and a plate heaped with melon, grapes, kiwi, figs, and a dollop of soft cream cheese. He shrugged and started eating the fixings himself.

Lila skirted the revelers, who were becoming well-liquored and less refined. The band was making a valiant attempt at "Satisfaction," and a perspiring, lurching dance floor crowd was yelling that it couldn't get none. Lila led Petey to a narrow doorway that opened to a set of steep stairs.

"Shit," said Lila once again, and she hoisted her gown to her waist and hurried up the steps. Her gams, Petey could not help but notice, were as sleek as everything else. Petey lifted up her own dress and stepped up.

Lila went to the captain's quarters, a cramped, windowless office next to the pilothouse. A second door led to the bridge, where a young man at the boat's helm eyed the two of them. They could hear the muted sounds from the festivities below. Lila leaned against a table and turned, arms crossed in front of her, to Petey. The two women were no more than a yard away from each other.

"You were the target—the one that druggie kid shot at under the seats," she said.

"That's me," Petey said.

"Duffy House's niece."

"Correct."

"If it happened once, you know, it can happen again. Ever think of that?"

"Constantly," Petey said.

She was nervous, trying to think fast, up against as forbidding an antagonist as any she'd faced so far in this thing.

"What has Red told you?"

"Everything. And nothing."

"I'm sure. Talk, talk, talk. It's always gotten that man into trouble, even on the air."

"How about Dean? What did it do for him?"

"My, my, go right for the kidneys," Lila said.

"For openers."

"They put a tongue in you, now didn't they, darling?" Lila said.

"Brought my best one along. I was told I'd need it."

Lila bared her teeth in a grudging smile.

"So what's your item? I can't leave my guests alone too long."

"You know about Dream's murder. You were his lover, so you had to. Something happened, things got out of hand. What?" Petey said.

"Red told you this?"

"No. Red told me he'd kill for you."

"Oh *my.*"

"Dammit, Mrs. Rohe," Petey said. "This isn't a social game. This is a kid's life. Or it was."

At that the blue vein reappeared, and Lila, almost absently, lifted a jeweled, manicured digit to her neck to camouflage its betrayal. Her expression went to stone.

"I know nothing of the murder. *Nothing.* I told the police that, and I'm telling you. Things happened with Dream. It was an affair, and a damn good one. George would have been livid if he'd known. His own golden boy, can you imagine?"

"You must really hate him," Petey said.

"At times. But mostly I'm past that. I like revenge better. With a little embarrassment and humiliation—those are the good ones nowadays," she said.

"But your husband would have been livid."

"To be sure. But then, George gets livid about the thought of any man in my life. He always did. Even the ones in my past. Even Red. He wanted to can Red so bad he could taste it, but the fans would have boiled him alive.

"But he didn't know about Dream. No, he couldn't have. If he had he would have exploded. Boom. All the seams. This hasn't been a good year for him, you know. He would have killed me. *Me,* I said. Not Dream. He'd never get rid of his golden goose."

"Even if that goose was laying more than just golden eggs?"

"Good. You're quick."

"Did he ever try?"

"Try what now, darling?"

"To get rid of you?"

"Daily. In more ways than you know. Our marriage has been ten years of attempted spouse slaughter. And yet he's never laid a finger on me," she said.

Then she curled her lip once again. It was a beautiful, treacherous sight.

"George is sexy when he's mad," Lila said.

Petey shook her head.

"I'll take your word for it," she said.

"You may do more than that," Lila said.

"I may?" Petey said.

"If you keep up your private-eye games."

Petey waited.

"Oh, yes," Lila went on. "George knows what you and your uncle are up to. The commissioner's office, as I understand it. George and the commissioner—that overblown pork belly trader—don't get along, you know. When George found out about Duffy he did what he does best, he put a shadow on your uncle. I should know. He's using the same guy he uses to follow me."

"You're kidding!" Petey said. It was her turn to raise her hand to her throat.

"I'm not a kidder," Lila said.

Petey suddenly felt queasy, as if she suddenly had to get off the boat, or, at the very least, over to a railing.

"Unk," she breathed.

* * *

If anybody was roused by my clatter, it was only in my imagination. But that was racing. Still, I heard no approaching footsteps, no movement, no jangling keys or dangling nightsticks. I stepped carefully into the Addison Street concourse, just across from the Stadium Club and beneath Aisle 223. The air was stale, the aroma of a loss, of used hot dog wrappers and empty beer cups.

My path was lit only by random lights of the night. I was surrounded by menus and billboards and signs of the ballpark, but I paid heed to none of them. I hugged the wall as if it were a ledge and I were forty stories up, and made my way over to the office. Though there were drips and creaks, pings and bumps, hums from fans and compressors, echoes in the night in this place which is normally humming by day, I saw and heard no one.

I ducked inside the open entry to the vendors' station, the storehouse where the beer and hot dog boys and girls come to reload, and came upon the door of the security office. I felt for the key and brushed the inside pocket of my sportcoat for the ushers' list. I felt like Jose Cardenal crossing himself on a 3–2 count.

The key slipped nicely into the slot in the door-knob. Clasping the key with one hand and the knob with the other, I shot a final glance toward the concourse. It was a move I'd seen sleuths make just prior to penetrating a locked office. I turned the knob and pushed in one motion. It wouldn't budge, and I bumped up against the door. I tried again. The key was like a sword in stone. No matter how I twisted and wiggled it, it still would not turn. *Dammit, Reulie,* I hissed.

I stood like a drunken spouse locked out of his own domicile—not that I'd had that experience before—stupid, obvious, vulnerable. The doggone door would not open.

* * *

By now the *Fromage* was well on its way back to Navy Pier, but that was not good enough for Petey. She knew what I was up to and up against, and she was certain she had to stop me. After Lila returned to her court, Petey quickly searched out a crew member.

"I *must* use your phone," she said.

"No phone. Just radios. Is it an emergency?" he said. He was a skinny kid with short hair and nervous eyes.

"Yes. No. I mean, to *me* it is," she said.

"We can call police boats or the Coast Guard. Or I can radio the office and have them call for you," he said.

"No phone?" she said.

"They're expensive. Plus, if word got out there was a phone on board these people'd be lined up to use it," he said.

"I can't believe this! This is the nineties!" she cried.

"Yeah, it is," the kid said, and shrugged.

Petey was frantic, but helpless. She rushed to the main deck to see where the boat was and saw that it was within view of the breakwater. She groaned. It had

taken the boat some time to travel this distance from
Navy Pier on the way out. She guessed it wouldn't be
any quicker coming in. The band was louder than ever
now. Jackets, ties, and high heels had come off and the
maple dance floor was shaking. So was Petey.

"So there you are," came a voice.

It was Henry Hanson's.

Petey smiled weakly.

"You don't look well."

"I'm not."

"Lila has that effect sometimes," he said.

"I've got to get ashore," Petey said.

"Swim much?" Henry said, and smiled like a
wasted Vienna choirboy.

Petey nearly strangled him.

"Can you believe there's no phone on this tub?"
she said.

"Oh, but there are many," Henry said.

"Where?" Petey exclaimed.

"Among the crowd. Personal cellular phones—dozens of them. The new high-tech jewelry," he said mer-
rily.

"Henry, could you get me to one? Please, I'm really
desperate," Petey said.

"Desperate women excite me. Come along,"
Henry Hanson said.

*   *   *

I wiggled and jiggled and twisted that damn key
until my fingers were about to drop off. I also used some
of the foulest language this side of Herman Franks.

Then, as if it were some kind of cruel game, the key
turned in the lock and the door opened. Just like that. I
was suddenly inside the pitch black office of Fingers
Brown, Cub security chief.

I didn't dare turn on a light, nor could I see three
inches in front of my nose. So I stood there breathing
hard and rubbing my sore fingers. Finally my eyes adjusted and by the light of a luminous wall clock I could
make out a few objects in the room. Like the desk. It
had to have a lamp. They always did. This one didn't.

Then again, Fingers Brown didn't have all his digits either, which is how he got his nickname and which meant the rest of this escapade was up for grabs.

A pro, a real operative, your garden variety Spade would have had a penlight with him. I wouldn't even know where to buy one of those things. I improvised. All ballpark offices have a little refrigerator in them. Fingers's was behind his desk. I opened the door and its light made the area bright enough for me to see what I was doing. I opened the desk and started going through folders.

All I found was vouchers and forms, the official detritus of a little ballpark general. And Fingers Brown was just that, a cantankerous guy who ran the ushers and the security guards as if they were his private army, *his* boys in pith helmets and the two-way radios, the guys who could keep the mayor and his horses outside the ballpark or look the other way and let a floozy in on nothing but her good looks, the gentlemen who showed you to your seat with a smile and the brutes whose job was to break up beer fights before innocent out-of-towners got hurt, the guys who talked tough but who, in the final accounting, were dependent on the civilized good manners of the crowd to keep order.

In the second drawer I found it. It was a clipboard with an inch-thick deck of rosters. I knew because they matched the one I had in my jacket pocket. I laid the clipboard on the floor, and by the light of the open fridge—which stank of snuff and salami gone bad—I flipped through the rosters until I found the one I wanted. I laid mine next to it and began to compare names. In the bad light and the fumes it took some time.

Then I saw it. A moniker that leapt out at me like Ronnie Santo spearing a foul pop in the third-base boxes. But this was no Santo, no spark plug of a third-sacker who could click his heels and drive in runs. This was a thug, a vermin.

"We have our shooter," I said.

I said it out loud.

I felt elated; I felt low. The second emotion won out. All was treachery.

Dammit.

At that, the office was ablaze with light and I was blinded.

* * *

In exchange for her phone number—in a crisis, Petey explained later, certain standards are compromised—Petey got her telephone. It belonged to a commodities trader who used it not to stay in contact with night trading in the Treasury bond pit but to call the sports lines to see how his bets were faring. Thinking on her sea legs, Petey dialed the one fixed port in the storm: the bar of the Cape Cod Room. There she found Red.

"Uncle Duffy's in trouble," Petey rasped.

"What happened? What's goin' on?" Red barked.

"He's at the park. With that key," Petey said, making every attempt to be too cryptic for those within earshot.

"Key? What key? Wait! Oh my God, *that* key! He's there now? Oh, for crying out loud—" Red uttered, the scene sinking into his still unpickled brain.

"You-know-who is onto him. And bad. I found out he's put a tail on Uncle Duf. I'm scared, Red," Petey said.

"Ho-ly cow! Where are you? What's all that racket?"

"I'm on your charity boat. With Mrs. You-know-who. We're just coming into the Pier."

"Criminy. That thing was tonight? So what do you want me to do?"

"Can you get inside the park?"

"Of course! Who do you think you're talking to?"

"Then wait for me at the Drake. As soon as I'm off this junk I'm in a cab and picking you up."

"Michigan Avenue side," he said.

"Wait for me. Promise," Petey said.

"Hey, whattaya take me for?"

"Whattaya got?" Petey said, and hung up.

By now the *Fromage*'s engines churned as the boat maneuvered toward its moorings. Petey raced over to the railing, looking as if she were ready to jump over, cursing through her teeth at the groaning ferry and its slow-motion progress.

"Come *on*, you bathtub," she hissed.

Just as she thought it was coming into port it went into a wide, slow U-turn in order to dock in the other direction. What Petey said is unprintable. I can only imagine that she was quite a sight, standing there dressed as she was, gorgeous, angry as a hornet, nervous, pounding the railing of the *Fromage* as if it were the wall of a jail.

Finally the boat swung near the Pier's concrete edge. Right then and there Petey made her move. She took off her heels, hiked up her dress, climbed the boat's railing, and leapt ashore. Those who saw her gasped.

She landed with a tumble and a rip, the already-slit seam of her dress giving up a few more inches. She recovered and scrambled like a thief along the pier, with her shoes in her left hand, toward the Grand Avenue entrance. Her long legs gracefully ate up the yardage. She cut corners and avoided benches and trash containers and kept her eye on the Pier's entrance as if it were a third-base coach and she were being waved home. In seconds she bounded onto the entry drive and nearly ran into the path of a taxi. Luckily, it had a conscious driver and a pair of functioning brakes; it was also passengerless.

"The Drake Hotel! Step on it!" she yelled.

The cab was a gleaming mustard-yellow Checker, that boxy, oversized relic and one of the few remaining on Chicago's streets since the Kalamazoo company went out of business years ago. This one groaned and rattled like a milk truck. Its interior was festooned with bumper stickers and promotional paraphernalia from a local radio station, including a wooden plaque that read:

You have entered the taxi of Osman,
Q-101's celebrity hack. Ride at your own risk.
You may be on the air, so
keep it clean.

"Osman at your service, lady. This is your lucky day," the cabbie said.

He was a dark-skinned, mustachioed Pakistani, his voice a pinched tenor, his accent laced with curry. On his thick head of dark hair was a black chauffeur's cap with "Osman—Q-101" in gold lettering above the bill. Below his head, all too visible to the unprotected eye, he wore a long-sleeved, double-knit shirt with a four-inch collar and an orange-and-brown houndstooth design that brought on instant astigmatism.

"Drake Hotel! Drive like hell," Petey gasped, unable, even in her frenzy, to avoid wincing at the sight of the shirt.

"In a hurry, lady?" Osman said.

"In a panic," Petey replied.

"Bad for you, huh?" Osman said, peering into his rearview mirror at Petey.

"Drive!" she roared.

He grinned brightly and, still looking in the mirror, goosed the boxy sedan down Grand and made the light onto Michigan Avenue.

Petey was sweating and out of breath, her henna haul of hair now collapsed around her shoulders. She grasped the frontseat and leaned forward. Through the windshield she could see the panorama of North Michigan Avenue as it sloped north toward the beach at Oak Street. She could also see the river of cars, buses, and horse-drawn carriages alternately stopped by traffic lights at every block and looming as a barrier between her and Red Carney in front of the Drake, and, of course, Wrigley Field.

"Hit it! Get around this guy! Don't get caught behind a bus!" she yelled.

"You telling Osman how to drive?" Osman demanded incredulously.

"Damn right," Petey answered.

He cackled and pounded the steering wheel.

"Go, Osman!" he yelled.

He gunned the motor and plowed through yellowish-red lights, switching lanes, cutting off rival cabs, and drawing rage from other drivers and upraised fingers from genteel pedestrians.

"Murphy, he will love you, lady," Osman said. "You listen? You hear Osman on radio with Murphy?"

"No, but I will. I will. I promise. You're doing great," Petey praised.

Osman grinned and nodded.

They hurtled past the side streets, Stuart Brent's bookshop, the Water Tower, Water Tower Place, Neiman's and Magnin's, Bloomingdale's, and the Hancock Building—until they came within view of the Drake.

"Get in the right lane. Pick up the guy at the corner —see him there in the green sportcoat—then haul ass to Wrigley Field!" she yelled.

"Haul *ass*, you say? Osman like that one."

"Good. Now do it."

"Wrigley Field? Baseball, lady?"

"Yeah, hardball," Petey said.

"Hardball? Oh boy, Murphy, he can love you, lady." Osman laughed.

Petey stuck her head out of the side window.

"Red!" she yelled.

Red waved and hustled over to the cab as Osman wheezed to a stop near the Michigan-Oak intersection. Petey flung open the door and pulled Red inside as Osman stomped on the gas, nearly clipping a top-hatted Drake doorman but making the light and racing into the underpass that leads onto Lake Shore Drive.

"Holy Cow!" Red crowed.

* * *

"House, you son-of-a-bitch!" came the voice.

I had been blinded by the light, but I didn't need my sight to recognize the presence of George Rohe, general manager of the Chicago Cubs Baseball Club. The words roared from his throat and banged against the walls of Fingers Brown's office like a line drive fouled into the dugout. I froze.

"You're about as good a private eye as you were a reporter. And that was crap," Rohe said.

"Everybody's a critic," I said.

Meanwhile, my pupils did whatever they do to readjust to light, and I faced my critic. Rohe filled the doorway like the reincarnation of Blimp Phelps, except that Blimp was a nice guy compared to Rohe. His hands were on his hips and he was steamed, seething, downright perturbed. I had not elicited such unbridled emotion from Cub management since I suggested in print that the franchise was more endearing in defeat than in victory. He was alone; at least, I didn't see anyone else.

"Breaking and entering. That the best you can do?" he said.

"Entered, but didn't break," I said.

"Forget the bullshit. How'd you get in here? How'd you get in the ballpark, for that matter?"

"I got a lifetime pass. Compliments of the club."

"Cut the smoke, Duffy. This isn't one of your shitbag columns. It could be a police matter," he said.

"Could be? Call them. Get Jimmy Slagle, the murder dick," I said.

"Whatta ya got there?" Rohe asked.

He picked up the clipboard with Fingers Brown's roster of Andy Frains. He studied it like a manager looking over his lineup card. And I studied him as he went through the roster of names, most of them, but not all, meaningless to him. And I can't be sure, but I think I saw something, something in that instant when Rohe read the name he did not want to see there. I believe I saw a tightening of the eyes, a slight inhalation, a momentary, involuntary spasm. Rohe was a bull of a man, more so right now than ever.

" 'Bert Tinker.' Of all the names he could have used," I said.

"Means nothing to me," Rohe said.

He said it firmly, with bravado, a look of steel, and a toss of the clipboard back onto the desk. But he was lying; the name meant everything to him, though he feigned ignorance. George Rohe was a Cubs general manager, one of a species that has made more Brock-for-Broglio trades than any in baseball history and then faced the press with flinty insistence that each deal would make the team a contender.

So I'm used to the mask. Cynicism is a sports columnist's daily bread, and my pantry never went bare. Yet I was lardered with much more than conventional skepticism in this case, and it was leavened with a piece of information that went down deep and way back.

It had to do with the story I did on Rohe when he was named G.M., the one where I found out about his first wife, the young divorcée and her no-good son. As I said earlier, I never used that information, but I never forgot it. Maybe that was because the woman's name was Tinker, in fact, it was *Bertie* Tinker. I remember chuckling about it then. Seeing that name on the roster now hit me like a ton of bricks.

Through all these years, with George Rohe sitting as the Cubs' G.M., I had never given his stepson a second thought. I simply never knew who the kid was. Not until he, George Whiteman, put his mother's maiden name on the ushers' roster.

And now that secret was staring me right in the eye in that suffocating little office in Wrigley Field. Bert Tinker—that *name*. And Rohe knew it. His code had been cracked.

Just then a figure appeared at his shoulder. It was a good head shorter than Rohe yet just as thick, and bearing no resemblance whatsoever to the G.M. In the dark, the guy was, however, a spittin' image of Burleigh Grimes, excepting a mug covered with stubble, which was Grimes's fashion. He was just as burly, if you'll excuse the obvious, and, when he came into the light, just as mean. In a flash I thought of Frankie Frisch, whom Grimes hated and who took more pitches in the back from Burleigh than any man alive.

But it was just a flash, for the figure was none other than Whiteman, now minus his obsequious veneer, expressionless, to be sure, with no helpful offers or polite phrases trickling from his lips as before. In fact, he looked altogether like a son of a bitch. My back started to ache.

* * *

Osman, grinning maniacally, his chauffeur's cap pulled down around his thick hair, goaded by Petey and the huffing presence of Red Carney in his back seat, drove the old Checker cab like a runaway stage. He knew the Drive was usually lined with traffic cops and their radar guns, and that cabbies were their favorite game, but Osman also knew that this ride, the redhead with the slit skirt, the TV baseball guy that even Osman, who was raised on cricket, recognized, Wrigley Field and all, was show biz.

"If we are in the morning I would call Mr. Murphy!" he shouted, raising his cellular phone in the air but, mercifully, keeping his other hand on the wheel and both eyes on the Drive.

The cab barreled past North Avenue and bore down on Fullerton Parkway. To Petey, even as she filled in the details for Red, the trip seemed interminable.

"Take Belmont! Go up the inner drive to Addison!" Red yelled.

"Go Osman!" Osman yelled.

* * *

"Leave everything right there, Duffy. All your lists and hunches and fancy footwork," Rohe said. "And George here will show you to the gate."

George. Just plain George. A name for Mitterwald and Frazier, but for a goon? Nevertheless, George advanced a few steps. He wasn't carrying a weapon; he didn't need one. He had arms like Carmen Fanzone but he wasn't as amiable and probably couldn't carry a tune.

"You screwed up coming here, Duffy. Somebody gave you a horseshit tip, and you bought it. That's not like you," said Rohe, another George, of course. He was suddenly more amiable.

His stepson came around the desk and stood behind me like a specter. His thighs rubbed together as he went. Only Ivan DeJesus had better ones.

"My big screw-up was sitting on a story a few years back, George," I said to Rohe.

"That wouldn'ta been your style," Rohe countered.

"You're old school, Duffy. No dirty laundry, no skeletons or black sheep, nothing but what's inside the white lines. I can appreciate that. You've been good for the game."

" 'The good of the game.' George, I can't remember when I've ever heard you talk about that."

I was jawing, stalling, maybe just a little edgy with George Whiteman, the human torpedo, the designated hitter, at my side.

"That Bill Veeck–Charlie Grimm lingo isn't up my alley," Rohe said.

"Better the wisdom of Steinbrenner, Finley, maybe Charles Comiskey if you go way back," I replied. "Or maybe I'm wrong. Your boy might be Ivan Boesky."

"That's more like it, Duffy. Take the usual shots. Come up with a few good lines and put them in the morning fish wrapper. In the meantime, guys like me have to run ball clubs."

"Makes me pine for the days of Salty Saltwell," I said.

"It would. You never much liked the changes around here. New ownership, lights, even winning a few ball games—they stick in your craw, don't they? For whatever difference it makes," Rohe said.

"You're right on two out of three, George. I do like to see the boys win. But you didn't mention a new wrinkle that doesn't cheer me."

"What's that?"

"Million-dollar insurance policies on starting pitchers."

Rohe said nothing, just stood in the open doorway and looked at me with the esteem he'd be likely to show a player to be named later.

"Everybody has insurance. It's part of the game nowadays," he said.

"Dental, disability, maybe even an HMO for the guys and the wives," I said. "But a life insurance policy? That's downright morbid. Or lethal."

I could not resist. Maybe I was fishing, or baiting, or just pissing him off. But I wanted some kind of murmur, some faint spark, some combustion—*something,* dammit. Here was the muckety-muck of the Cubs, the CUBS, a treasure that belongs to no man and no corporation, the same individual who had witnessed hearts rent by the ghastly murder of a strapping young ace inside these hallowed grounds, and from whom, at the very least, I wanted some faint trace of response. I would tempt fate—my own—to get it.

"A lousy policy. So what? The movie studios take them out on their warm bodies all the time. Why not us?" he said, his ego too obese to ignore a salvo.

"Just one? And only on Weaver," I said, and thought: Frank Schulte, don't fail me now.

"Yeah. He was a reckless son of a bitch."

"How reckless?" I asked.

He braked. The line of chatter wasn't going his way, and Rohe liked to control the flow.

"How much did it take to seal his doom? One bad outing? A string of them? Maybe a few remarks during arbitration? A needle here and there? How did this kid get under your skin?"

"Didn't happen, Duffy. You're playing newspaper games again. Bold type, big headlines," he said.

"How reckless?" I repeated.

The pause seemed eternal.

"He crossed the line," Rohe said.

"Or did *she*?" I said.

I had no more trump cards. I didn't need any more.

There was no fuming, no steel-eyed glare, no bellicose veins standing out. In George Rohe's tiny yellow eyes there was only desolation. And Red Carney's refrain played silently, elegiacally on our lips, *Lila, Lila, Lila*. . . .

Then Rohe snapped to.

"Conversation's over, Duffy," he murmured. "Thanks for the memories."

With that, his goon put a vise grip on my arm and yanked me out of the office.

Rohe walked ahead, swiftly turning into the concourse and heading toward the front office. There was no discussion, no parting words, no directive for his heavy. That was fine. I did not need fanfare while being shown the door.

Except that as Rohe took a right and proceeded, I presumed, back to his office, his thug jerked me to the left. Fine, fine, I thought, I don't need to leave the front way. The ballpark offers hosts of convenient exits.

But none on the second deck. Suddenly I realized I was being pulled, pushed, and quite efficiently manhandled up the ramp toward the ozone seats. The view at this time of night, I was certain, was dreadful.

* * *

Screaming up the inner Drive, Osman narrowly missed two joggers, a pair of Pekingese attached by leash to a retired but fiercely litigious personal injury attorney, and a college kid struggling with an empty Dove Bar pushcart. It wasn't until much later, Petey told me, that she thought of the possible consequences of being party to vehicular manslaughter.

At Addison, Osman wrenched the cab into a left turn and popped a hubcap, which rolled and hopped along the pavement and up against the door of a candy-apple red BMW.

"Stop at Clark!" Red yelled.

To Petey he said, "We go in the front door."

"The front?" Petey cried.

"Only key I own," he replied. "Just stay close."

Petey clutched her heels, then decided to leave them behind. Then she had another thought, and she quickly rifled through her purse.

Osman ran a red light at Broadway, but got the green at Halsted in front of the Town Hall police station.

"Almost there, lady and gentleman!" he crowed as the park's walls came into view.

"Great job!" Petey yelled.

"Thank you, lady! Osman a bat from hell!" He cackled at himself.

With that he floored the cab through a mustard-colored light at Sheffield and struggled to stop the rattling machine at Clark and Addison.

"If we're not back out in ten minutes, call this number and tell them to get over here," Petey said, handing Osman a note with Detective Jimmy Slagle's number on it.

Osman raised his phone again.

"Osman can do!" he yelled.

In the shadow of the main gate and the famous red-and-white sign overhead, Red and Petey deplaned onto the sidewalk, leaving the red-hot hack and its unpaid meter at the curb, and sprinted for the steel-door entrance just north of the advance ticket windows.

* * *

With the hood's iron hand still locked around my arm, I half-shuffled, half-skipped up the demanding zigzag grade of the ramp leading to the second deck along first base. It was a trek, and I started to breathe heavily.

"Ease up a little. Ease up a lot. In fact, let's go to the bleachers instead," I bleated. "I'll show you where Charlie Grimm's ashes are strewn. I'll show you where the Babe pointed his homer. I'll show you Swish Nicholson's greatest blast. Did you ever know that the left-field bleachers were so small they used to call 'em the 'jury box'?"

I was blathering like an idiot. My voice echoed through the empty steel girders like the ghost of Pat Pieper. Worst of all, the mug wasn't buying it. He was as mum as Rick and Paul Reuschel on a good day. He was a cold, unsentimental torpedo, and he pushed me relentlessly up to where the foul flags fly.

* * *

Once inside the door, Red waved at the front desk man and, with Petey close behind, was buzzed inside. He hopped the stairs leading to the second-floor offices. Petey began to follow, then stopped, seeing the entrance to the stadium straight ahead. She went for it, rushing into the dimly lit concourse, then stopped, unsure of just where to go. From her most recent Wrigley Field adventure, she knew where the security office was located. Yet she did not know if I was there or, indeed, just where I might be.

Her first impulse was to go to the door leading to the clubhouse along the third-base side. Unlike on Weaver's fateful day, it was locked tight. She groaned, then sprinted—barefoot, silent, swift as a woman in distress—for the nearest entrance to the grandstands. There was no one to guide or impede her. Rohe had dispatched the night security crew to the parking office near the players' lot on Addison Street, where they sat and watched bad reruns on a local TV station. Petey turned into the wheelchair tunnel and emerged in the open air of the box seats behind the home plate screen.

The park was deathly still, moonlit, the vines whispering in the summer breeze, the pale green scoreboard a dark shroud in the northeastern sky, the skeletal light towers extinguished and harmless. A few lone bulbs illuminated the recesses of the stands, and Petey searched them for me.

Instead of seeing me, she heard me. Not the scrape of my steps on the concrete, or my wheezing lungs, or, in my wildest fantasy, the tattoo of my fists against the goon's sternum. No, Petey heard me trying to jabber my way to freedom.

"Give it a rest a minute, pal. Hoo boy! Smell the roses a minute," I yelped in between gasps. At the rate he was hustling me up the ramp, I'd drop dead without his having thrown so much as a brushback.

"You're a fan, aren't ya?" I kept on. "You got a feel for some of the great ones who played here. Come on, give me one of your favorites.

"Hey, did ya know the great ones who *ended* here? I mean, Wrigley Field is one of the great waiting rooms of the big leagues. Why, Jimmy Foxx—the *Beast,* Double X—he landed here! And the *Rajah*! Hornsby. He put on the Cubs' flannel.

"I can go on, George. Hold it here a minute, let me catch my breath. Whoa. Rabbit Maranville—yeah, he played a little shortstop right here—"

I was racking my brain.

"Then there's ol' Diz. Dizzy *Dean,* for crying out

loud. When he got here his toe was shot and his arm was worse. Threw his 'nothin' ball.' Yeah, right here, George. Right here!"

My stall had an effect I hadn't counted on. Petey honed in on the location of the chatter. She spotted me and the thug as we arrived at the entrance to the second deck. Instantly deducing that I was not up there on my own whim, she looked around for some kind of equalizer. She saw it on the field in the form of a groundskeeper's rake holding down one edge of the home plate tarpaulin.

My cries became Petey's cover. "Lou Burdette! Now there's one few people remember. Was close to forty years old when he toed that rubber right there!"

In a second she was down behind the screen, over the wall, and hotfooting it to home plate. She picked up the rake and turned to retrace her steps when she saw yet another object lying near the Cubs' dugout. It was a bat, a fungo, taped at the top end and cracked in the middle, yet still in one, relatively solid piece as fungoes go. Billy Williams had broken the thing hitting rainmakers to the outfielders and had given it to a groundskeeper, who had gone home without it. Petey discarded the rake and picked up the fungo, not pausing to note that it was a Peanuts Lowrey model.

"Or Ralph Kiner! Him too. You ever a Kiner fan, George?" came my squeal.

Like a midnight gazelle, Petey leapt over the wall, up the grandstand steps, into the tunnel, across the concourse, and up the same ramp my executioner and I had just traversed.

"Richie Ashburn! Oh, we could have used him in his prime. Covered center field like the dew. We get him and he can't even reach the gaps, for godssakes!"

The bum wasn't buying it. He either had no sense of history, no love of the Cubs, or he was simply a virulent bastard. He yanked me down the steps toward the railing just as I thought of somebody with whom he could truly identify.

"Joe Pepitoooo—!"

I never got it out because he started to roughhouse.

He twisted my arm behind my back and slammed me with his hip. I returned the struggle. I threw my remaining elbow, hooked a foot on a seat, and put up as much of a physical fuss as old wordsmiths are capable of. My flailing caused him to lose his balance and together we toppled against a bank of seats. I'm a hefty bag of bones with a lot of lumps, and the jumble of limbs was considerable, like Barry Foote jumping Tim Stoddard.

The tussle took some time and pissed the guy off. *Really* pissed him off, and he straightened up and threw a punch at me. I saw it coming, ducked, and still caught it in the neck. My head snapped, my eardrum exploded, and little fiery bugs flew around my eyeballs.

I was a wet throw rug as the goon dragged me down to the railing.

That's where I held on. I grabbed that bar like an editor clings to a deadline, like a true Cub fan who pines for the days when a game could be called on account of darkness. My manhandler, on the other hand, came at me like a crazed cleanup hitter, sweating, grunting, his teeth bared.

He grabbed one of my legs and lifted me into the air like a bag of bats. I was going over. I was going to dive like a Texas-League foul ball, plummet like the output of Steve Bilko at the end of spring training, swoon like the Cubs in September, or August, or July, or June . . .

"Uncle Duffy!!!"

The cry came like relief from the bullpen. It was Petey at the top of the deck. At her voice the bum turned, took a wild kick in the thigh from yours truly, and then dropped me. He bounded up the aisle, retracing our steps and going right at Petey. He saw that he had two of us to dispose of now, and he apparently judged—correctly, from my way of thinking—that Petey was the greater threat at the moment.

Except that he didn't see her ash. As he lumbered up the steps like Dave Kingman trying to run down a line drive, Petey reached back, timed her swing, and swung with everything she had. Her form was magnificent, a vision of Ernie Banks sending an inside fastball onto Waveland Avenue, the epitome of every technique Lou Fonseca tried to impart to Cub swatters: a compact, level, angry swing. It tagged the son of a bitch in the knees. The crack of bat on bone shot through the ballpark and made even me wince. The goon bellowed —his first utterance all night—fell, and writhed in a kind of agony he had only given before, never received.

"Bingo!" I yelled.

"Cubs win!" Petey exulted.

21

Box Score

While Petey and I were engaged with the lethal
George Whiteman, Red had gone to the general manager's office for George Rohe's throat. The confrontation
must have been epic, and not a little bit sad. Here were
two men who had spent their lives worshipping in the
temple of baseball, and one of them had defiled it almost beyond repair.

Red, of course, raged out of control, a condition
which put his diction somewhere between that of
Harry Caray with too many cold ones and Dizzy Dean
in the heat of a rally. Gleaning from his days around Leo
Durocher and Herman Franks, drawing deeply into his
stockpile of Lee Elia, Red hurled every insult and
epithet imaginable at Rohe. Rohe indignantly feigned
ignorance and accused Red of being blind drunk. He
also tried to alert security. The stadium's night crew of
gendarmes, however, had been put on hold by Rohe
himself in order to let his stepson choreograph my own
little leap of death.

What must have been something was that frozen
rope of a bond that tied Red and Rohe, which was, of
course, Lila. She had possessed both of them, driven
them, haunted them, and, ultimately, ignited emotions
so strong and volcanic in one that a gifted young man
lay cold in his grave. To be sure, Red had nothing to do
with that. His weakness was passion, misplaced no
doubt, but passion as hot-blooded as any poet ever

dreamed. Red is that kind of guy, and he knew the awful pain that may have cast the wretched Rohe adrift.

But that squishy stuff can be taken only so far. When all was said and done, Rohe was a greedy and vengeful bastard. He was a bastard apart from or because of Lila—I'll let the pundits figure that out. He was a bastard to a kid, that golden kid, he thought had wronged him. And, finally, he was a bastard to the whole community of baseball.

Red knew it, and it steamed him something awful. In those heated, furious moments when the two men confronted each other in the low nighttime light, Red wanted to do what Leo Durocher once suggested be done to a futility infielder: "He ought to be taken out behind the barn and shot."

Once he laid eyes on Rohe in his office, Red tore into him, calling Rohe a "rotten sonuvabitch" and a "horseshit general manager," and incidentally accusing him of avarice and murder, citing the life insurance policy brought to light by Frank Schulte. Then he tired of the oratory and went directly for a sock in the eye. He stormed around Rohe's desk and grabbed the general manager by the shirt. Rohe was no little man, so the fisticuffs were a toss-up. A poor punch selection and a lot of pushing followed, all of which made a good deal of noise and did little damage. But it was a venting good try for old Red.

The two of them might have battered each other indefinitely had they not been interrupted. Osman, the crazy cabbie, knew he had a live one, and he could no more sit on it for ten minutes, as Petey had ordered, than he could allow a bus to merge. After only a few moments, he telephoned Jimmy Slagle with Petey's message, then he dialed his cronies at the radio station and told them something big was going on at the ballpark. Osman loved a party, and he was soon to have one on his hands.

In no time Jimmy Slagle and a pair of his plainclothesmen hurtled up to Clark and Addison in an unmarked but unmistakable police car. With Osman trailing clouds of glory behind them, they rushed inside the stadium. There was plenty of racket to guide their pricked up ears. Red and Rohe were going at it like a pair of drunken moose in Rohe's office, and Petey and I were accosting and assaulting Rohe's hired killer in the upper deck.

With their gats drawn and Osman hot on their steps, the dicks split up and sought out the brawls. One went for Rohe's office; Slagle, a partner, and Osman dashed for the upper deck. I could hear their huffing and their heels as they charged up the ramp toward Petey and me. Petey stood over a cowering, writhing George Whiteman, measuring him like Andre Dawson eyeballing Eric Show, threatening to swing again and take him downtown. She was a sight in her torn evening dress and bare feet, the fungo bat poised above her coppery and very tousled hair, a look of such extreme glee, determination, and not a little mayhem on her face as to make an uncle weep.

Slagle was clearly confused. He cuffed Whiteman and ordered Petey to drop her bat. The cabbie lit up with a grin the size of home plate and crowed, "One for the good guys, huh, lady?"

Slagle growled and told everybody to return to ground level and decent illumination. He lowered but did not holster his cannon. He looked at me, wrapped as I was like a discarded hot dog wrapper around the upper deck railing, and just shook his head.

Whiteman could barely walk. I didn't feel so chipper myself, especially after having so recently anticipated my head meeting foul ground at thirty-two feet per second squared. Petey and Osman, on the other hand, bounced along as if they were going out for peanuts between innings.

We were met in the main concourse by Slagle's partner, his weapon also drawn, with Red and George Rohe in tow. The police officer was somewhat intimidated by both men, two big shots in the city's sports fishbowl, but he was taking no chances. He also had his hands full trying to keep them apart. Red was still looking to poke Rohe; George, ever arrogant, demanded that Red be arrested. Slagle scanned the three of them, then turned and took in the rest of us.

What followed was a few extra innings of accusation and denial, fingers pointed and heads hung low, and the anatomy of a despicable deed. We were motley: eight players in all, a starting lineup comprised of a grizzled and aching veteran; a chatterbox; a fleet, red-haired rookie; three plainclothes fielders most competent at the Alphonse-Gaston routine; a foreign-born, good-hands-weak-stick utility man; and two hit men. All we needed was a starting pitcher, a flame thrower, a whirling virtuoso of the hill who could compensate for our inadequacies by shutting down the opponent: a Dream Weaver.

Slagle was not thinking on that level; he wanted to know who was who and what in hell was going on. To his credit, he gave me the floor. I quickly introduced George Whiteman and revealed his twisted relationship with Rohe. I then recounted the mechanical details and intricacies that led up to the murder of Dream Weaver, complete with background, motive, an inference or two, and a few nicely turned phrases about George Rohe's ruthless methods and pathetic character.

For his part, Rohe stood still, glowered, and said absolutely nothing. It was an uncharacteristic but, I presume, appropriate response. Things were now, he knew, in the hands of the best litigator his money could buy. Slagle hesitated only briefly after hearing my tale, and that was to get a look at Whiteman. The hood's grimace had been replaced by a scowl, a slit-eyed, contemptuous expression that exuded generic evil. And the brunt of it was directed at George Rohe.

It was at that moment that I felt a genuine pang of emotion, of deep-seated hurt for Dream Weaver. He truly had been caught in a rundown, a punishment more vengeful than he ever could have imagined. In those stunned seconds before he absorbed that molten slug in his heart, in this Wrigley Field, a place where he felt secure from any harm worse than an occasional bad outing, he must have been as frightened of this monster who stood in our midst as of anything in his short life. I ached for him then, and I do to this day.

Apparently Slagle recognized the same quality in Whiteman, not to mention George Rohe, and it was ample cause for him to arrest the two of them, even though his own investigation had scarcely led him in their direction at all. He nodded at his partner, and the junior detective handcuffed the general manager. Rohe hissed a few threats at me and Slagle, but they were little more than an attempt at face-saving. You don't get thrown out of the ball game in your home park without putting up a fuss for the fans. Only this time there were no diehards to give George a hand before he hit the showers.

It was Red, now resigned to the fact that Rohe's fate was out of his hands, who got in a few parting shots.

"He never did belong in the major leagues," he said as Rohe was led off. Red was still flushed and raging. "He belongs in a factory somewhere or in a mine digging coal. He's been about as valuable to the Cubs as a batbag."

Petey snuck an arm around the broadcaster.

We emerged from the ballpark to see the beginnings of a media mangle. The cabbie's calls to Jimmie Slagle and to his radio station had soon been relayed across the city. Slagle's car had been joined by a gaggle of blipping blue-and-white squad cars parked at odd angles throughout the intersection and completely blocking traffic down Clark and Addison. There were cops everywhere, and a crowd that had poured out of nearby saloons as if the Cubs had just clinched the pennant.

Osman's cab was pinned at the curb, its door open, its two-way radio bleating, and three guys standing on the hood trying to get a better view of the proceedings. The sight of them was enough to dislodge Osman from Petey's side, but not before he turned to her, grinned, and said, "We do a job, huh, lady?"

As he sprinted off to whatever fame he could reap, I

spotted the TV minicam trucks on the perimeter of the traffic jam. In no time Weigel and Morris and those other on-camera sports birds would be running up. That was Red's playground, and he stood by looking like he was ready to go live.

I was elated about how the evening had turned out, but I had had my fill of thrills and acclaim for one night. I grabbed Petey, who looked as if she was ready to adjust her makeup, primp the hairdo, and join Red in the media show, and gave her a look that said in no uncertain terms that we weren't going to stick around.

"Look," I said to Red and Petey, "let's let Slagle handle the TV guys and the reporters, and let's us get the hell outta here. We'll have plenty of time to tell our tale later."

Red was torn, and so was Petey. Red, of course, was so much a part of live broadcasting that his adrenaline gushed at the very flicker of a camera's glowing red light. And many of them were about to glow. But he knew what he had just gone through, that he had been a choice part of this breaking news and was presently in no condition to call the play-by-play. As for Petey, the blush of being an instant media princess was not yet off her rose. She coveted the lights, the mikes, and the glare.

"We could get you back to the Drake, Red," I proposed, "and over a couple of nightcaps try to sort through the box score on this thing."

My common sense was unassailable, Red knew, especially since he was a little the worse for wear after his tussle with Rohe. And yet he stared somewhat wistfully at the TV minicams descending on Slagle, his two cuffed malefactors, and a group of uniformed cops behind them. Petey eyed the melee just as longingly. But I had to prevail. It wasn't going to be in the interest of my future with the commissioner's office if my mug and Petey's showed up on the 10 P.M. news on every TV set from Chicago to Phoenix and back in connection with the Weaver case.

The two of them grudgingly walked away with me. With Petey's arms thrust into those of her two favorite uncles, we slipped behind the thickening crowd. At Waveland Avenue we found a taxi with a driver actually in attendance, and we directed him to reverse the path of what would become Osman's legendary transport of the reinforcements—only at a more leisurely pace. He didn't seem to mind, nor to recognize his passengers, and simply looked into his rearview mirror at the maddening crowd and whistled.

"Lot of fuss around that ballpark these days," he said.

Little did he know.

"Rohe and Whiteman . . ." Red said, as if the very mention of the perpetrators was too much to contemplate.

We were back in the comforting environs of the Cape Cod Room's lounge. Red was nursing a potential shiner administered by Rohe, I was nursing what was left of a bicep bruised by Whiteman's grasp, Petey was nursing abrasions on the soles of her feet, the result of running the ramps with no shoes, and we were all nursing glasses of champagne brought by Red's bartender after Red told him of our conquest. Again it was late, all but a few customers had left, and the management was more than willing to let us sit there and wind down while they cleaned the place up. Not only that, but several of them paused now and then to listen in.

"Vermin. There's no other way to describe them," I said. "But first I want to know how you two showed up just when you did. You saved your uncle's considerable rear end, young lady."

I leaned forward and kissed Petey on the cheek.

"Lila Rohe told me that her husband had a tail on you," Petey said, "and I knew what you were up to. You're about as sly as an intentional walk, Unk. My problem was that we were out at sea when I found this out. I called Red on a cellular phone and was lucky enough to get him. Then I hailed a human torpedo of a cabdriver who got us both to the ballpark quicker than you can say Tinker to Evers to Chance."

Tinker, I thought to myself.

"I sensed immediately," Petey went on, "that Lila knew who killed Dream. I'm sure George never told her, but she must have known. She's a quick study if I ever saw one, and I can't see any man keeping too much from her."

"I'll drink to that," Red said.

"A wronged woman, that was your theory from the start, Red," I said.

"Duf, I was mistaken about who pulled the trigger but I had a feeling a dame was in there somehow," Red said. "I didn't want to believe it was Lila. Petey here never had that problem."

"Once I got her affair with Dream straightened out —no help from Unk here—"

"Guilty," I said.

"—of course, when half the world says it's true and half says it's bogus, it's a hard nut to crack. I think Lila liked it that way. But hey, if it was hard for us to get a handle on the thing, imagine how hubby George tied himself in knots over it," she said.

"That was the shiv in his gut. Enough to combine with his greed and his arrogance and his—ah, dammit, the guy is evil, I'm convinced of it—to kill the kid," I said.

"So what was that insurance stuff Schulte brought up all about? And how did Obie Blintstein play out in the whole thing?" Red asked.

"A lot of smoke. Rohe the machinator working behind the scenes, mostly. He figured Weaver and Blintstein were so dirty with underworld types that his own shenanigans wouldn't be noticed. And they almost weren't. Thing is, none of those leads rang true to me. It just took a long time for me to admit it.

"Truth is, when the commissioner told me Rohe had his own investigation going, it left a rotten taste in my mouth. Where in hell did they get off dogging me? And now I wonder how much they knew. I got the tip from Eddie Reulbach while the two of us were in a men's room at the ballpark, and for all I know someone could have been in a toilet stall overhearing our whole conversation.

"Whatever, at least I was in the ballpark. The murder was committed in the ballpark, in Wrigley Field, and something kept pulling me right back there to find out how and why."

"You got a nose for these things, Unk. Could be a whole new career for you," Petey exuded.

"Yours isn't so bad either, kid. Even though you almost got it sent to kingdom come by those lowlifes you scraped up against."

"Who was that Key character, anyway?" Red asked. "I don't like any sonofagun who takes potshots at this lovely lady."

"He's a dope supplier. A bad guy," Petey said.

"What I wanna know is how do all these birds get in the ballpark with guns?! For crying out loud, it's preposterous! And I'm not one of these antigun guys, but it seems to me that some places are off limits to firearms. Wrigley Field is one of them," he bellowed.

"Yeah, yeah!" chimed the bartender and several waiters.

"I don't know about Howard M. Key," I said, "but Whiteman made a careful study of it. He had to. Most importantly, he put in the fix on the security assignments in the tunnel. He actually saw to it that the spot nearest to the scene of the crime was vacant. He did it by assigning a phantom usher to that post. That's what Eddie Reulbach tipped me to.

"After pulling that off, it was easy. Whiteman was a familiar sight around the park, every part of it, so nobody thought his presence was out of the ordinary no matter where he might be. He even unlocked the door to the concourse so it would look like anyone from the outside could have gotten in. Then he waited for his chance. He slipped in the tunnel, confronted and shot Dream before the kid even knew what was going on, then slipped off in any one of a number of convenient directions.

"As far as the mechanics were concerned, it was as smooth as a well-delivered spitter. Otherwise, it was nothing but bloody murder committed by a hood at the behest of his boss. Something Rohe would put under the category of 'control,' which I'll tell you all about one day."

"God Almighty . . ." Red said.

"You know, I feel worse than ever for Dream right now," Petey said. "All the smears that his reputation took. And Obie's too. A lot of people hung the murder on him."

"Obie was no angel. He was supposed to keep Dream straight," I said, "make sure his contacts didn't turn on him and so forth. In a way it was just the opposite: Weaver was a cover for Obie and all the stuff he got into. The man should have known better."

"We all should have known better," said Red.

At that the bartender motioned us to the TV console above the bar. The local stations had cut into the late-night gabbers and reruns to go live at the ballpark. ". . . in a dramatic development at Wrigley Field just moments ago," the anchorwoman said, "police have made an arrest in the murder of Cub pitcher Dean Weaver." Then he went directly to live coverage—the scene we had escaped not long before. As an on-scene reporter spoke we could see the heads of Jimmy Slagle and his boys in the background. Then Jimmy came on, looking very authoritative when only moments before he had looked quite addled, and announced pending charges against Rohe and Whiteman.

I hardly listened to the rest, knowing Slagle could not say much more. My thoughts were drowned out by Petey's outburst. She pointed at the screen where Osman, the loony hack, was gesturing victory signs in the background and mouthing, "We got 'em!" Even Red, in his increasingly mellow condition, laughed out loud.

I suddenly realized it was time to make a telephone call, and I found a phone booth near the Room's entrance. It was late, but he had told me to call at any hour.

"Mr. Commissioner . . ." I ventured into the phone.

"What!?" barked Grand's voice. I knew I hadn't

awakened him, only disturbed his reveries or one of those Elmore Leonard novels he favored at this time of night.

"House," I said.

"Heard of 'im," he came back. "You got anything other than speculation and some niece of yours in trouble again?"

"The case, that's what. Cracked wide open and its rotten insides spilled out all over Clark and Addison. You're gonna be waging damage control on this one, I'm afraid."

"Start from the beginning, Duffy," he ordered, and I did so.

"Rohe!" he hissed.

When I finally got to the wrap-up, having been interrupted often by the commissioner's profane outbursts about Rohe's character and pedigree, he congratulated me.

"How obvious are you on this thing?" he asked.

"The evidence is there. I have a feeling Whiteman will flip on his boss. There's not much love there. In the meantime, I think I can stay out of the glare," I said.

"Good. I still need you. Some rumblings here in the Bronx give me the queasy feeling that it's going to be a long, hot summer."

"Just send proper remuneration for this one," I replied. "Anything else and we renegotiate."

"You're a good man, Duffy. Full of shit, but a good man. And how's that niece of yours?"

"On her way to law school," I said, and meant it.

"Oh by the way," I said, suddenly remembering something, "how did you know George Rohe was investigating the murder?"

"I got a phone call. Lila Rohe. I'd like to meet that lady sometime," Chambliss said.

"No you wouldn't," I countered.

Chambliss chuckled, the first time this conversation, and we rang off.

When I returned to the lounge, Red's eyes were heavy. He'd been through more in this evening than even he could handle. Still, he perked up and called for another bottle of bubbly. Once again we saluted each other. This was no clubhouse celebration, but it was a toast to a sweet moment, to scrapes survived, doom avoided, and an assignment completed with shining colors. We could hoist the Cub flag of victory up the pole.

Petey, having shaken off the excitement of the chase and the capture, actually shuddered. She was exhausted, and just now coming to grips with the danger we both had courted. The glass quivered in her hand; the lady runs on fire, not ice. God love her.

Then she beamed, that fresh, enchanting, sparkling smile of youth, and turned to me.

"We did it, Unk," she said.

"Came through in the clutch," I said.

She clinked her glass on mine.

The music we faced in the days that followed was soft compared with the clamor raised on behalf of George Rohe. The Cubs, you see, were on a roll. With Carl Lundgren anchoring the pitching staff, some uncharacteristic clutch hitting, a string of days where the wind blew out, a bevy of breaks and good bounces, and even a few Kenmore Avenue home run clouts, the team won twelve in a row and broke into first place. The fans and the press once again went wild, branding Rohe, who was free on bond after his indictment for murder but barred from baseball by the commissioner, a genius. They railed for his reinstatement, yapping the "Nice guys finish last" bromide as if it came from the Sermon on the Mount.

And who could blame them? After all they've been through, I once wrote, Cub fans will embrace an ax murderer if he can get them a pennant. I wrote that, but I didn't mean it. So help me, Dream, I didn't mean it.

Maybe the Cubs' surge was a tonic, a way of putting the murder in Wrigley Field to rest. The ballyard looks better in green, or in red, white, and blue playoff bunting, than wreathed in black. The fitting phrases of the many Weaver eulogies—lo, the saddest of possible words—are best replaced by those tried, true, and famous Wrigley Field exclamations:

"Back she goes. . . . Way back! . . . Back! . . . Back! . . . Hey! Hey!"

"It might be, it could be, it is!"

"Holy mackerel!"

"No doubt about it."

If you enjoyed Duffy House's first baseball adventure, you'll be happy to learn that there will be two more Duffy House mysteries coming from Bantam this summer.

The following is a preview of **MURDERER'S ROW,** wherein Duffy takes on a case even more treacherous than his first.

MURDERER'S ROW will be coming from Bantam in July, '91.

The Boss

"So I'm feeling a little smug, Duffy," Chambliss said.

"Don't," I said. "At our age smug is getting through a day without Metamucil," I said.

For me this hadn't been one of those days. The night, however, given what was looking up at me from the dinner plate, was more promising. Lamb chops laced with mint butter, asparagus spears as thin as pencils, and a Caesar salad I came to praise, not bury.

"Let me bask a little. The game's going good," he said.

"Don't go soft on me, Grand," I said to Granville Canyon Chambliss, the high commissioner of baseball who was sitting at his throne across the table and letting the fumes of some stellar veal chops affect his thinking.

It would be temporary, I knew, because Chambliss was an old soybean trader from the Chicago pits who was made lord of baseball when the game needed a guy like him. And though it meant that he took up residence in Manhattan and worked in the mahogany and low light of a Park Avenue office instead of the throng of a La Salle Street futures pit, he was still Grand, a torpedo of a guy who dressed badly but had his head screwed on straight. At the moment, his tie was loose, his sleeves were rolled up and he had bleu cheese dressing on his chin.

The dinner was on his expense account because we were on his turf: a well-appointed chunk of W. 59th Street just around the corner from the Plaza Hotel and just across the street from horse-drawn carriages and the heel of Central Park. Why, we passed that young actress Miss Angie Dickinson on the sidewalk as we came in and she smiled a smile at us that brought the term *femme fatale* to my lips.

The joint was called Mickey Mantle's, and while I'm the last guy to darken a spot with an old ballplayer's name on it—though I'll go out of my way to clink forks at Rusty Staub's—Mick's place was okay. My druthers would have had us in the Carnegie Delicatessen on Seventh Avenue. I can't begin to say how many hours I spent and how many pounds I amassed there through the years, and the Stage Delicatessen before that. The Stage was a required pilgrimage from the old Sheraton Hotel on Seventh and 54th, where the visiting teams and scribes always stayed. Besides pudgy writers gorging themselves on the corned beef, you'd often see Mantle and Bill Skowron in there. Roger Maris, was a regular, too, and before them Moe Berg haunted the place. Skowron and Maris used to dip their hands into the pickel barrels because they thought the brine toughened up their paws. At least that was the idea. That was before the Stage was sold to gentiles, who right away put a bar in. Even this gentile knows you can't sell whiskey in a delicatessen without eroding the place, so most everybody moved over to the Carnegie, with those sandwiches that are twice as expensive and too big for one mortal to consume at a single sitting. Oh my, how we tried though, and I had a taste for one of them right now.

But Chambliss, who is no stranger to the Carnegie, felt at home here on the wooden chairs and round tables of Mantle's place. Rouged waitresses in black pants hovered around him like clubhouse attendants, and the bill of fare contained provender that Mickey himself would chew on. The walls were hung with baseball decor, to be sure, but classy, provocative stuff: paintings and prints in and out of Yankeedom. They leaked the memories of old sportswriters.

"To hell with ya then," Chambliss went on. He was eating with his fingers, strip mining an inch-thick chop. "I'm not a cheerleader but attendance is up, revenues are up, and we got about fourteen teams still in the race —and it's only the first week of September."

"The rich get richer," I said.

"You want otherwise? Drugs in the clubhouses? Managers putting down bets? Fans with bags over their heads?" he said.

And he was right. Before Chambliss was invited in around, big-league baseball had tried its damnedest to shoot itself in the foot. It was a time, Grand had declared, "when everyone thought they could do anything they wanted." Whenever the league called a press conference, you didn't know if it was to give out the Cy Young or announce that it was cooperating with a grand jury.

Then Chambliss stepped in, saw the enemy was us, and started spanking. He took up Bart Giamatti's refrain and took it right to the ballplayers themselves. "You guys have a privileged life that most people can't even dream of," he admonished everybody from starting pitchers to batboys, "so live up to it and *obey the damn rules.*" Then he set the rules and smacked anybody who bent them. It was something to see.

I watched intently, even in my semi-emeritus condition within the sporting press. I've personally been around long enough not only to remember when George Herman Ruth was swatting them, but to have had the pleasure of witnessing several of the Bambino's proud prances around the bases. Frank and Estelle House probably would have preferred their son to have pursued a more honorable profession, just as Mr. and Mrs. Stengel of Kansas City once wished that young Charles Dillon had gone into dentistry. It was baseball's good fortune that Casey had knuckles unfit for drilling teeth. I don't remember what I was unfit for.

At any rate I was fifteen when I started with the old

Chicago *Daily News,* getting an infusion of ink in my veins that never thinned. My beat wasn't the front page, (and I knew that Hecht fellow before he went Broadway), except when the boys of summer or autumn won grand championships and we bannered the results. No, I chronicled the stuff of pastime, a diversion, the kiss of a ball on red clay, young men cutting and darting on green grass; games.

I was never anything but a sportswriter and never aspired to be anything else. I liked the spectacle and enjoyed reporting it. I've always relished the company of sportsmen, true and otherwise—those who played and those who spectated. As plebeian as it may sound, I echo Will Veeck's sentiment that there is no sight more beautiful, no sound more sweet, than a ballpark full of fans. That won't put Veeck and me up there with Voltaire, but that's all right, too.

The bulk of my toil was in the fields of a daily column called "On the House." Thirty years of it five days a week. That wasn't too original a head and the column wasn't dictated by the Holy Ghost. What it was was mud-in-your-eye sports as I saw it, and you could frame it or let the parakeet daub it. But you always got the gist of things athletic, who won and why and how the weather was. And the people must have appreciated that, otherwise the editors would have had me writing recipes.

Then it came time to surrender the column to a young Turk, a barb-tongued younker who venerated a well-turned phrase more than the straight dope, a guy who'd rather talk to the player's wife than the player, who didn't like to travel and moaned like hell when the game went longer than two-and-a-half hours. But I won't get started on that. That the *Daily News,* an institution I worshipped, folded shortly after my retirement was, in my most charitable view, only a coincidence.

So I went out to graze, but not completely, since the papers still ask for a piece now and then, usually when some old, once artful dodger passes. Plus, Mr. Spink's *Sporting News* will still print anything I throw at them; and another publisher, for a sum of money that will not endow my relatives, wants my memoirs. I was working hard on that last item—I mean *memoirs* now, called "One More on the House," not just a bunch of wormy columns and moldy anecdotes about same—when that Wrigley Field debacle turned me into a gumshoe.

My meal with Chambliss this night was partially to fete that interlude.

"Hell, I don't think things ever got lower than when the Weaver kid got whacked in Wrigley Field," Chambliss said. "Good Lord—the best pitcher in baseball smoked right there in the ivy and the sunshine. Now that depressed me no end."

He tossed the bone on his plate and used his linen napkin like a paint rag to wipe his digits.

"Saw Red Carney the other day," he continued. "He started in again on the whole thing. What a big hero he was and your niece—Petey, isn't it? The old barker is crazy about her. I couldn't shut him up."

I held up my knife and fork lest he go on. We both knew the tale, about Carney, the legendary mike man of the Chicago Cubs, and Petrinella Biggers, my lovely carrot-top niece from Cincinnati who spent that summer's weeks before commencing law school as my assistant bloodhound in search of the Wrigley Field killer. The sleuthing was Chambliss's idea: he wanted a baseball man on the inside of the investigation. He wanted a point man to tell him unfiltered versions of what people —cops, players, owners—were saying under their breath in the ballparks and the clubhouses about the murder of one of the game's brightest stars. And I went along with it. And Petey, well, she went along with me. We got lucky, unraveled the unsavory affairs of the Cubs' den, nabbed a fiend before he dispatched us, and restored the element of friendly to the Clark and Addison confines.

But that story is well told elsewhere. Meanwhile, I was in Manhattan as a guest of the Commissioner, and his gratitude and baseball's pockets went deep. My real mission in New York, however, was to attend the funeral of a fellow scribe. For some reason—who am I kidding?—because of too much booze and nicotine and room service food—the roster of my former colleagues was going down like starting pitchers in August. And, as ever, there was no cheering in the pressbox.

This one was Hugh McGrew, an old Ebbets Field beat man who wrote tighter prose than Red Smith and played the harmonica better than Phil Linz. I always liked Hughie, but hadn't seen much of him in later years because he wouldn't ride in airplanes and wouldn't admit to the existence of the Los Angeles Dodgers. The man despised Walter O'Malley.

"Why didn't you bring that doll along with you, Duffy?" Chambliss asked. "I ain't dead yet, you know."

"Enough's enough, that's why," I replied. "Petey's a sweet kid with a big brain, and she's on her way to law school where she belongs, dammit."

"I say something made you want to chew on me?"

"Ahh criminy, Grand. The kid got infected with that Wrigley Field whodunnit. Worse case than Red, who put her on the air and slobbered all over her. She just lit up to the attention like a rookie on opening day.

"Now it's time for her feet to touch down," I added, putting the last of the lamb between my chops.

A long-fingered waitress snatched our empty plates and replaced them with cups of steaming coffee. Chambliss gave her some kind of hand signal and she returned with a pair of brandy snifters. In them she poured a golden elixir that coated the crystal and sent the smell of fresh peaches aloft.

"I should have such charming problems," Chambliss said.

"Oh-oh. Here comes the baseball-is-horseshit-ever-since-those-two-Yankees-swapped-wives routine. So give it to me, and don't ignite that thing."

Chambliss was unwrapping a panatella and lolling the business end of it on the wet of his lips.

"Stopped smoking them years ago," he said. "Doesn't mean I can't suck on them."

"Love 'em and lave 'em," I said, and wished I hadn't.

"All right, you want horseshit? Well, there's horseshit right here and right now in my own backyard. The Yankees and that goddamn Rupert Huston," he said, poking the cigar into the air for emphasis. I could see he wanted to unlimber.

"I'm a Chicago guy and I always thought I'd enjoy an era where the Yankees were a doormat. After all the beating up they did on the other clubs all those years. I don't have to tell you the record of that franchise is something else.

"Now they're not only down, but Huston is grinding his heel into the club. The whole organization. Doing his best to make the pinstripes and that NY logo that flapped on the chests of Ruth and Gehrig and DiMaggio into a laughing stock. A cheap decal."

"Sounds like you got a new perspective, Grand," I said.

"Oh yeah, Duffy. Being Commissioner and being east I see it a little different now. When baseball in New York is down like it is now, it isn't good for baseball in general. I'm convinced of that. And I never thought those words would pass these lips.

"He's *using* the franchise, Duffy. Using it like a toy, an ego toy, instead of caretaking a ballclub with a great legacy. All of his tantrums and hiring and firing are one thing. How he publicly embarrasses his people—some good baseball people—that's his prerogative because he owns the show. I know that, too. But dammit, he's—he's —he's tampering! He's contaminating. He's eating away at the guts of baseball ownership worse than all the oil tycoons and real estate hustlers and cowboys that went before him.

"Ah, horseshit, I don't have to tell *you* what he's doing. I'm just blowing off steam. . . ."

With his left hand Grand upended the snifter and drained its sticky contents into his coffee cup. Then he drained the cup. With that he abruptly got up, pushed his chair back, and drew glances from adjoining diners who already knew who he was and seemed to be enjoying the show.

"Excuse me while I patronize the little boy's room," he said, and rumbled off, the still-whole, wet cigar sticking out from the knuckles of his right hand.

Chambliss hadn't told me anything new. Like every baseball writer in the land, I'd watched and lamented and written nasty paragraphs about the spectacle of Rupert Huston, the Yankees' egomaniacal, mad czar. Bad press collected like spitballs at Huston's feet, and he stepped through it like a plant owner driving through a picket line. You couldn't faze him, couldn't humiliate or rile him, and you certainly couldn't stop him.

Nobody in New York expected Huston, a beer and real estate sharpie who had bought the Yankees more than a decade earlier at a bargain basement price, to be a statesman. He was simply a rich son-of-a-bitch, a wheeler dealer operating in a town full of them. And Huston came out swinging the moment he got here. As young Casey Stengel had exclaimed upon being traded to the Giants, "Wake up, muscles, we're in New York now!"

Yet nobody in Gotham expected Huston to do what he did to the Yankees. Nobody expected him to pervert the organization of the baton and top hat, to make it a temporary hitching post for rented players and managers at exhorbitant rates, players brought in like mercenaries only to be scorned and excoriated a few years later by Huston himself if they did not perform to his liking. Apple barrels rot from the top down, and it didn't take long for the premises to teem with fruit flies. Despite their fat paychecks, Huston's players soon grew surly and disgruntled. The glow they felt from first becoming a Yankee, *New York Yankee,* was quickly tarnished by the toxic tactics of the boss, no matter how many times the scoreboard beamed Movietone footage of past legends and the loudspeakers blared Sinatra's "New York, New York." And these players from the provinces, from Oklahoma and Kentucky, wished only to leave. There were no smiling DiMaggios, no shy young Mantles, no grinning Berras. Finally, the imports were sold off like unwanted penny stocks.

Huston was the current bane of Commissioner Chambliss' existence. Every time he picked up a tabloid or tuned in the 11 o'clock news, everytime he looked in baseball's mirror he saw Rupert Huston. Huston was the ogre of New York, a bigger villain than whatever masochist was posing as mayor, a character so well chronicled the papers did not even use his last name. And yet Chambliss worked for the owners, which included Huston, and while he currently enjoyed support from cooler heads, there was no telling when Huston would marshal the support of incoming owners, the pizza kings, fast-food earls, blue jean dukes, and real estate counts who would back him because they had bought into the game the way he had and appreciated his way of doing things.

Chambliss returned with the cigar in his teeth and his hands pink from the blow dryer.

"I put a bug in your head, didn't I? Just bring up that bastard's name and it gets you going," he said as he sat back down.

"Actually, Grand, my eye caught that pose of Roberto Clemente over there on the wall. Lost myself wondering how long it's been since I saw Bob run in right field."

"Nice thought," he said, "but you're a liar."

"October 1972. Pirates lost the playoffs to Cincinnati on a wild pitch."

"What I've not done, if you're still paying attention," Grand continued, "is take the jackass head on. Kuhn did that with Finley. Both of them were mud wrestling in a courtroom before it was all over with."

"I've got the complete transcript of that trial. I ever tell you that?" I said.

"I never asked. Can you imagine me telling Huston he couldn't unload a ballplayer like Kuhn did with Finley? Look what Rupert did with Bill Wolfe yesterday. Gave him away to Pittsburgh for what—?"

"Three minor leaguers and change. Huston said Wolfe 'wasn't contributing' . . . said he had a bad attitude. I read all about it on the way in. Last year's RBI leader for chopped liver. Couldn't believe my eyes."

"You and the rest of this city," Chambliss said. "They're ready to lynch the bastard. People even call my office, for cryin' out loud. They always call my office."

"What'd John Brush said about the trade? He wasn't even mentioned in my paper," I said.

"Yeah, well, after Huston stalks off the pulpit, his general manager has to stick around and pick up the pieces. I saw a little of the press conference and Brush looked like he'd been hit by a street cleaner. Which is tough in this town because we don't get much street cleaning."

"Poor sonuvabitch," I said. "How'd you like the job of explaining Huston's deals to the world?"

"He tried. Said the Yankees were out of the race and Pittsburgh was willing to part with some good young kids for a power hitter in their stretch drive. The Yankees were building for the future and all that stuff he knew was horseshit. By that time Huston was long gone."

Grand sucked on his dormant tobacco stick.

"And you know, I see the guy all the time. We make the same rubber chicken affairs and he treats me like his goddamn roomy. Slaps me on the back and says 'What say we play some porkbellies, Grand?' Jee-zus! I got all I can do to keep from decking the guy!"

I laughed out loud and belched, my belly telling me to stop with the peach brandy already, my waistline pounding at my belt like an angry landlord.

Just then a young fellow brought a phone to the table. It was a portable affair, with a retractable antenna, the Flash Gordon kind of gear that everybody but me takes for granted nowadays. Chambliss threw a suspicious look at the kid, whose hair was parted down the middle and clipped high around the ears, and he snarled at the phone. The commissioner didn't wear a beeper and he didn't take calls when he was eating dinner. I liked that about him. Somehow, however, he knew he had to take this one.

"Yes, Marjorie," he said, knowing who was on the line.

He listened briefly, then fairly spat the cigar from his mouth.

"Good Lord . . . !" he said, his voice trailing off. His expression dropped somewhere between nonplussed and stupefied; his free hand covered his open ear. He looked at me then looked away as people do when they're captive to that device.

"Who?" he barked. "Yeah, the Bronx guy. All right, a few minutes. Yeah. Yeah. Yeah. Marjorie, c'mon now . . ."

Then he lowered the phone from his ear, not sure of what to do with it, and turned to me with an expression I had never seen on him before. If I were to guess, I would say he looked like that at birth of his first child and at the onset of his first kidney stone. His mug was a stew of conflicting emotions, a battleground of exploding capillaries, and he was starting to perspire.

He spoke in a controlled hush, wanting only me to hear what he was saying.

"They just found Rupert Huston," he said. "In Yankee Stadium. The sonuvabitch has been shot to death."

ABOUT THE AUTHORS

CRABBE EVERS is the pseudonym for the partnership of William Brashler and Reinder Van Til, a pair of boxscore devotees who admire the poetry of Franklin P. Adams and have spent long hours at the feet of Duffy House.

WILLIAM BRASHLER is the author of eight books, including his novel about baseball in the Negro Leagues, THE BINGO LONG TRAVELING ALL-STARS AND MOTOR KINGS, which was made into a popular motion picture. He has also written biographies of Josh Gibson and Johnny Bench. He lives and works in Chicago.

REINDER VAN TIL, a long time book editor and free-lance music and art critic, has published a book on regional history and numerous magazine articles. He lives and works in St. Paul.

CRABBE EVERS has recently completed two more Duffy House baseball mysteries which Bantam will publish during the summer of '91: *Murderer's Row* (July) and *Bleeding Dodger Blue* (September).